SKOKIE PUBLIC LIBRARY
31232002197632

DIRTY SWEET

DIRTY SWEET

JOHN McFETRIDGE

ECW Press

Published by ECW PRESS
2120 Queen Street East, Suite 200, Toronto, Ontario, Canada M4E 1E2

LIBRARY AND ARCHIVES CANADA CATALOGUING IN PUBLICATION

McFetridge, John, 1959–
Dirty sweet : a mystery / John McFetridge.

ISBN 1-55022-717-3

1. Title.

PS8575.F48D57 2006   C813'.6   C2006-900295-9

Editor for the Press: Michael Holmes
Cover and Text Design: Tania Craan
Cover Image: Luc Beziat / Getty
Typesetting: Mary Bowness
Printing: Friesens

This book is set in Sabon and Bubba Love

The publication of *Dirty Sweet* has been generously supported by the Canada Council, the Ontario Arts Council, and the Government of Canada through the Book Publishing Industry Development Program.

DISTRIBUTION
CANADA: Jaguar Book Group, 100 Armstrong Ave.,
Georgetown, ON L7G 5S4
UNITED STATES: Independent Publishers Group,
814 North Franklin St., Chicago, IL 60610

PRINTED AND BOUND IN CANADA

For Laurie, always

CHAPTER ONE

"The cars were stopped on King, right there, waiting for the light to change."

Roxanne Keyes lit another cigarette and told the detectives exactly what she saw happen then. "A guy got out of the Volvo, the passenger side, walked back to this one, and shot that guy in the head. Then he walked back to the car, got in, and it drove away."

She didn't tell them she was pretty sure she knew the driver of the Volvo.

"He just walked?"

She was about to say, no, he swaggered like you guys, but she said, "Yeah, he just walked."

That was half an hour ago. Since then, the uniformed cops had closed off the street, the crime scene guys had taken thousands of pictures and thrown a tarp over the corpse in the SUV. The crowd that had gathered on the sidewalk was already starting to drift away. People on the Starbucks patio, the witnesses who'd given their driver's license information to the uniformed cops, were restless waiting for the detectives. Half an hour, and the feeling of being part of a special event, a big deal in Toronto, was gone. They were complaining about places they had to be, even though they hadn't been there much longer than it would have taken them to drink their coffees.

Roxanne had made one more phone call to Maurice Abernathy, lowering the price again, Jesus, to seventeen-fifty a square foot for a lousy 20,500 square feet in the only listing she had, a half-empty reno they called the Toy Works. He still wouldn't take it, but he wouldn't turn her down, either. Just wasting her time. She told him what she'd seen, right there in front of her, and he'd said, "That's a great scene." Maurice produced cheap action movies, using Toronto to look like some American city, but his business was going down steadily as the Canadian dollar was rising.

He'd said, "I might be able to use that," and Roxanne was going to tell him about the driver, about how she thought she knew the guy, but then she started to think maybe she could use it, too.

What she'd wanted to do was reach into her purse, get one of the joints out of her tampon case, and fire it up. Get lost in the moment, all this activity. Let everything going on all around her turn into one dull hum and just float on the buzz. Forget about the deep, deep shit she'd gotten herself into. But she never was very good at just letting things happen. So she wondered, how could she make this work for her?

But the detectives arrived and now she was telling them everything.

Almost everything.

"They weren't arguing, shouting at each other?" The

younger good-looking detective was asking all the questions. He looked to be early-thirties, the same as Roxanne, and he looked like he went to the gym a little more often than she did. The other one, the black one with the shaved head who looked like a football player whose name Roxanne couldn't remember, didn't seem too interested.

"No, not that I noticed. I was just sitting down."

"Did they seem to know each other?"

"I don't know."

"So, for no reason, this guy just got out of his car, walked to the next one in line, and blew some guy's head all over King Street?"

"Most of it hit that bike courier," Roxanne said. Then, "I'm sure he had a reason, detective. People have all kinds of reasons for what they do." Like Roxanne had a reason for not mentioning that she was pretty sure she knew the guy driving the car. Maybe if she could remember where she knew him from.

"Yeah, we'll ask him."

"Did he say anything in another language?"

"Now that you mention it." She looked at the black guy; she'd almost forgotten he was there. "He might have."

The younger detective said, "This is Detective Price. I'm Sergeant Loewen."

Price said, "Russian maybe?"

Roxanne took a drag on the cigarette and exhaled slowly. "Maybe."

"Just one word, or more?"

"I wasn't really listening. I was on the phone." She motioned to her Blackberry on the table. She was still wearing the ear bud.

"Okay, thanks very much," Loewen said closing his notebook. They'd already been through this with the other witnesses. No one knew anything, really. Some people thought the driver was the shooter. Some people thought the guy was walking on the sidewalk, pulled the trigger, and then jumped into a moving car. Loewen said, "We really appreciate it."

But Price wasn't going anywhere. "Did the other guy say anything?"

"If he did, I didn't hear it."

Price glanced over his shoulder at the car under the tarp only a few feet away. "So they weren't shouting at each other?"

"Not at each other."

"Each other?"

"The guy who got shot was yelling. It might have been Russian or something, when I came out of the café. By the time I got to the table and sat down, he'd stopped and that's when the other guy walked back and shot him."

"But the other guy, the shooter, he didn't say anything."

"Not that I heard."

"Can you describe the man with the gun?"

She took another deep drag and exhaled smoke. "Older, maybe mid-fifties, black hair — I remember thinking it was probably a dye — broad shoulders, cheap blue sports coat. Walked with a bit of a limp."

Loewen had his notebook open again and was writing as fast as he could. "This is great, thanks. Anything else."

"He was wearing sunglasses."

"You mean glasses like those?" He pointed to the trendy optometrist shop behind Roxanne, next to the Starbucks.

She barely glanced at the display and pushed her own D&G's further up on her nose. "No one would put these in the window. They must have been ten years old, and they weren't exactly stylish when they were new."

Loewen nodded and looked at Price.

"Did you happen to notice what kind of car he was driving?"

"Well, he wasn't driving, but it was a Volvo. S80."

Loewen nodded, wrote it down. "You sure?" It was at least the third make of car offered by the witnesses.

Roxanne took another drag on her cigarette and said, "I'm thinking about getting one."

"What colour?"

"I don't know yet, I'm not even sure I'm going to get one. They have a new SUV I'm looking at, too, but SUV's are kind of out these days. They've got a convertible, too."

"I mean the car the shooter got into."

"Oh, blue. They call it 'midnight blue.'"

Price said, "Can you describe the driver?"

Yeah, the driver. Roxanne looked like she was thinking about it for a second, then shook her head. "Not really. He didn't get out of the car." She could picture him sitting in the car. From a different angle, from the front, where she could see his face.

Loewen looked at his notebook, read something. "Was he about the same age as the shooter?"

No, Roxanne thought, he was at least twenty years younger. "I'm sorry, I didn't really see him."

"Well, anyway, I gotta say, Miss Keyes, you're very observant, especially under the circumstances."

"It was eerily quiet, Detective," Roxanne said. She looked past him at the tarp-covered Navigator. "And slow.

He seemed to raise his gun and fire in slow motion, but when I went to move, to turn my head, it was like I was in slow motion, too."

"It's a shocking thing to see," Loewen said and Roxanne nodded slowly, but that wasn't it. It wasn't the shooting or the guy's head exploding all over the bike courier at all. It really should have been a lot more for her, more to get involved in, get lost in, but she was still thinking what she could do with it.

She said, "So, this wasn't road rage, was it? Is it like some Russian Mafia hit?"

Loewen smiled and didn't mean for it to be so patronizing, but after talking to so many witnesses who watched too much *Law and Order*, that's the way it looked. "It's a little early to say what it is."

"Of course."

"Well," Loewen said, "you've been very helpful."

Shaking his hand, she squeezed it a little too hard. "If there's anything else."

Loewen said, "Yeah, we might need to do some follow-up."

Roxanne reached into her purse and pulled out her little leather folder. She handed him her business card from Downtown Real Estate, the one with her picture on it, with her longer hair before she got it cut for the summer. "You can always reach me on my cell, detective."

"Commercial Services?"

"Leasing. We have a few renos in the neighbourhood. Old factories and warehouses turned into office space. This neighbourhood is really taking off."

"All right. If we think of anything else."

"That'd be fine."

• • •

Some days, you just can't believe your luck. Once Boris decided there was just no way to deal with Anzor and that they were going to have to kill him, he brought his "Uncle" Khozha up from Brighton Beach. They went over half a dozen different ways to get to the guy, and then on their way to his office to check it out, who should pull up behind them but the man himself?

Idling at the red light on King Street West, Boris watched the tall, good-looking woman in the business suit, the one with the skirt a little too short and the heels a little too high, come out of the Starbucks with a cup of coffee in one hand and a cell phone in the other, wire going right into her ear. He was pretty sure he knew her, but he wasn't sure from where. Something about her was different. Her hair was shorter? He almost turned completely around to watch her find a seat on the patio, and when he did, he saw Anzor in the Navigator behind him.

He said, "I don't fucking believe it," and Khozha said, "So, go through the fucking light, who cares?"

"No, I mean I don't fucking believe that prick bastard Anzor is right behind us." Boris hadn't spoken this much Russian in a couple of years, and even then it was diplomatic school Russian. He couldn't talk like that in front of Uncle Khozha.

Khozha turned right around in the leather seat of the Volvo s80 — brand new and a nice car, great stereo and one of those computer map things — and looked at the guy stopped behind them. The light changed to green and Anzor started to yell right away, waving his hands. With the tinted windows, he couldn't see into the Volvo.

"Fuck him," Khozha said, and got out of the car.

Boris wanted to wait, to follow him, do it quiet someplace. He wanted to hear Anzor beg for his life after the trouble he'd caused, flaunting it in front of everyone, making Boris look weak. And he really wanted it to be more dramatic, more like in a movie. But what happened was so matter-of-fact and straightforward. Khozha walked back to the car, both front windows were down, raised his gun and fired, *pop*, *pop*, *pop*. Anzor's head exploded. Then Khozha walked back to the Volvo, got in and said, "What are you waiting for, it's still green." The fucking light hadn't even changed. Boris stepped on the gas and they went through the intersection.

"Now I'm going to have to get a new fucking car."

"So, it's what you do, isn't it, steal cars?" Making it sound like he was some Jamaican kid sneaking around in the middle of the night.

"I like this car."

"So keep it, who gives a shit?"

"She saw you."

Khozha took a pack of Camels out of his sports-coat pocket and lit one. "Who?"

"That woman at the coffee shop, she watched you shoot him and walk back and get into my car."

He said, "Fifty people saw," opening the glove compartment and tossing the gun inside.

"Doesn't that worry you?" They were still driving east on King. At Spadina, Boris turned right and headed for the Gardiner. He hadn't heard any sirens. As soon as they pulled away, everything in the world went back to being the same as it always was, like nothing happened.

Khozha was looking out the window at a golf course and a high fence around a driving range, right there in downtown Toronto, in the shadow of the Tower. "No, it's good," he said. "The more people see, the more stories there are, no two alike. It's good."

"That woman with the phone, though, she didn't even blink."

"She didn't see anything. She'll say, 'Oh, I don't know, it all happen so fast.' Say the car was red or green, maybe black. Maybe a Lexus, maybe a Honda."

Boris said, "A fucking Honda?"

Khozha shrugged.

He was probably right. This was more Khozha's territory, that's why he brought him in.

"What kind of gun you use, blow his head off like that? That a Colt?"

"Is Tokarev, Russian. It's not the gun, it's the bullets. Hollow-point steel. Guy makes them in Staten Island, does good work."

"They work all right." The traffic was heavy, as always, on the ramp up to the expressway and they inched along, the SkyDome to their left, high-rises blocking out Lake Ontario in front of them, like the city was embarrassed to have a waterfront. Somewhere under the expressway and between warehouses was "historic" Fort York.

"So, you take me to the airport?"

"I was going to take you to my club."

"What for? I'm going home. The job's done. You can pay me now."

Suddenly it seemed like it was 10,000 dollars too much, but that was the deal and Boris Suliemanov was determined to establish himself as honourable all the way.

"I don't have the money on me, I didn't expect it to happen right away."

"You don't have my money, Biba?" Always so short-tempered, Boris thought, and the only guy who still calls me Biba.

"I have it at the club. Come on, we'll have a drink, celebrate."

"I want to be back in New York tonight."

"Yeah, sure, no problem, tonight. Flights every hour to New York."

"Yeah." They were on the expressway then, moving. "That's the best thing about this city."

CHAPTER TWO

Roxanne thought he might have been one of the Russian guys looking to buy some waterfront land last year, the guys who said they could bulldoze over the homeless in their tent city in an hour. Could she just call him up and say, "How've you been? Killed anyone lately? Driven any getaway cars?"

After the detectives had left and traffic was moving again on King Street, Roxanne walked back to the Toy Works, a couple of blocks west of Spadina. A hundred years ago it had actually been a toy factory. By the fifties it was mostly sweatshops churning out cheap clothes, and by the end of the eighties it was mostly empty. Five years ago, Roxanne had convinced Angus Muir, against what he called his "better judgement," to buy the building and renovate it for the booming high-tech industry. It was all open concept, high ceilings, exposed beams, hardwood floors, but fully wired with T1 connections, backup power, and constantly monitored and controlled air temperature.

The shooter had been calm, walking up to the Navigator, raising his gun, and firing three shots. The cute detective said he'd hit the guy with all three, even though the first one probably killed him. Roxanne tried to focus on the driver. Younger than the shooter, better dressed, good-looking. Was he really, or was she imagining that, hoping? He was pretty cool, though, no screeching tires racing away from the scene. The light changed and he drove away. She was positive she'd spoken to him. More than once. She was sure he had an accent.

The Toy Works was on the wrong side of Spadina, away from downtown and not far enough to be Liberty Village, but for a while there, the area was looking good. A lot of the old warehouses and factories were renovated into condos, a lot of old row houses just bulldozed into the ground. Art galleries were opening up, film companies moving in. Roxanne had no idea what movies they made, but a lot of big Hollywood movies were being shot in Toronto, and people kept telling her that animation and digital effects were huge in Canada. Software companies. Some decent restaurants opened. Rodney's Oyster Bar even moved over from Adelaide and Jarvis.

Then the high-tech bubble burst.

In the polished wood and marble lobby there was a huge mural of Norman Rockwell kids playing with toys on one wall, and beneath that, the mostly empty building directory. While Roxanne waited for the elevator, a woman came in. She was wearing a suit like Roxanne's but a little more conservative, and she was talking on a cell phone, saying, "Because I said so, and that's just got to be good enough. Put Rosalie back on. . . . Jordan, I'm not going to tell you again," rolling her eyes with that tired mother look and getting onto the elevator as the doors opened. "Yes, it's final. Final, Jordan."

The elevator doors closed and Roxanne was alone in the lobby. She saw the elevator stop at three and checked the directory. Three quarters of the third floor, 37,500 square feet, was VSF Online Services. Could be anything. Roxanne had to think to remember a white guy in his early forties. Good-looking. She remembered he was never in a hurry or upset by the delays. Moved in the month they opened.

Almost three years ago. She wondered if he might want the rest of the floor. No idea what VSF Online Services did, these guys all gave their companies meaningless names. Meaningless, or inside jokes no one else ever got. Roxanne got onto the elevator thinking he was probably barely holding on, and she should be lucky he wasn't looking for less space.

But what's luck got to do with it?

She had that song in her head, changing love to luck, when she got off the elevator on the completely empty fifth floor and finally fired up that joint. Pulling it deep into her lungs, she felt the pleasant light-headedness right away as she looked out the windows facing south and west. Rooftops of other old factories, some renovated, some not, some stopped halfway through the process. A giant neon Kentucky Fried Chicken bucket, and dozens of huge billboards all lit up in bright flashing colours, some with TV screens playing commercials, trying to catch the eyes of commuters escaping downtown Toronto for the suburbs.

You make your own luck. From the day she started as the receptionist, nineteen years old and hired for her looks, she knew. Greet the customers with a smile and something low-cut and tight. She made her own luck. She got to know the leasing business, got to know a few brokers and some developers, and she started making her own off-market deals, handling some shadow vacancies, lining up customers with stuff that wasn't officially listed yet. At twenty-five, she took the course and got her license. Sitting there, another classroom where she just didn't fit in; all those housewives on one side, looking for a hobby, something to keep them busy between Regis and Oprah now that the kids were in school all day, the commercial guys on the other side. And they were all guys — older, with plenty of business experience, but looking for a change of pace, no one caring about what the others had to learn, and Roxanne in the middle. A few bumps on the road, hell, a few bumps and grinds, but she was driving a Jeep Liberty with the full sport package, Mopar roof rack with the four lights across, and living in a Queen's Quay condo before she was thirty. Met Angus Muir, and she was making her own deals from the ground up.

Her high heels clicked on the completely resurfaced hardwood floor as she walked towards the north side. She sat down on the windowsill, looked out, and took another hit on the joint. It was decent dope, but she still couldn't let go and just drift on the buzz. More factories, old three-storey brick buildings that were once the mansions of Parkdale and now were either divided up into rooming houses, or boarded up and abandoned, squats. Low-rent high-rises, instant slums. One of the 9/11 hijackers had lived in one of those apartments for a while, or so desperate-to-be-in-on-anything-important Torontonians wanted to believe.

She was sure as shit not going to lose everything now, burst high-tech bubble or not.

She knew the driver of that fucking Volvo.

She took another hit. Young guy, her age or a couple years older, no more. Clean-cut. When that black cop mentioned Russian, she thought she could hear the guy saying something with an accent. What was he saying?

If only she could place him. He must be some kind of big-time criminal, stops at a red light and kills a guy. Or the passenger kills a guy, but the driver was so cool about it. A guy like that must have something going on. A guy like that makes his own luck.

Another song came into her head, Madonna, her hero from way back. When she was a wannabe, showing off her flat tummy and her belly button in grade seven. Yeah, he could be her lucky star. He could take her far.

"That's a sweet smell, takes me back."

Roxanne looked towards the elevators. She didn't jump or react in any obvious way, she just squinted through the rising smoke at the guy walking towards her.

"Another victim of misspent youth?"

"I guess you could say that."

He was easygoing, dressed casual, khakis and a blue shirt buttoned up halfway over a grey T-shirt, as if he'd bought page twenty-nine of the Eddie Bauer catalogue. She thought he could be the catalogue model.

She said, "It worked out okay, though," and took another deep hit from the joint.

He shrugged. "The right place at the right time, I guess."

He waited for a moment, but Roxanne didn't say anything, so he said, "You're Roxanne Keyes, right? The real estate broker for the building?"

"That's right." She finally turned around a little on the windowsill and looked right at him. Close up, he wasn't quite as clean-cut and smooth as the catalogue models.

He might have worked construction back in the day, and he never wore makeup in his life. He looked a little like Kevin Costner in that baseball movie — not the one in Iowa, the one with Susan Sarandon.

"Somebody said they saw you come in. I've been looking for you. I lease the third floor."

"VSF Online."

"That's me. Vince Fournier."

"Is there a problem with the lease?" She was hopeful for a second. "Do you need more space?"

"Yeah, a little. Just storage really, we're putting in a few more servers."

"Okay, sure."

He was wondering how come she just sat there smoking the joint, like nothing unusual was going on. She looked maybe even a little more spaced than the dope alone would manage, so he asked, "Are you all right?"

She looked at the joint in her hand like she just noticed it. "I'm fine." She took one more hit, inhaling long and slow, and holding it for quite a while before exhaling. "I was on King Street before."

He nodded, not pretending he didn't know what she was talking about, but not freaked out either. He said, "That was quite a scene. You saw it?"

"Yeah."

"It's on the news, CityPulse 24. They're saying it was road rage. What's this city coming to?"

No reaction.

"I can see why you need a little break." He motioned to the joint, and she dropped what was left to the floor and stepped on it.

"So, how much more space do you need? There's not much left."

He laughed. "There's the rest of three, and two more floors."

She didn't laugh. "It's going to be the same rate."

"But it's just for storage."

"It's for servers, you need all that dust-free, reinforced floor, extra secure doors and stuff."

He was going to say that he didn't need any reception or offices, or anything that looked too good, but why argue? "Same rate."

"How much do you need?"

"I don't know, 10,000 feet, I guess. The rest of the floor."

"That's twelve-five. I can draw up a new contract, or have your existing lease amended."

"Let's do a new one, I might put it under a different company name."

They started walking towards the elevator. Vince said, "You were supposed to have an office in this building by now."

Yeah, well, this building was supposed to be fully leased by now, she thought, but all she said was, "It's just as easy to work out of the Lake Shore building," which, even as she said it, sounded lame, as the place was all the way on the other side of downtown. Then she realized she'd have to go all the way there to get a copy of the lease and take it home to work, because she didn't want to be in the office if Angus came in. So she asked Vince if he had a copy of his lease.

"In my office. You want a copy?"

"That'd be great."

As soon as Roxanne saw the naked woman, she knew how she recognized the driver of the Volvo. Boris Suliemanov. Yeah, he was Russian all right.

• • •

The naked woman was lying back on an old couch, one foot up on the coffee table and absently fluffing the tiny patch of hair on her puss, tugging on the silver ring through her navel. Roxanne figured she was close to thirty. She was saying, "You used to be able to make a living working the lunch rush downtown."

Another woman — Roxanne realized she was the one in the suit she saw in the lobby, the one arguing with her kid on the phone — was sitting up in an armchair. Now she was wearing lingerie, supposed to be sexy, like the stuff the live models wear in the windows of Miss Behav'n on Queen West on the weekends. Too expensive, and Roxanne never knew a man who cared about lingerie, only that it came off fast.

The naked woman was saying, "It was different then, you could make a living working lunches. And Josh — you know he's handicapped, Downs, so I need to spend a lot of time with him. I used to work a four-hour shift, lunch, on Bay Street and that would be enough, you know?"

There was one other woman in the room, what Vince had called the "employee lounge" at the very back of the building. The windows were open, overlooking the fire escape and the parking lot. The third woman, looked like a teenager, was wearing a white bra and cut-off jeans, unbuttoned and unzipped, hanging open.

They were relaxing, hanging out. The naked one lit a cigarette and said, "Back then, people had martinis, or some drink before lunch, and a full course and then another drink after. Now, shit, now people have water, Evian or Perrier, it's still water, then a salad, maybe something else but probably not, and nothing after."

Vince had been showing Roxanne around his place, VSF Online, which turned out to be Internet porn. When they passed the lounge — which was really just unfinished space with the same hardwood floor, beams and posts as on the empty floors in the building with some couches and chairs tossed in — a young black guy stopped them and wanted to talk about someone named Garry.

While Vince stepped away to talk to the black guy, he called him Suss, Roxanne watched the women on their break. It was the casual way they sat around talking, the teenybopper picking at the threads where the waistband of her jean shorts used to be, saying, "So? That's easier, less to do." That's how she knew Boris Suliemanov.

They looked just like strippers, the casual nakedness, sitting around at work, smoking. And strippers made her think of Boris.

The naked one took a drag on her cigarette and said, "But tips are based on the total, a percentage. Used to be the average lunch bill could be forty-five, fifty bucks, that's 200 for four guys, an average tip on that is twenty-five, thirty bucks. Now, same restaurant, same shift, same guys, the average bill is like thirty bucks. Takes the same amount of time to serve. You can't make a living on tips from that."

"But you can here?" This from the other one, Miss B. Haven.

"Sure, the same four hour-shift while Josh is in school, I can take home 300 a day. Sometimes two, still that's usually at least three grand, twenty-five hundred a month."

"And you get to be home when your kid gets home."

"Yeah. Well, actually, they cancelled his bus, so I have to drop him off and pick him up, so that's another reason I need these kind of hours."

"You could work at a peeler bar, though."

The teenybopper said, "You ever do that? Fucking bikers and Russians, bringing in all these chicks from Romania and fucking Upper Slobodia and shit. They'll give blow jobs for ten bucks, you can't make any money with them around."

"And they treat you shitty, always on your back about being late or taking time off for doctor's appointments. Josh has a lot of doctor crap. They call it freelance, but you have to be there when they want you there."

Roxanne saw Vince was trying to finish up with Suss, but the guy wouldn't drop it. He looked like one of those tough-talking rap singers, or like he was trying to look like one, with his casual slouch, baggy clothes, sunglasses, and a grey ballcap with a black G on the front. Vince turned and was walking away, but Suss was still talking.

"It's okay here, though, Vince is a decent guy," the naked one said, and the teenybopper agreed.

Miss B. Haven said, "This could really work. I have my kid with a babysitter but he starts school in September. It's really that steady here? And you don't mind the work?"

"Well, I'm not saying if I could get a good shift for business lunches, you know, in out, decent tips, I wouldn't take it. But this is a lot better than some high maintenance ladies-who-lunch crowd, you know?"

"I guess so."

"It's more play-acting than sex. Hell, anybody can fake an orgasm."

"I don't." The others looked at her, and Miss B. Haven said, "I mean, I can, I used to. Then, I was breaking up with this guy, this jerk, and I told him, threw it in his face, you know? I faked it every time."

Yeah, they knew.

"Then he says to me, 'So what, you fake orgasms. I fake whole relationships.'"

Boris had wanted to lease the first floor of the building for a strip club. A classy, "gentleman's club," he called it. "Very upscale, European," which she'd thought meant good-looking white chicks. Like the Russians and Romanians taking the jobs away from these women here talking daycare.

Angus didn't have a problem with it, said they could call it the Toy Box, but Roxanne said they'd never be able to lease out the rest of the building with a peeler bar in the lobby. Not like it would make any difference now.

Vince finally said something and Suss laughed. Vince came back to where Roxanne was standing in front of the lounge.

"Sorry about that." He saw her looking into the lounge and went back to telling her about the online porn business. He said they hosted a lot of adult sites, mostly amateur, webcam stuff, but, "We're also a content provider, shooting a little video here and running live sex shows."

Roxanne didn't know what content provider meant, so Vince explained that people start up adult websites as a small business, something they can do from home. Pictures of the girlfriend or the wife naked, they sell monthly memberships and sign up as many customers as they can, but there's a huge amount of competition these days and they need more content than they can shoot themselves. So companies like VSF Online, in addition to hosting the site on its servers and handling the credit card payments, sells content — video modules, ten-minute porno movies to download, access to live strippers, interactive sex shows, archives of hundreds of thousands of pictures.

"Here we go," he said opening the door to his office. "Lot of fetish stuff, but it doesn't generate as much revenue as you'd think."

The office was big, with a desk by the windows, one wall filled with a bookcase — and a lot of books, paperbacks and hardcovers that all looked read — and a sitting area with a couch and a big armchair. There were three computers set up around the room and some filing cabinets.

"Have a seat. Would you like a coffee, or have you got the munchies?"

"I'm fine." Roxanne sat down on the couch and said, "So business is good?"

"Well, you know, sex sells." He looked through the file cabinet, saying, "Turns out the whole dot-com boom was just dot porn."

"And you were in the right place at the right time."

He shrugged. "Here's the lease, hang on." He picked up the phone on his desk and asked someone named Ella to come into his office. "When VCRs first hit the market twenty years ago, the whole industry was driven by adult films. It's kind of the same for the online stuff. The rest of the industry will catch up, maybe just not as fast as people hoped."

The office door opened and a woman in her mid twenties came in. She had blond hair in pigtails, wore black-rimmed glasses and a short cotton dress, and Roxanne figured she was at least seven months pregnant.

Vince handed her the folder and asked her to make a copy of the lease and she left.

Roxanne said, "Were you in the computer business before this?"

"No, I was in the entertainment side of things. More the supply. Had to learn the tech stuff. It's getting easier."

"Do you think things will pick up soon? In other parts of the high tech field?" She was trying to be businesslike, to act like the professional she always saw herself as, but now that she remembered where she knew Boris from, she was trying to figure her next move.

"Could be. I heard Amazon made a profit last quarter. Anything's possible. I'm not really convinced people want to do much shopping online, except for this kind of stuff, the thing you don't want your neighbours to see you buying. But you never know."

Ella came back into the office with the folder and a photocopy of the lease on top. She said, "Garry called again. Wants you to call him."

Roxanne watched him shake his head a little. If he was annoyed it didn't show. He was calm, in control.

He said, "I just talked to Suss about him."

"He's persistent."

"Tomorrow."

Ella said, "He'll call again at five-thirty, and again at nine tomorrow if you don't call. He's got some actors he wants you to look at."

"Actors. That what he's calling them? All right, I'll talk to him." He looked at Roxanne and said, "Guy shoots the video modules we license, ten-minute movies. He's really a terrific filmmaker, but he only wants to spend money on the gay stuff."

"Is it a big market?"

"It's pretty much the only growth area left."

Roxanne put the lease in her bag and said, "So you might need even more space?"

They walked out of the office, Vince saying, "Let's not rush into anything."

But Roxanne was thinking of Boris and her opening line.

CHAPTER THREE

"She was in shock, man."

"She was a lot of things," Price said. "But shocked wasn't one of them."

"C'mon, you see a guy's head get blown off right in front of you?"

Price took his spicy sausage from the guy behind the cart and started loading on toppings. "Most of it hit that bike courier, that's what she said."

"She was in shock."

Sauerkraut, onions, black olives, corn relish — the corn relish makes it — Dijon mustard. They were standing on Spadina at the corner of King. Traffic was moving again, crawling down Spadina towards the Gardiner. Loewen already halfway through his hot dog when Price got his, walking back to their car, saying, "No way. She was not in shock."

"She's got great legs," Loewen said.

"She's got a great body," Price said, "but she ain't in shock. I doubt anything ever shocks her."

"She's a real estate agent."

Price leaned on the hood of their car and looked up Spadina. Another block and Chinatown started, vegetable stores out on the sidewalks. There were a lot of people set up on rugs and towels on the sidewalks, too, selling colourful scarves and incense and beaded jewellery. Mostly girls who looked like they stepped out of 1968, except they showed a lot more skin and had tattoos all over — their arms, their backs, even their necks. Price couldn't imagine what they had where the sun don't shine. And every part of them was pierced.

He said, "She's a lot of things."

Loewen said, "Yeah," drawing it out enough for Price to roll his eyes.

"Oh man, you going after her?"

"I've got to do some follow-up."

"You know this is going I.S. That guy was Russian mob."

"He was Russian, we don't know mob. We can work this."

"We don't know mob, yeah right. Come on, we don't have to do anything. We file our IR's and move on, be glad about it. We'd never be able to put together anything on this."

Loewen said, "What are you talking about, there's plenty. Crime Scene hasn't even finished, we've got witnesses. We can't just walk away now, the only thing we know about the dead guy is his name. We're just assuming he's mob."

Price gave him a look, like why would you want to bother. "Well, we got his Russian name and the fact that he got his head shot off waiting for a light to change. No argument, not even a scratch on his brand new Lincoln Navigator, which we're going to find out was stolen in Edmonton. Maybe he was a doctor back in Moscow, but over here, he's the mob."

"So that's why we should keep going."

"Going? Going where? Ten witnesses can't agree what kind of car it was five feet in front of them."

"It was a Volvo s80, midnight blue. You know it and I know it."

"What about the ones said it was a Lexus? Or a Honda?"

"Come on, we've got to be able to get something. Hit a guy in the middle of the day on a busy street?"

"I doubt that was the plan. They just saw their chance and took it."

"Okay, that's it. So this is my chance."

"What?" Price turned sideways a little. He couldn't believe this guy.

Loewen finished his dog. "Come on, when is Maureen getting back?" Price's partner, Maureen McKeon, was off on maternity leave. He told Loewen she'd been off a month and she was taking six, wouldn't be back till September.

"Okay, so this is a real chance for me. I've only got a few months to get noticed, go for a full-time transfer."

"Why you want to work homicide?"

Loewen looked at Price. So cool in his thousand dollar lightweight summer grey suit, baby blue shirt, and red-and-silver striped tie. His shades. Leather shoes. His whole demeanour, showing up on the scene, people freaked out, traffic backed up, uniforms running around everywhere, and he takes charge.

"Come on," Loewen said. "Homicide's where it's at."

Price chewed on his sausage, took his time, cool as always, before saying, "Guys killing their wives, sitting in the corner sobbing, drunk, when we get there. Wannabe gangbangers up in the jungle, think they're tough, shooting each other for shoes. We clean up the mess. It's not glamorous."

"Come on, I've been partnered with you for two days, we already got a Russian mob hit."

"If it is a mob hit, you think we'll get anywhere with it? Better to give it to the big boys, let the pony patrol take it."

"The fucking Mounties?"

"Task force."

Loewen was shaking his head up and down. "Now you're talking. Maybe we can get on the task force."

"Be what, gophers?"

"Look at this as what it is, man. This is a great opportunity, this guy getting whacked in the middle of King Street."

"Look at you," Price said. "Two days on the job, you're saying 'whacked.'"

"Two days in homicide, I've been on the job ten fucking years. I know chances like this don't come along every day."

Price walked back to the hot-dog cart and bought an iced tea. He waved the bottle at Loewen, offering him one, but he shook his head. Price came back to the car, leaned back on the hood, put one expensive leather shoe on the bumper. It was true, what Loewen was saying about opportunity. When Price had been on the force less than a year, working bullshit public relations jobs and standing next to the mayor every time a TV camera was on because he was black, they called it "Community Relations Officer," he had his first conversation with an inspector and changed his whole career path.

He was working a party at one of the hotels right behind City Hall. Big developers, the mayor, a bunch of city counsellors, the deputy chief and some inspectors. Most of them headed upstairs as soon as they could get away, to the top floor, where the hookers were stashed. By two in the morning, the press was gone and Price had had enough of showing off the force's cultural diversity, so he went to the City Hall parking garage across the street to smoke a joint and found Inspector Alistair Nichols.

The Inspector was so drunk he'd gotten about ten feet and slammed his Crown Vic into a post. Price found him sleeping with his face on the airbag, his pants around his ankles, and the girl nowhere to be seen. Inspector Alistair Nichols, so high up in the force he still had his Scottish accent, said, "There's a good lad," when Price pulled up his pants and helped him into an unmarked car and drove him home. Came back and got the Inspector's car to his brother-in-law's body shop. There wasn't much damage, and they charged some asshole lawyer for an airbag replacement, told him his wasn't working. The next day, Price took the totally repaired Crown Vic to the Glasgow Rangers Supporter's Club in Scarborough. No paperwork, no reports, nothing. Just Inspector Alistair Nichols looking out for him.

Since then, Price figured he did everything on his own. Made detective and was on his way. Still, when an opportunity presents itself, you gotta take a look. "I guess we could ask around a little."

"All right. You'll talk to Nichols, get us on the task force?"

"Slow down, man. We don't want to show up empty-handed, begging to be on the team. Maybe if we knew a little more about the dead guy."

"Now you're talking. I'll run him through CPIC, see what the computer has to say."

"No, hold up. I know a guy."

And Loewen thought, of course you do.

• • •

What Roxanne remembered, it was right after Boris Suliemanov tried to lease the first floor of the Toy Works that her Jeep was stolen. She was in the building late one night. The T1 lines had just been hooked up, she was making sure everything worked, got lost on the Internet, and when she came out the lot was empty. It was on a lease and fully insured, so she got another one, but it was still a pain.

Now she was trying to think if there was a way to work it. CityPulse 24 was still calling it road rage, all the anchors whining about what has our city become? It might just disappear, another unsolved homicide in a city with more and more unsolved homicides. She could call him up and say, "Hey, Boris, this is Roxanne Keyes, you tried to lease some space in the Toy Works building down on King? Remember, I didn't want a strip club in the lobby? Well, anyway, I saw you drive the getaway car in a hit yesterday and I wondered . . ."

What? What did she wonder? Would he just give her money? How much? How would it work? She promises not to go to the cops, and he pays her?

Because she really needed the money. Angus was tired of waiting. If she couldn't come up with something by the end of the month, he'd . . .

She remembered seeing Angus on a building site take on a guy twice his size. Angus said the guy was stealing from him. The guy was denying it, waving his arms around, shouting, and Angus wouldn't back down. All the other guys on the site were watching by then, and the guy says to him, "You calling me a liar?" trying to turn it around on him, and Angus just told the guy to get the fuck out and when the big moron wouldn't, Angus shoved him up against the side of the office trailer, almost knocked the thing off its blocks, and that's when Roxanne saw the hammer in his hand. She hadn't even seen him pick it up, he must have had it when he first confronted the guy. He smashed it against the side of the trailer, put a big fucking dent a couple of inches from the guy's head, and told him to get the fuck off his site. Then he just dropped the hammer and turned around, saw Roxanne. He kind of shrugged and they went into the dented office to look over some numbers.

Now he was just about done with her.

But Boris. This was a guy who drove a Volvo downtown and watched a guy get his head blown off. From the frying pan into the fire.

Then an image of Vince from the online porno place came into her head. She couldn't believe it, he was sexy all right, but it wasn't really the time. Then she realized what she was seeing was how calm he was. She could be that calm.

She got the vodka out of the freezer, in there beside a stack of Weight Watchers entrees and a tub of Chapman's ice cream — chocolate fudge — poured half a glass, added orange juice, and lit a cigarette. She looked out the windows of her condo at Lake Ontario, big and dark on one side, and downtown Toronto, steel and glass and all lit up on the other.

Maybe just run into him, like a coincidence. Meet him somewhere, say, "You look familiar," something like that. Feel him out, see if he remembered her.

Then she thought, what did he do after the Toy Works wouldn't lease to him? She remembered he said his club would be classy, upscale, very European, professional dancers. "International," he'd said.

Roxanne finished her drink and found the yellow pages in a cupboard under the sink in the kitchenette. She sat on a barstool at the breakfast nook and looked under "entertainment," and saw ads for belly dancers, Strip 'N' Tell, clowns, and Hollywood look-alikes. Flipping pages, she saw twenty or more full page ads for escorts and remembered something about most of the ads all being for the same place, a house on Coxwell, some guy and his wife who got arrested last year. Or else entirely new ones were already in the phone book.

She looked under clubs, and found the Blue Jays fan club and a bunch of tennis clubs, and then she looked under nightclubs. She found the Exotica Cabaret, Cheaters Tavern featuring Las Vegas style dancing, Treasures Nightclub, House of Lancaster, the Landing Strip, and Club International.

That would be Boris: Club International, Dixon Road. Looked like he'd opened up out by the airport. Roxanne thought maybe she'd stop by. Then what? Ask to see the owner? The manager? Look in the parking lot for a midnight blue Volvo s80? What if she found him?

What if he remembered her?

What if he'd seen her this afternoon?

That stopped her. Staring at her own reflection in the

condo's windows. It was possible. What if, while she'd been trying to figure out who he was, he'd been figuring out who she was. Thinking, that woman on the patio, I know I've seen her some place, but where? Going over everything. She wondered how long she'd had the skirt she was wearing, and the blouse, the Dior. No, it was new. So was her hair, shorter than it had ever been and a lot blonder.

But he'd looked right at her.

Say it would take him a while to realize she wasn't a stripper. Then he'd go over the professional women he'd met. That's what she was, and he probably hadn't met that many. Would the breweries send a female rep to strip clubs? Maybe, they might like that better.

Maybe he'd come looking for her. Could she play it cool like Vince would? Could she say, "Boris, hi, how've you been? I see you opened up near the airport. That's a much better location. I guess you don't get downtown much."

But if he did look her up, Roxanne wondered, would she play it cool so he wouldn't think she was a witness, or would she play it cool so that he'd know she was, but she could be reasonable?

Really, though, what could she do? Call the cops and say, "Oh, I remembered something. It turns out I know the guy who drove the getaway car?" It was possible, but it sounded lame. She didn't want to turn him in, but she had to have something on him.

The license plate.

Not the whole thing, but what if she could call the cop — what was his name, Loewen? — and say she remembered part of the license number.

He'd say, hey that's great.

Or maybe he'd say, just like that?

Or, isn't that lucky.

What did Oprah say, luck is a matter of preparation meeting opportunity?

So here's some opportunity.

• • •

Khozha said, "Do they all have those big fake tits?"

"If they don't, they're hitting me up to pay for them."

Boris closed the door of the safe in the floor of his office. There wasn't really anything in it, a little walking-around money, maybe twenty grand, but enough to let someone think he'd found the cash. Boris knew no one would ever find the other safe, the real safe, in the change-room behind the lockers, still he was pissed fucking Anzor had been such trouble. Made him nervous, that much cash just sitting there.

Khozha'd come out of the VIP room. The real VIP room, with the big couch and the lock on the door. This was his third girl since he'd said he wanted to go straight to the airport. Boris couldn't believe the old man could get it up that many times. Later, he'd ask the girls what he did in there.

"Why don't you take two of them in there at the same time," Boris said. "We won't have this line-up."

Khozha sat down on the couch across from the desk and said, "And all those fucking studs; navels, eyebrows, fucking studs all over their cunts, their nipples, their faces. Tongues."

Boris said, "That can be good, on the tongue."

"They gonna leak out all these holes."

"They dance naked, they have to decorate themselves somehow."

"And the fucking tattoos. Teddy bears and flowers and barbed wire and Chink writing. What's with the Chink?"

Boris said, "I don't know, it's spiritual or something." Then he said, "There's only a couple more flights tonight. You ready?"

"That one with the really short hair, the crew cut, and the redhead? They go together?"

Boris said, "If you want."

Khozha said, "Yes, I want," as he stood up.

The office door opened and a big guy walked in. Over six feet, close to 300 pounds, he looked like a biker trying to look straight in his blue suit and white shirt. He still had his long hair in a ponytail, though, and there were tats on his hands, a spider web and a knife dripping blood.

Boris said, "Khozha, this is Henri, my manager." He said it the French way, "On-ree," and the big guy stuck out his hand to shake.

Khozha turned and opened the door to the VIP room. He said, "And bring me another bottle."

Boris watched the door close, and didn't want to look at Henri. He moved some papers on his desk and said, "The redhead, what's her name? Angie, and GI Jane. Send them in together."

Henri said, "He's going through every girl we got, your uncle."

"Yeah, he is."

"I thought he was going straight to the airport." Not a question, the way Henri said it.

Boris said, "He likes my club," letting a little pride show, finally looking up at Henri, waiting for him to say it was his club, too, or some shit like that. Before Boris took it over, the Club International was a sleazy tittie bar called the Galaxie run by Henri and his biker buddies. The chicks were always stoned, and had plenty of attitude. The customers were delivery drivers and raghead cabbies and security guards from the airport. Didn't even have a VIP lounge.

Now the place was classy. Two main stages, flat screen TV's running top European skin flicks, and Internet connections in the booths. The clientele was a lot more upscale businessmen — not just guys waiting for flights, a lot of local office guys, regulars. Boris brought in chicks from Poland, Slovakia, Hungary, Romania, all over eastern Europe, good-looking white chicks who knew what their job was and were good at it.

Henri said, "You didn't have to bring him in, you know."

There it was, Boris figured. Henri had it so good he didn't like it. It confused him. He stayed on as the manager, ten per cent owner, booked the girls, kept them in line, and with what Boris paid him plus dealing speed and weed, he made more than he ever had in his life. Still, he was pissed off all the time.

"I need a new car."

"I know, fuck, it was all over the fucking TV. Middle of fucking King Street."

Henri had wanted to do it. Said he could take care of that prick bastard Anzor and be done with it. That's what Boris couldn't figure. Here was Henri in his thousand dollar suit, taking care of business, paying fucking taxes he was so clean, and he *wanted* to go and pop some prick when he didn't have to.

"Saw a chance, took it."

"Guy from fucking New York, what does he care?"

What do *you* care, Boris thought, but he shrugged it off. "I want another Volvo, or an Audi."

was young and trying to make an honest living as a street dealer, he sees one of those trucks driving down the street, guy inside ringing a bell, that sharpens knives."

"We don't get them much on condo row," Loewen said.

"You missing out, they do a great job. Anyway, Willis here, being the criminal mastermind that he is, figures this guy drives around all day, people pay him in cash, so there's plenty in the truck. Hard to find a place has more than fifty bucks in the till these days, right, Willis?"

"This Anzor, he had a lot of enemies," Willis said.

"So Willis gets himself a dull knife and jumps in the back of the truck. Says to the old guy, 'Give me all your money.' That what you said, Willis?"

"Fuck you, I'm not telling you shit now."

Loewen was already starting to laugh.

"Old Stanislaw Woceski, he pulled out a cleaver and cut Willis's hand clean off."

"I guess," Loewen said, "he had some good sharp knives in that truck."

"That came as a bit of a surprise to the genius here."

"Knife that sharp, though," Loewen said, "couldn't they get the hand back on?"

"You'd think, wouldn't you? But it fell out of the truck and a dog got it."

"Fuck you both. This Anzor, gets his head blown off in the middle of the fucking day on King Street, for fuck's sake. Do you want to know why or not?"

"Someone told you why?" Loewen said.

"No one told me, asshole. I know why."

Loewen grabbed his one good hand and pulled the fingers back hard.

"Ow, motherfucker, let go."

Loewen kept up the pressure. "You be nice, Willis."

"It's on the way already."

Boris nodded, pleased. He couldn't tell about this Henri. Here he was doing everything right, but talking like a hotshot. Maybe he was all talk. Maybe he was glad they brought in Khozha. Really, though, Boris thought, what the fuck do I care? Another year, have a few legit businesses going, and dump this club right back in his fat fucking lap.

• • •

Price swaggered into the bar on Queen West, way past the trendy part of Queen, way out in Parkdale. Crackdale. The place was almost empty, one strung-out hooker in a booth with a skinny guy covered in tattoos, some U of T

"Ow." He looked at Price. "This what you teaching them now?"

Price said, "What do you know about Anzor?"

"Let go my fucking arm."

"What do you know about Anzor?"

"Ow. Fuck. He's an agent, he brings in dancers from Europe for the tittie bars."

"Just dancers?"

"And hookers. Natashas."

"Teenagers."

"Picks them up in Bosnia, or wherever the fuck. Tells them they're going to be nannies. Puts them to work in massage parlours and trick pads."

"What else?"

"Ow. Fuck. Deals a little speed and some heroin."

Loewen kept on pulling the fingers back and Price kept nodding.

"He gets his supply from the bikers. You know, the mayor's friends? But word got out he was moving more than they were supplying him."

"We got a new mayor now. And word got out, did it?" Price said.

Loewen said, "It wasn't bikers who killed him, though."

Price pulled his sunglasses down on his nose and stared at Loewen.

Willis said, "I know that, asshole." He looked at Price, "Where'd you find the rocket scientist?"

Loewen let go, and Willis pulled his hand right back to his chest, draping his stump over it for comfort.

"Look, Price, if I know he's doing this shit, lots of people know. Some of the clubs who used his girls kept them after their work visas ran out, set them up as whores.

He got a piece of that. And I heard something about him taking big bags of cash with him when he went to Moscow to get more chicks."

"So he was skimming from what he laundered?"

"What I'm saying. He had a lot of enemies."

Loewen started to reach for Willis' hand again, but he pulled away.

"If all you got is thug man, you not going far. You got to learn some new technique."

Loewen took his hand again and pulled the fingers back. "Whatever the situation demands."

"Hey man, I can't do all your fucking work."

Price said, okay, that's good and as they were leaving, Loewen turned back to the table and said, "They ever find the dog?"

Willis didn't look at him, and Price said, "Tell him."

Willis said, "It was my own fucking dog."

"He brought home, what? The little finger and part of the thumb?"

"You're so fucking funny."

Loewen said, "So now, when you jack off, it always feels like your own hand, right?"

"So fucking funny."

Price looked at Loewen and rubbed his thumb over his fingers. Loewen dropped a twenty on the table as the waitress finally brought Willis his beer.

CHAPTER FOUR

MADONNA BLASTED OUT of the Jeep's stereo. Pushing her over the borderline. Roxanne sang along, tapping the steering wheel with both hands, the red glow of her cigarette bouncing in rhythm. So long ago, this song. Fourteen, living with her mother in the Masonettes, the public housing up by the DVP and the 401, hating every minute of it. Sent to school, with all those fucking snobs across the overpass at George S. Fucking Henry High School, because she was so smart, instead of Vic Park, the tech school with the rest of the welfare kids. But it's not like she could go on the ski trips to Mont Tremblant, and then all the Masie kids hated her. And everything she saw or read told her what was wrong with her: too fat, hair too dry, boobs too small, or the wrong shape, or some shit, and her attitude. Holy shit, she heard a lot about her poor attitude, young lady.

Then she saw Madonna.

Not perfect, she doesn't look like one of those stick-figure models always pouting and looking sad, or like they're too fucking tired to walk to the fridge. Madonna had her shit together, she was doing things and she liked herself. Push me over the borderline. Roxanne didn't even know that song was about an orgasm till years later, she just knew something was going on. People were always saying Madonna's a slut or a whore.

Roxanne got that a lot, too. Whore. High school assholes following her around singing that song about the hooker, about you don't have to sell your body to the night. Roxanne. Jesus, what was her mother thinking? But she knew people were just scared of Madonna because she didn't need anyone else to make her happy. She does whatever she wants. She makes her own luck.

Roxanne hadn't listened to that first Madonna CD since she was wearing a big crucifix on a gold chain, a dozen bracelets and crop tops, and getting kicked out of that snob school and she stole it from the CD store in Fairview Mall. But as she turned her Jeep off the 401 and onto Airport Road, she sang along and wondered. Would Boris Suliemanov be her lucky star? Could he take her far?

• • •

The one with the crew cut, Amelie, but she called herself Martina — all the Czech girls did — came out of the lounge, naked except for her high heels and white tennis socks, walked up to Boris at the bar and said, "You uncle," and shook her head. She asked the bartender for water, and the nice Canadian girl in the white shirt and black vest screwed off the top and handed her the bottle.

Boris said, "He's leaving soon."

"Soon? I don't think so." No matter what their first

language was, most of the eastern European girls spoke a little Russian, but Boris always had them speak English. Better to be able to talk to the customers.

"What does he do in there?"

Amelie drank from the water bottle and said, "What do you think he does?"

"That's four times tonight."

"He watches a lot. He's always with the orders, bossy. Kiss her more, now you go on top, turn around. Is hard to keep up."

Boris nodded, looking around, the place half full on a Wednesday night. He was proud of his club, he just wished it actually made money. Even paying the European chicks practically nothing — they got such good tips and he knew they skimmed more than he should let them — and with such markups on the booze, the place was still no cash cow.

Amelie said, "He wants something to eat."

"What?"

"How do I know? He say to get him something." She turned around and walked back to the VIP room.

Boris was shaking his head when Henri came up to the bar and asked, "What's wrong now?"

"Nothing, what could be wrong?"

Henri looked at him, knowing Boris was pissed off about something but let it slide. He said, "Your new car's here."

"Volvo?"

"Saab."

Boris nodded, pleased, and Henri said, "I don't know why you've got such a hard-on for Swedish cars," and Boris told him it was a northern thing, snow and ice like back home.

"Yeah," Henri said, "we got plenty of snow and ice here," but Boris smirked at that, like you don't know snow.

Henri said, "No reason to drive a piece of shit box on wheels. You want, I could get you a Range Rover or a Jag."

They walked through the club, and Boris saw Amelie come out of the VIP room and motion to Marie-Claire, one of the few Canadian dancers, to go back in with her.

Boris stopped at the small bar and told the girl working there to get a pizza for Khozha.

• • •

Roxanne was about to leave. Her window was halfway down, and she flicked her cigarette out. She'd seen the Volvo; it was definitely the same car. She wrote down the license plate and she had her hand on her key ready to start the Jeep, when a black BMW pulled into the lot. It stopped right behind the Volvo, blocking it in next to the dumpster, where it was in the loading zone in front of the no parking sign. The door opened, and loud hip hop pounded out into the quiet lot and a young black guy, clean cut with short hair, got out. Then a yellow Saab convertible pulled in behind the Beamer, and another black guy got out, this one with long dreads, bright yellow. Roxanne watched them walk around the Volvo, saying a couple things to each other, nodding. These were young guys, early twenties at most, but very serious.

Roxanne let go of her key when the side door to the club opened — not the door the customers would use, there was no handle on the outside of this one — and Boris Suliemanov came out. There was a big guy with him, a bouncer, but wearing a nicer suit than most bouncers.

Boris said something, and one of the black guys closed the Beamer's door and the lot was quiet again.

The black guys lit cigarettes, bright white against their dark skin, and the bouncer had one of those little cigars. Boris walked around the Saab, not looking too happy. He touched the rag top and motioned with his hands.

The black guys shrugged. They didn't seem to give a shit one way or another what Boris had to say. The one who drove the Saab handed Boris the keys, and the other one jumped back into the Beamer and pulled out of the lot. Then the one who drove the Saab got into the Volvo and started to back it out. Boris stopped him before he took off and opened the passenger door.

Roxanne saw the light come on inside the car, saw Boris open the glove compartment and take something out. The door closed, the light went out, and the black guy drove off in the Volvo.

The bouncer was still holding the door of the club open, and when Boris got close to it, under the light, Roxanne saw him put the gun in the inside pocket of his suit jacket.

She started her Jeep.

Madonna blared from the stereo: "Burnin Up." The window still down.

Boris looked over.

Shit.

Roxanne put the Jeep in gear and took off, not looking anywhere near Boris.

She was on the 427 heading south before she started to breathe again. She could feel her heart pounding hard, Madonna's voice still blasting, singing about you don't even know I'm alive. Yeah right, Roxanne thought, let's fucking hope not.

• • •

Boris said, "Did you see that chick?"

"What chick?"

"In the parking lot, in the Jeep. She drove away when we came back inside."

Henri shook his head, didn't see a thing. He said, "What's wrong with a convertible?"

They were walking back through the club, the place almost empty now, and the redhead, Angie, stopped them. She said, "I finish now, my shift over."

Boris looked at Henri who said, "Yeah, so, go home."

She said to Boris, "You uncle — he say no leave."

"Fuck him. You want to go, go."

She turned on her high heels and walked to the change room.

In the office Henri said, "I could have got someone to handle it for you."

Boris wondered why he wouldn't drop it. "It's done."

"We could have picked this asshole up and dumped him in fucking Lake Ontario. They never would have found him."

Boris held his hand up for Henri to be quiet. He hated talking so openly about business. And, he thought, you would have shot him same as Khozha did, or a drive by. It's on the news all the time, fucking bikers acting like it's the Old West. Or Moscow.

Boris said, "You think anyone in this city cares about some Russian pimp got killed? They calling it road rage for fuck's sake. It'll be off the news tomorrow."

"I hope so."

"What do you care? It got done, you didn't have to be involved."

"You think I'm fucking scared to do it?"

Boris was sitting behind his desk drinking vodka straight up and thought, is that it? Always trying to prove he's so tough, thinking that's why the bikers will always be run by the real mob, always be nothing but foot soldiers. They can't put business first, always so worried about their fucking rep, their tough-guy look. Boris looked Henri in the eye and waited.

Henri shrugged, like he didn't really care.

Boris said, "She looked like a professional."

"A pro? You mean a hooker?"

"No," Boris said, "I don't mean a prostitute." That's all they know about, these bikers, hookers and strippers. "I mean a professional woman, like a lawyer or a doctor. No, not a doctor."

Henri didn't care. "Some chick thinks she's going to be a dancer, she comes and looks the place over, gets scared, and leaves. What do you care?"

"I don't. Not at all." Boris waved his hand dismissing the idea, but really he was sure he'd seen her before, and not that long ago. He knew she wasn't a dancer. He'd spoken to her, he knew it, he could hear her voice. She could be a cop, he thought, they had all kinds in this country, you could never tell. Women, men, even niggers. They look like bikers and bankers. They speak Chinese and Italian and Russian.

He remembered this woman, whoever she was, talking about something she knew a lot about. Confident, in control.

Boris was tired. A long day. Another long day. And now Khozha still here, which means he's going to spend the night and probably sleep half the day tomorrow, and not be on a plane till after six. The good news, he'd cleared up the shit with Anzor. The bad news, someone was going to have to do Anzor's job. He looked at Henri.

"How many pieces have they got?"

"You mean cars? Ten, twelve." Boris held up his hand and Henri said, "For fuck's sake, this place isn't bugged."

"Don't take chances."

"That's right, my nephew never takes chances, always plays it safe," Khozha said, coming into the office and slumping on the couch next to Henri. "That's why he's such a big success in Canada. Three years, and he has this pisspot club doesn't make any money, and some jigs stealing cars probably make more than he does."

"Where's a Russian learn to talk like that?" Henri said, "Jigs?"

"Why, what you call them here?" Khozha said, slurring the words, the vodka finally getting to him. "African Canadians?"

Boris said, "Come on, I got you a room at the Constellation."

"I'm not staying with you, Biba? Don't you have a villa?"

Boris wondered again why he'd brought Khozha in. He'd actually thought he was doing the old man a favour. Well, and he was so totally expendable. He told him the hotel would be more comfortable, have room service, he could sleep in and then go right to the airport.

"Bring the redhead," Khozha said. He looked at Henri. "I like to wake up with a blow job."

Boris said, "She went home."

Khozha stared at him, big drunken eyes looking like Rodney Dangerfield, not getting no respect. "I told her to fucking stay."

"I sent her home. You want, we'll send someone over in the morning."

"I want you to send someone with me now."

Boris shook his head, and then nodded to Henri. "Can you get someone to tuck in my uncle?"

"You *asking* him?" Khozha said getting to his feet, swaying, almost falling over. "You fucking tell him what to do. No wonder these fucking lumberjacks don't respect you."

Henri was on his feet pounding his finger into Khozha's chest, saying, "Shut up, old man, I'll fucking mess you up."

"Listen to big ape." Khozha turned away, not even noticing the finger, and said to Boris, "Let's go, Biba."

Boris stood up. Shit, he was so tired.

• • •

Amelie and Khozha were in the back seat of the Saab, Khozha running his hands over her crew cut, telling her he liked it so short, it would never get in the way. He asked her about the tattoo on her neck, the Chink writing, and she told him it meant strength.

In the front seat Boris felt like a chauffeur, a fucking driver. He imagined himself in a monkey suit with a stupid-looking hat. Never should have brought in Khozha. Should have let Henri take care of it. Except that lately, he was getting worried that he looked exposed, especially to Henri and his biker pals, like a guy cut loose, on his own. Like what he was. And asshole Anzor telling everyone Boris was soft, weak, couldn't back it up. He wanted it to look like he was part of an organization. He couldn't do anything about what he was. Since his brother got himself killed in Moscow, Boris really was out on his own, but calling in Khozha from New York made it look like he was still plugged-in, still connected to something big.

So now the asshole Anzor was gone. It looked good on the news, like Boris could do anything he wanted, in the middle of the fucking day. Except now he was getting ready to ship a dozen cars to Latvia and he had no way to deposit the money. Forty grand a car, half up front. Before, Anzor would have taken the cash and deposited it in a friendly bank in Bosnia while he was getting more girls. It would have made its way around the world and ended up in Boris's account, nice and clean.

Fuck. They'll have all the cars by the end of the weekend, ready to go.

Boris pulled out of the parking lot and looked at the empty space the Jeep had been in. She could be anything, that woman.

If only he could remember.

• • •

Roxanne couldn't figure out why she was so freaked out by the gun. She'd seen it before — hell, she saw it used to blow a guy's head off not twelve hours ago. But it was different in the parking lot. It was definitely Boris Suliemanov, taking it out of the glove compartment of the Volvo, so casual. Dropping it in his pocket and looking over at her when she started the Jeep. The stereo so loud.

The fact that it wasn't a big deal made it a big deal. Like he used one all the time. So, Roxanne figured, okay, forget it, just drop it, these guys are serious. Whatever they're into, there's nothing here for me, it's not worth it.

But it did feel like a rush, her heart pounding.

Like when she was eighteen years old and going out with Sammy. He'd pick her up at George S. Henry High in his Camaro and squeal the tires pulling out of the lot. It was even better when one of her asshole teachers was there, left in the dust. Then they'd pick up the "product" — actual cocaine, she'd never seen it before in her life — and make some deliveries. The T-top open, the stereo blasting Poison or Bon Jovi. Sometimes Sammy would do a couple of lines with one of his better customers, one of the Bay Street boys, or the lawyer. Sometimes they'd do it off Roxanne's stomach and her heart would just pound. One time, the Vietnamese girlfriend of a Bay Street boy did a line off Rox's stomach, then just pulled off her own top and laid one out between her perky breasts.

Yeah, Roxanne thought she was so cool. Or at least she finally thought she was alive, she could finally *feel* something.

Like she could feel something now.

Turning off Lake Shore onto Queen's Quay and into the parking garage under her condo building, she knew she didn't want to give it up. Overdrawn, credit cards maxed, she was never going to cut them up again, and Angus ready to do something drastic. She needed something big. But Boris?

I'm not a kid anymore, God. Not eighteen years old, thinking I'm cool.

Angus was pissed, but this little deal with VSF Online would keep her head above water for another month or two, and by then she'd have something else.

Anything else.

The next morning, she printed out the contract and drove over to the Toy Works.

• • •

Loewen said, "I heard Martin Sheen say that he feels more human when he comes to Canada, because we aren't all armed and dangerous and we don't shoot each other."

"You want to show him this," Price said. "Don't you?"

They were standing over the body of a dark-skinned guy, maybe twenty-five years old, four bullets in his chest, blood all over his unbuttoned silk shirt. Could be Latino, maybe Middle Eastern, hell, maybe even Tamil. Hard to tell with the blood all over him and Toronto being so multi-ethnic. Half an hour ago, the club was packed, more than a hundred people. Now the place was empty except for the dozen or so cops and crime scene people.

"Let him have a look, see we can shoot just as well."

"I don't know about that," Price said, "took four shots."

The place looked like everyone there had just beamed up. Nice leather jackets still over the backs of chairs, half-full glasses and beer bottles on the tables. Even the DJ and the wait staff were gone. Not a single witness of any kind.

"Look at the tat." Loewen shoved the dead guy's arm with his shoe. "S-Dawgs."

"Snow Dogs. 'Cause they import cocaine."

"And they export weed. You know Canada is now a marijuana-exporting nation."

"Impressive for a country with such a short growing season."

"Yeah, and with such expensive electricity for indoor growing."

Loewen took a couple of steps towards the back door of the club, now open, with crime scene guys going in and out. "So, they come in the back door, shoot him in front of all these nice people, and walk out. Probably another gang. Christie Boys around here, right?"

Price said, "Now you want to work a gang homicide?" and walked out the back door of the club.

Loewen followed. A few cops stood around the parking lot drinking Tim Hortons coffee.

Loewen said, "I'm only going to be here a while, I just want to clear one case."

"Yeah? Which one?"

Loewen thought he'd like it to be the one where there was at least one witness. One good-looking witness, Roxanne something. He'd call her in the morning.

Inspector Nichols stepped over the yellow tape and asked what they had.

Price said, "A tragedy. Young man cut down in the prime of his life."

Loewen couldn't even tell if he was joking or not. Nichols wasn't laughing, but he didn't look too broken up.

The detective and the inspector stepped away, and Loewen didn't know if he should follow or not. Shit, what a day. Then Price waved him over, saying, "This is Loewen. He's with me till McKeon gets back."

"Ah yes. Has she had the little tyke yet?"

"Couple of weeks ago. A boy, they call him Nathaniel."

Inspector Nichols nodded. Loewen thought the guy looked like he'd come from working in a bank. Two in the morning and he's wearing a clean suit, no wrinkles, shiny tie. And then Loewen wondered how much inspectors get paid.

He heard Price say something about the "other thing," they had.

"Our Russian friend," Nichols said, and nodded.

Loewen wanted to jump right in, say how they should keep it, work for a while, but he watched Price, looking like he was taking out smelly garbage, saying, "I guess it's going I.S."

Nichols shrugged. "The Intelligence Service is very busy."

"We did talk to a guy," Price said, "knew the deceased."

Loewen watched Price glance up at the Inspector, all casual like, and then look away again.

Nichols said, "Never hurts to have more information."

And Loewen thought, it's like these guys are talking in fucking code. First rule of police work: CYA. Cover. Your. Ass. Nobody says anything that can come back and bite them.

"Felt he was involved with some other Russians, but also some bikers."

Nichols nodding, interested, maybe, but not showing anything Loewen could make out.

Price saying, "The task force'll be interested in him."

Nichols: "No doubt."

Price: "Drugs involved, the Mounties will want to know."

Nichols: "Of course."

Price: "It is our city, still."

Nichols: "Certainly."

Price: "We could ask a few more people."

Nichols: "I suppose Mastriano and Dhaliwal could have a look into this."

Price: "He is Snow Dawgs. Ray knows them," meaning Rahim "Ray" Dhaliwal, another homicide detective a couple years older than Price who had worked the murder of a Christie Boy and his girlfriend a few months back. One of the Snow Dawgs shot the guy and threw the girlfriend off a tenth-storey balcony. Claimed she fell, said he was taking her home as a trophy, wouldn't hurt something that fine. Said to Dhaliwal, "Don't your people take home prize bitches from Kashmir?" Ray said he thanked the Gods the punk was a month past the Young Offenders Act.

Inspector Nichols said, "I'll see that copies of your reports get to the right people."

And then Price glanced at Loewen and he wanted to say, what? What the fuck are you talking about? But Price seemed pleased. He thought.

Then Nichols said, "Ah, here are our friends from the television." He put on a serious face before stepping into the light coming from the video camera.

Price stepped up beside Loewen and said, "Okay, you got your chance. Don't fuck it up now."

Right, Loewen thought, that's confidence.

Price said, "I know somebody we should talk to."

And Loewen thought, great, what now, a one-legged purse snatcher?

CHAPTER FIVE

Vince knew the guy wasn't going to get violent. No matter how much he was stomping around reception, threatening, pounding on the desk. Ella was just sitting there, staring at the pens the guy had knocked out of her mug, not making a move to pick them up, even though Vince knew it was driving her crazy.

The guy must have started yelling at Garry as soon as he got off the elevator, because he was backed right up against the wall, the big jerk pointing at him as Vince came into reception saying, "What the fuck's going on?"

The guy turned on him, and Vince knew everything would be okay. He'd seen this type way too often, used to scaring people smaller than he was, intimidating people in a nice office. He hadn't had to back it up since grade three.

The guy, trying hard to look in control but all red in the face said, "Like I told the faggot here, three months and we're still paying you, you said we were gonna be making thousands by now, you said —"

Vince cut him off. "What's your name?"

"Gord Shepherd. My girlfriend, Emily and me, we spent three grand on one of your fucking amateur sites, and we're still spending over a grand a month." The guy, Gord, was at least ten years younger than Vince and he was a lot bigger. Looked like he worked out a lot, and hadn't started to go to pot yet. The girlfriend was even younger, maybe twenty-one and kind of mousy, but with a good enough body in her tank top and miniskirt, what she probably thought of as dressed up. Vince saw them as rural, or from the further suburbs out past Brampton, Orangeville or something, making their way in the big city. Toronto's full of them, uneducated white kids who think the city is their birthright and don't understand how come all the foreigners have it so easy.

Vince didn't have much patience for them. If their parents sold the farm to some developer and now they had a shitty house in some subdivision full of Pakis, too bad.

He said, "What are you doing here, Gord?"

Gord balled his hand into a fist and said, "I want my fucking money back."

"Our money," the girlfriend said.

"How long have you had your site up?"

The elevator door opened, and the real estate woman got off. She stopped one step out of the elevator, looking around, seeing that she'd walked into the middle of something. Some big guy, like so many jerks she knew from hitting on her at the gym, standing in the middle of reception just looking for someone to punch, and everyone else standing around scared.

Everyone except Vince. He was walking right up to the

guy in his calm way, saying, "Gord, how long have you had the site up?"

Slam. Gord pounded his fist down on the reception desk. Ella jumped back, Garry moved closer to Roxanne, and Gord looked a lot more comfortable with people scared of him.

Except Vince was still as calm as ever. He said, "Gord? Over here," and got right in the guy's face, waited till he was looking at him before he said, "Which site is yours?"

"Sexy Sarah," the girlfriend said.

"Sexy Sarah. Well, we host hundreds of these sites, you know, so we can't keep track of all of them, but Garry here will be happy to look up your records, see how the memberships are coming. Emily here *is* plenty sexy." Vince looked at her, and she smiled and tried to look sexy.

"I want my fucking money back."

But Vince kept looking at Emily and said, "I'm sure when the members find you, they'll stay loyal. You are the real deal." Vince made it look like he could barely tear his eyes away from Emily, and looked over at Garry. "Why don't you get these people the intro package you and Suss put together?"

"We got that," Gord said.

The girlfriend said, "We followed it," and Vince nodded, so understanding, and said to her, "With all these amateur sites, anyone can put one up. It can take awhile to find a diamond in the rough."

She liked that. "Some of them are so skanky," she said. "We want it to be more classy."

With Emily talking details with Vince, he knew the scene was done.

Gord knew it, too. As soon as well-dressed Vince started talking nice to Emily, it was over. Gord knew that was how easy it was to get her to do just about anything, by telling her how sexy she was, pretending to listen to her. Show-off little bitch, that's how he talked her into starting the site in the first place.

All the tension in the room was gone now, and Ella started putting her pens back in the mug.

"Well," Vince said, "Emily here is a babe, so you just need to give it some time. An angle. Classy is good."

Emily said, "But maybe we need more . . . something."

"It's always good to have an angle," Vince said. He nodded, like the meeting was over, but then said, "You could add a little something, you know, something different. Do you have any friends who could join you?"

Gord said, "I don't know, man."

Vince could see right away that would be too much work for Gord. Making a quick buck off naked pictures of his girlfriend sounded easy, but now it was starting to look like work, and Gord wasn't interested in that. Vince figured only in this world's biggest hick town could a guy this thick even get this far, not having any idea it was all just because of where and when he was born.

Emily, though, seemed a lot more interested. She didn't want to give up on this that easy. Vince said to her, "Yeah, that market is pretty saturated." He looked like he was thinking about it. "There's a lot of good locations in town. You could stick with solo stuff, but take it further."

Gord didn't see the point, that was obvious, but Vince saw the look in Emily's eyes, the little bit of excitement.

She said, "The flashing pictures get a lot of hits."

"All right," Vince said, walking her to the elevator and pressing the button. "That's a good start. See where you can go with that." Gord was making his way to the elevator, still looking pissed off but not even knowing why anymore. "It's just like any small business," Vince said to him. "You have to give it enough time to get going. Remember, post pictures to plenty of bulletin boards and get onto as many webrings as you can. Have you contacted Carla Cox yet?"

The elevator door opened and Gord said, "That old broad in Montreal?"

"She's got the number one amateur site in the world. You want to know how it's done, she's the one to talk to. She works it."

Emily was smiling and nodding, back on course and ready to go. She said, "Thanks," and smiled at Vince as the elevator door closed.

• • •

"Just another day at the office?"

"Work, work, work."

"I really thought he was going to hit you."

Vince said, "So did I."

They were walking through the halls towards Vince's office, past a studio with fake moans coming out real loud.

"No you didn't," Roxanne said. "Not for a second."

Vince glanced over his shoulder, then turned into his office.

Roxanne sat in the chair across from the desk and watched Vince sit down. Like he owned the place, she was thinking, but of course, he did own the place.

She said, "You sure you don't want a new security system? I know a guy, can get you a deal," and thought again how there might be more to this guy with his Eddie Bauer casuals and his calm approach, which Roxanne was starting to realize didn't mean he was soft at all.

Now he was leaning back in the chair, putting one foot up on the desk and saying, "This isn't the same rate."

"It's the current rate."

"We agreed on the same rate as I have now."

"No, we agreed on the same rate the building is leasing out at now."

She watched him to see what he'd do. When she'd printed up the lease she thought she'd be able to get the new rate out of him. Now she wasn't sure at all.

It didn't look like he'd get all whiny or self-important, like pretty much every other tough-talking guy she did business with.

"No, this is bullshit and you know it." He dropped the file on his desk and looked at her, not pissed off, just not going to do it, and Roxanne thought, okay, this is different, this is straight up like we're equals, a couple of business professionals.

Still, she said, "But you need the space, this is still way cheaper than moving to a whole new building."

He said, "Don't bother, I'm not going to play. The old rate or nothing."

She liked him, liked the way he respected her and didn't bullshit with some story about cash flow and the bad economy, just told her the way it was. She said, "How did you know you could talk to that girl instead of the guy?"

"'Cause he's just an asshole, but she's into something and she likes it. She likes the attention. Same as all these amateur chicks. It's why they do it."

"I thought the boyfriends pimped them out."

She said it to see what his reaction would be to a nice white woman in a Donna Karan business suit talking like that, letting him know there was more to her.

"You think that moron's running the show? No, it's the girls, there's so many of them we can't keep up. They're like the buffalo before the white man. Coming in here in their PornStar baby tees, can't wait to start showing-off."

"Oh come on, they wear that stuff with irony." Still testing him, see if he knew what it meant.

He said, "You need money to have irony. You need a nice safety net of mommy and daddy's house in the burbs. These girls, it's for real. The boyfriends might talk them into it, or they might let the boyfriends think they talked them into it, but once they start making money and the emails start flowing in: 'You're so sexy,' 'You're so beautiful,' 'I love you.'" He shrugged.

"So you just prey on their low self-esteem."

"Yeah, I'm the bad guy here."

"You just see an opportunity to make an easy buck."

"I wish it was easy. There are over 60,000 amateur sites up now, more every day. You get five thousand hits a day, you think you're doing something, turns out that gets you about 1500 bucks a month. You have to update everyday, always have the latest software. It's a lot of work."

"You said they sell memberships. They must sell them pretty cheap."

"Most sites are really just click-through farms, a few free pictures then links to pay sites. They get a kickback for everybody they redirect, but it's pennies."

"It adds up to billions every year, though, doesn't it?"

"So they say, I don't know. Supposedly eighty to ninety per cent of all online transactions are porn. It's like any other business, though. The top five per cent make eighty percent of the money, the rest come and go. There's a big turnover, like selling real estate."

"Bored housewives, looking for something to do," Roxanne said. Sitting in that classroom taking the exam, she remembered them, wondering could they just as easily have set up a camera on top of their computer and played with themselves? Some of them, maybe. Would be a lot easier than hustling for listings.

"It's the same thing." Vince said, "People like Gord and Emily there, they try it for a few months, lose some money, and get out."

"But there's always more to take their place."

"One born every minute, the man said. Chance at easy money, and getting told how sexy you are."

Roxanne heard the door open and turned to see the black guy, Suss, standing there, saying, "Garry's ready with the numbers." This time his ballcap was burgundy, with a white M on the front, pulled low over his eyes.

"Okay, I'll be right there." Vince picked up the file and handed it to Roxanne. "The old rate."

"Sure. You want, I can bring it back in an hour. Give you a chance to cut a cheque."

"I'm going to be busy all day. Garry's making movies. Ten minutes each, high-speed download takes less than a minute. He's good, he went to film school. How about after work, around six?"

She told him, sure, and gave him a sexy smile and walked out slow, knowing how good her ass looked in the little plaid skirt.

And wondering about him.

• • •

Amelie opened the hotel room door wearing nothing but a red thong. She said to Boris, "You uncle, he's in shower," speaking English like Boris wanted, and walked back into the room.

Boris watched her in front of the TV, singing along to a Pink video while she put on earrings. The sun shining into the room glinted off the studs in her nipples and the crystal teardrop hanging from her belly button.

He said, "You get any sleep?" and she looked at him, rolling her eyes.

"He passed out as soon as we got here. But he woke up early."

The place had a nice view of downtown Toronto in the distance, the tall shiny buildings. The Royal Bank building, TD Canada Trust, Scotiabank — they were all banks — the Tower sticking up out of the bunch. Everything looked so new, Boris thought, like a fresh start. No history. That's what he liked about Toronto, that and all those banks so eager to take his money, no matter where it came from. He'd slept well himself, and was anxious to get Khozha to the airport and get back to work. It was a relief Anzor was gone, that'd take some pressure off, but someone still had to do Anzor's job, and Boris really didn't know who that would be.

Amelie pulled on a white T-shirt and picked up her jeans from the bed. Boris watched her, noticing only one bed had been slept in, and started to wonder if she actually liked Khozha.

"If you want," he said, "you can take today off."

"Is okay." She pulled on her jeans and sat down on the bed, looking back at the TV.

Before Boris could say anything else, his cell phone rang and he started talking to his mother. Or really, he listened and his mother complained.

While she was going on about the rude people in her

building, and how all the kids were stealing from her and the people in the butcher shop were so stupid, they couldn't understand the simplest things, Khozha came out of the bathroom.

Boris said, "Yes, mama," and nodded at Khozha, looking for some understanding.

Khozha was already dressed, wearing nice pants and a clean white shirt, clean-shaven and looking years younger than he was. He winked at Boris and threw his shaving kit in his bag. He was smiling, rubbing his hands together, and he stood in front of Amelie and said to her in Russian, "You eat yet? Order something."

Boris was going to pick up a donut in the departures lounge, he waved at Khozha. "So, he's an idiot, just ignore him. Ma, I'm telling you," he said into his phone. In Moscow, his mother had spoken fluent English, and French, but now in Canada, she refused. Boris shook his head, holding the phone away from his ear, looking at Khozha and Amelie.

Khozha was looking at him now, serious.

"Okay, ma, yeah, I hear you. Okay." Man, she could go on forever, he thought. Everything was wrong, everything a problem. "Yeah, okay. I'll call you later." He flipped the phone closed and said, "We don't have a lot of time till your flight, let's go."

But Khozha wasn't going anywhere. He said, "How is your mother?"

"Fine, she's fine. Come on."

"There's no problem?"

"No, no problem, let's go."

But Khozha looked at Amelie, gave her a knowing look like they knew something was wrong, and why wasn't Boris telling them. "Sounds like something's wrong, Biba."

"She just doesn't like it here, this city. She's homesick. Everything's a problem."

"What's the problem now?"

"Now? Always. Can't get decent food, everything's too far, everything's too expensive. When she first came over, I bought her a place near here, but it was too far from everything. I don't even know what *everything* she's talking about, all she does is sit in the house and watch TV. Now, suddenly, she's Jewish again, I never heard her mention it my whole life, now she wants to go to temple, so I buy her a place on Bathurst, two blocks from a synagogue. Then that's no good, those people are such snobs, so she finds a temple with people who speak Russian, okay? So I buy her *another* condo, right on the fucking lake, costs a fortune, and all she does is complain."

"Your mother is a strong woman, Boris."

He'd never heard Khozha say anything about his mother before, and he'd never called him Boris. What was going on? Even Amelie was paying more attention, looking at Khozha, seeing something was happening.

"Yes, she's very strong, she's just homesick. And there was an idiot in the park."

"What idiot?"

Boris knew he shouldn't have gotten specific, he should have just left it at homesick. He could see the flight leaving in his head, and knew it would be another hour and a half till the next one.

"She walks on the beach, there's a boardwalk and parks. It's nice, you know, should make her happy." He shrugged. "People walk their dogs, they let them off the leash, they chase squirrels."

"What happened?" Khozha wanting to get to the point.

"Mama says they shit everywhere, she doesn't like that,

walking in a dog's toilet, she says. People are supposed to pick up the shit, you know? So, this morning, there's a bunch of people standing around drinking coffee, the dogs run everywhere, and Ma tells one of them his dog just took a shit and he should pick it up."

"Yeah, so?"

"So the guy says to Ma, 'Fuck off, I'll pick it up, shove it up *your* ass.'"

Khozha was coming around the bed now, saying, "You let someone talk like that to your mother?"

"So he's an idiot, so what? Fuck him, just let it go, you know? We don't start trouble here."

"We didn't start it."

"Khozha, we got a chance here, okay. We got a real opportunity to make something. We can't shit it away on assholes."

"Yeah, okay, I see what you mean." Khozha was nodding like he understood, but Boris knew he didn't. Even Amelie on the bed looked a little worried, like, what was he going to do?

"Let's go see your mother."

Fuck, Boris thought. He said, "You can still catch your flight."

Khozha said to Amelie, "Come on, Biba will drop you at home." He turned to Boris. "I need a car."

"No, you have to get on the plane."

"Boris, come on, I want to go home, you know that. I hate this fucking city, always trying so hard to be something it's not. But I haven't seen your mother since your father's funeral. I feel bad I didn't go to Mikhail's, but you know, I can't go to Moscow."

Yeah right, Boris thought, you don't feel bad about a fucking thing, all smug and pretend-innocent.

Amelie was pissed off too, looking like a jealous girlfriend.

Boris couldn't see a way out. "We'll go to the club," he said. "Henri will get you a car."

Pulling out of the parking lot behind the hotel onto Dixon Road, a plane took off right over their heads. Boris watching it go, up into the clear blue sky, the sun shining on its metal belly, a beautiful sight, thinking, Fuck, Khozha should be on that goddamned plane.

"Stop."

Boris hit the brake hard. He'd just about hit a Jeep. A black Liberty with the four lights across the top, just like the one he'd seen the woman driving last night. A fat bald guy was driving this one, and he gave Boris the finger as he pulled a U, heading back towards the hotel. Boris stared after him, and saw a huge billboard with a man's face on it and a slogan, something about meeting all your leasing needs.

And then Boris knew where he'd seen the woman in the Jeep. Where he'd talked to her a couple of years ago. Two blocks from the fucking Starbucks, where she'd been sitting on the patio watching Uncle Khozha shoot Anzor in the face yesterday afternoon.

The same woman who was in the parking lot of his club last night.

The real estate lady. He still had her card in his desk.

• • •

Roxanne parked on Kingston Road and saw how much the neighbourhood had changed in only a couple of years. The old Italian grocery store was gone, and another building she couldn't even remember was gone and condos were going up. North Beach, or Upper Beach they called them, and she thought, Shit, real estate agents will call something miles away "the Beaches" in Toronto. She didn't even understand why. It was an okay draw if you were pushing a baby stroller or walking a dog, but it was no place to live if you were young and single. Even if the condo ads all had sexy people playing volleyball on the beach. They all drove in from downtown.

Now a few new restaurants looked okay, and a bar called Paddy O'Farrels had a few tables and chairs on the sidewalk they were calling a patio. The junk stores were calling themselves Antique Boutiques or even Folk Art Galleries, but at two o'clock in the afternoon, there wasn't much pedestrian traffic.

Roxanne walked into The Feathers, a holdout from the time when the whole neighbourhood was working-class WASP. English beers on tap, pictures of Scotland on the walls, and 300 different kinds of single malt on the menu. The menu brought to you by one of the cast of *Coronation Street*. Some of the people inside had changed in the last fifty years. There was what looked like a middle-aged softball team eating chicken wings at the bar, talking loudly and drinking Blue Light out of bottles. Most of the people, though, could have been sitting in their local in Paisley. There was even a soccer game on the TV.

Angus waved Roxanne over to his table in the corner. He was by himself.

"Where's Giselle?"

"I don't know anyone by that name," he said.

"You mean your wife doesn't know."

The waitress came over with a menu but Angus waved it off. "You're no' eating are you?"

"Glenlivet."

"And another one here," Angus said, and finished off his shot.

Roxanne said, "The neighbourhood's really changing."

"About bloody time. Hasn't been a build here in fifty years."

"All the houses are getting renovated, though."

"Nickel and dime. No, now there's finally some real buildings going up."

"You getting any of them?"

"Some."

The waitress brought their drinks and left without saying anything.

Roxanne looked at Angus and didn't see anything, the guy always so cagey and secretive, as if small talk was too much. Never saying anything about his business.

"And a lot of condos," Roxanne said.

"Aye, like the last time. The go-go eighties. You were too young."

Roxanne took a drink of her Scotch, thinking, story of my life: wrong place, wrong time.

"But then the bottom fell out," she said. "Fast. Lot of people lost money."

"Lot of people made money."

She noticed how his accent floated in an out, depending on his mood. How it got classier depending on the company. She knew if she spent a night with him and his Glasgow drinking buddies, she wouldn't be able to understand him after the second round.

"I got something from the Toy Works."

Smiling now, Angus held up his glass. "The movie man came through?"

"No."

"No?"

"He won't say yes, but he won't say no. I just leased out the rest of the third floor."

"At the current rate?"

"At the original rate, nineteen-fifty."

"That's no' much."

"Three full floors are leased now, only four and five left."

"We were supposed to be fully leased by now."

Roxanne knew she couldn't bullshit him, give him a lot of crap about high-tech bubbles bursting and economic slowdowns. He was just looking at her, waiting.

She really didn't know what he'd do if she said that was it. She was out of leads, out of chances. Giving up her Jeep and selling her condo, she could buy another couple of months, but it would be digging such a hole she'd never get back out. She'd never get another chance.

She said, "I've got something else."

"Oh."

"Yeah," thinking, this is it. And feeling her heart beat. "You remember there was a guy, a Russian, wanted to lease out the first floor for a strip club."

Angus nodded, looking interested. "That's right, maybe some office space, too."

"Yeah." She'd forgotten about the office space, he had some other businesses he said, he might want to put in the same building. Some kind of booking agency for the European strippers and something . . . shit, she wished she could remember. "That's right. Well, I saw him yesterday and he's still interested in the office space."

"You saw him?"

"Yeah." She could feel it now, the back of her neck, getting all twitchy. She sipped her Scotch and tried to stare down Angus, but he always knew.

"You know I want my money."

"Yeah."

"But you be careful."

"Sure, right, it's just some office space," she was trying hard to be casual but Angus held up his hand.

"Don't bullshit me, Roxanne."

"What? You think I'd get involved with Russian gangsters?"

"Who cares where they're from."

She drank some more Scotch, warm going down, smooth, but she wasn't getting any of that light-headed feeling. "I'm just going to lease him some space."

"Right. You remember that."

"Sure."

Then Angus leaned in a little close and said, "I know you will. You can take care of yourself, can't you?"

"Sure."

He nodded. "But a little more office space isn't really going to help out our cash flow problem."

"I don't know how much he wants. It could be a lot."

"How much are you leasing it for now?"

Shit, she thought, I'm not leasing it at all. "We're getting nineteen-fifty a square foot."

"So, say twenty bucks. What's he looking at, 5000 feet?"

Roxanne nodded, might as well agree seeing as how the Russian guy doesn't even know he's looking at any.

"So that's a hundred grand. Will he go for twenty-five?"

"Maybe."

Angus was nodding, working something out in his head, trying to decide. Roxanne wanted to rush him — what is it, what are you working on? But she waited. Finished her drink and waited.

"So, maybe you could write up a lease for fifteen dollars a square foot."

"I'm sure he'd go for that." She was confident, thinking it was a great deal for the building, if you were actually looking to rent some space.

"No' for him. His says twenty-five." He looked at her moving his finger back and forth between them. "Mine says fifteen."

"So, fifty thousand difference."

"A year."

"Yeah, or a little over four grand a month."

"That comes to me."

Now Roxanne was nodding. "In cash?"

"Cash."

That'd be easy enough — deposit the Russian's cheque into the company account, then take out four grand and give it to Angus. If that'd make him happy, fine. It was better than getting her head caved in with a hammer, or whatever else Angus came up with. She was always glad he never made any suggestions about how she could work it off, not that he ever really paid for pussy, but he knew plenty of guys who did. Four grand a month worth, though, that would be a lot of work. And when would it end? He never said anything about a total, about any debt being paid off. In fact, Roxanne never knew how much Angus had actually put into the Toy Works. All she knew was that she'd made a lot of promises about leasing out the whole building at thirty bucks a square foot and hadn't come close. Now she was going to be on the hook forever.

Fucking Angus, really was the Scottish mob.

"Okay," she said. "I'll talk to him."

"Let's have another round, then." He waved the waitress over.

Chapter Six

Khozha took the Saab south on the 427. All these expressways with numbers, 401, 403, 407 — which was the toll road, owned by some private company, they couldn't even get away with that in Russia — raised up over the streets but still packed with traffic. He drove to the very end of the Gardiner Expressway, just like Biba said, and onto Lake Shore. If there was a lake nearby, you couldn't tell, just old factories, a power plant, sewage treatment plant, the stench was everywhere, and a huge smokestack.

But then, just after the Tim Hortons and the Burger King, across from the back doors of the postal sorting warehouse, Khozha saw the sailboat masts in the little bay. Then, past the parking lot — this fucking city always put the cars first — there was a beach.

Sand, lifeguard towers, blue water. Khozha was amazed to see it all so close to downtown and so far from the ocean. They really are Great Lakes, he thought, couldn't see the other side.

He pulled into the new development. Biba said there was a racetrack here before.

Khozha parked on the street in front of a brand new ten-storey condo building. Didn't look too bad. Nice view of the lake, if she had one facing that way. Could have been a lot worse. Mikhail getting himself killed in Moscow could have left her with nothing. No one had expected Biba to actually get anything going in Canada.

Still, she'd always been a tough woman, difficult to please. Victor and Khozha working all those years, smuggling, dealing, paying off. Every day a risk, and she always expected a little more. Khozha used to wonder why Victor put up with her.

In the lobby of the condo building a woman came in carrying a small dog, fumbling with her keys trying to open the door, and Khozha held it for her. They rode up five floors together on the elevator and then she got out, not saying a thing, never looking at him. Khozha stayed on, up to the top floor, thinking, everyone says this city is so friendly. Assholes.

Her place faced the lake and west, towards the city. A great view, a great location, and these places aren't cheap. Maybe Biba's right, maybe she's just impossible to please. Maybe he's just taking over from his father and Mikhail. Shit, Khozha thought, what the fuck am I doing here?

He knocked on the door.

"Khozha Starshii. What a pleasant surprise."

All Khozha could think was she still looks like Ingrid Bergman.

And everything made a lot more sense.

• • •

"That's pretty good," Vince said. "He clears four grand a month clean and leaves you hanging out there with nothing."

She said, "What do you mean?"

"Well, it looks like it was all your idea. You've got the two leases, you're the one skimming. If something ever happens, it'll all fall on you."

He took another piece of bread from one of the baskets hanging on ropes from the ceiling and looked at her.

She said, "But I'm giving him all the money."

"So you say. He's not writing you a receipt, is he?"

The waitress came to the table and Vince ordered a cassoulet. Roxanne asked what the soup of the day was, then ordered the endive salad.

"I haven't been here in years," she said, "it hasn't changed at all."

They were in the Select, a French bistro on Queen West doing a hopping business on a Thursday night. Mostly people out on dates and a couple of tables taken up with what looked like people out after work, mostly women. These days, there are a lot of good restaurants in Toronto, they're just spread out all over the place.

"Okay," Vince said. "So this is the first time he's done this? And then you tried it yourself with me?"

She looked at him, sitting there buttering his bread, looking all innocent even though it had taken him less than three seconds to see through the scam. That was back at his office, when she decided to just tell him the truth because he still wasn't pissed off at her. Nothing seemed to get to him. She'd brought him the new lease and tried to tell him that by taking the whole floor he'd get a "discount" working out to about a thousand bucks a month.

And he'd looked at her and said: "Which you don't tell

the building owners about and put in your pocket."

After that, she told him about Angus and the scam he wanted her to pull with Boris. Before she got too far, Vince suggested they should go out to dinner.

Now she was saying, "It looks pretty straightforward. He pays me ten grand a month, I put six in the building account and give Angus the other four."

"And you don't even get a single point for yourself."

"I told you, the whole building reno was my idea, and when it didn't work out . . ."

"Yeah, I know, but that's business. You take a risk."

"I guess I didn't know what kind of business Angus was really in. That kind, they don't take too many real risks."

"No," Vince said. "But he can spot an opportunity. Do you know what kind of business Boris is in?"

She just said, "Yeah."

The food arrived, and Roxanne picked at her salad while Vince ate. She asked him where he was from.

"How do you know I'm not from Toronto?"

"No one's from Toronto."

"You are."

"How do you know? Anyway, you're right, I am. I didn't realize it showed."

"It doesn't look bad. Not on you. It's just you don't often meet someone from the centre of the universe."

"It's the centre of the country, anyway, so what?"

"It's the way you lord it over everyone."

"You know why? It's 'cause everyone we meet is from somewhere else. Montreal, Vancouver, the States, Italy, England — god, the Brits — China, India, somewhere. All we ever hear is how much better they do everything. No matter where someone's from, they always tell you, 'Oh no, in Somalia we treat people so much better.'" She poked at her salad. "So we have that inferiority complex and we take it out on our family, like people do."

He was looking right at her, interested, so she shrugged it off. "So, you didn't tell me, where you from?"

Still looking at her, he said, "All over. I've lived in a bunch of provinces," and she said, "You could try opening up a little, you know, it won't kill you."

He said, "You never know what might kill you."

When he reached across to get a piece of baguette from the basket hanging on her side of the table, Roxanne held his hand and got him the bread. She didn't let go of his hand.

A half an hour later, they were back at her condo on the lake.

• • •

When they finished and Roxanne rolled off and they were both lying on their backs she said, "Wow, you really do work in the sex trade, don't you?"

Vince didn't say anything and watched her stand up.

She stood looking down at him, her hair seeming longer than before, falling over her face, and her tits looked great. He'd wondered about them in her expensive push-up bra, tight silk blouse and sexy skirt. They could have been disappointing, but they were round and stood right up. Then he wondered if they were just a more expensive job than the ones he was used to in the office.

"It's good to be with a professional." She tapped his foot as she walked out of the room.

And Vince thought, a professional what? Then he was thinking how everyone can be a pro sometimes. This Angus guy, this builder who reno-ed the building, he was probably an honest guy, probably took a lot of pride in his work. But he gets into a jam, or he doesn't make as much as he thinks he should, and he sees a chance and takes it. He's not a pro, he's not the mob, but he can do it this one time.

Sounds like every escort Vince ever drove, every chick coming into the office. Just this one time, just till I pay off these bills, get back on my feet. Vince had never seen a plan work out. Just some people who could see a chance and take it.

Coming back into the bedroom wearing a short red silk robe, Roxanne was saying, "What is it?"

"I got a song in my head, can't think of what it is. 'See a chance, take it.'"

"Find romance. Fake it," she said, climbing up and sitting cross-legged on the bed, dropping a big glass ashtray between her feet and lighting a cigarette. "Steve Winwood. You faking it?"

"It's the 'see a chance' part."

She took a drag and held up the pack to Vince. "You think I'm not taking the chance? You think I should hold out for a cut?"

And he was thinking, what about this girl? Professional in her business suits, even if the skirts are a little short and the blouse a little tight, but that's just style. She's not a pro, she's just getting out of a jam. Now she's talking about getting in deeper, and she doesn't even realize it. He took a cigarette out of the pack and she tossed him her lighter.

Or does she?

"What do you think, ten per cent? A thousand bucks?" She blew smoke up towards the ceiling.

Vince said, "Just what you were trying to skim from

me." He inhaled deeply. It felt so good. He hadn't had a smoke in almost five years.

She slapped at his foot, playful-like, flirting, and Vince thought, yeah, there's more to this girl. She's smart and she's independent, she takes care of herself. More like the women he used to try and date in the straight world: the lawyer who did the corporate work for him, and the broker who tried to get him into mutual funds. Women he thought he should be with. But it never worked out. Oh sure, for a while they liked the "danger" or the thrill in being with somebody doing something "edgy," something they thought was edgy, even if it really was boring, more like running a daycare. But the real classy women, educated women, independent women, women Vince was always attracted to, at the end of the day, they'd rather be with a lawyer or a stockbroker, some safe guy, the wildest thing he ever does is grope her in the parking garage, maybe make out in a hot tub.

The funny thing, though, Vince knew, was that he was the only guy who didn't picture every woman naked as soon as he saw her. It was like taking his work home with him.

But this Roxanne, she looked like she lived in the straight world, but she came up with the scam so fast.

He said, "He's gonna say maybe ten per cent of his cut, which is 400. It's a big risk for something that won't cover your car lease."

"My lease is three-eighty."

"You need a new car."

"It got you here, didn't it?" She smoked and looked around the small room. Vince followed her eyes. No pictures on the wall, no art at all, the curtains looking like Ikea.

"Okay, so maybe I can get Boris to take more space, a higher rate, and take a decent cut."

"You really have some leverage on this guy?"

She hadn't told Vince what it was, just that Boris was a sure thing, he'd lease almost anything she asked him to. Now she just said, "Yeah, some."

Vince took a drag and blew rings. She wasn't going to tell him what kind of leverage, and he wasn't going to ask.

"He wants to put in a peeler bar," she said, "The Toy Box."

"Can't open a new strip club downtown, you know that."

She'd forgotten. She looked at Vince and said, "Shit yeah, since the new bylaw. The old ones get to stay, but when they close, that's it. I guess Boris didn't know."

"I bet he knows now."

"Shit. But he also wanted office space. For some kind of booking agency."

"There you go."

Vince had seen this before, too. Someone looking at a score so good they couldn't let it go.

Slow drag on her cigarette. Tilt of her head. "Maybe he'll want a whole floor."

Well, Vince figured, what's it to me?

"You think he's your answer?"

"He could be my lucky star."

Vince didn't get it.

She stubbed out the smoke, dropped the big ashtray on the table beside the bed, and snaked her hand up along Vince's leg, over his thigh, and said, "Let's see what kind of a pro you are."

He figured this time would be better, getting to know each other more, but they went through it exactly the same.

Maybe the next time.

• • •

Boris ran his hand through her thick, dark hair. It was soft and long, hanging loose over her shoulders, and wondered if it would feel gay, someone doing this to him with a crew cut.

She lifted her mouth off him and said, "Something wrong?"

"No, honey, that's good, keep going." He relaxed and went back to stroking her hair. Okay, if Khozha wants bald chicks, that's fine. Shit, Boris, don't let him get to you, he'll be gone soon. It was taking longer than usual, though, even with her long, thick, soft hair. He'd thought a quick one before he went home, but he just had so goddamned much on his mind.

Khozha was still in town, another night at the hotel. He'd come back from seeing Ma and didn't want to talk about it. That was more like Khozha, but he seemed happy, and that didn't. Took Amelie with him.

Took the Saab.

Boris wanted to ask him about the asshole with the dog, did they see him? Did Khozha say anything? But he didn't want to know. He just wanted it to go away.

Henri bugging him, wants to know if he needs another car. Fuck. He can't tell him yes, that makes it sound like Khozha is staying. And he can't tell him no, because he does need a fucking car.

And that real estate lady.

He stared at her card sitting on his desk. It had her picture on it, but she was different now. In the picture she had longer hair, darker.

Not as dark as this girl face down in his lap. He stroked her hair again, pulling it through his fingers, the different shades of black and brown and, he was pretty sure, some blue. She was good; this wasn't her fault. She kept trying different things.

Roxanne Keyes. What the fuck does she know? She was sitting at that Starbucks, she watched Khozha shoot fucking Anzor and get back in the car. She saw. And then she was in the parking lot last night. She saw again. So what's she up to?

The girl mumbled, "Mmmm, yeah."

Boris leaned back. Yeah.

She must have talked to the cops he saw on TV, the bald Negro and the young guy, looked like a Slav, saying yeah, sure, it could have been road rage, but knowing perfectly well it wasn't. So what? They won't waste any time on a Russian pimp, Boris knew that.

Unless it was easy for them. Unless some real estate lady told them who was driving the car. One reliable witness was all they needed.

He had almost a full load of cars ready to ship to Riga. But no Anzor to pick up the cash and get it into a bank. Why did that prick have to be so greedy?

Well, why did he have to tell everybody how much he was taking, that was the real problem. Making Boris look weak and vulnerable.

Like he was.

Shit. Clear your fucking head, Boris. Think about this girl right here and her silky hair and her lips and her small hands.

If the real estate lady is going to be a problem, just shut her down. Henri is begging to be a tough guy, so let him. Yeah, she's nothing.

"Mmmm, yeah, that's it."

Boris smiled, stroked the girl's hair. Yeah. It's gonna be fine.

He was thinking about the real estate lady when he finished, thinking he could look her up, or get Henri to do it.

And then the next morning, she called him.

CHAPTER SEVEN

"RIGHT, SO WHAT WAS THE question again? Oh yeah, how did I become a pimp?"

"How did you become the world's worst pimp, was the exact wording."

They were sitting in the breakfast nook of Roxanne's condo. A small glassed-in balcony with a great view of the islands, the small planes taking off from the airport and the ferries on the big lake. Vince was wearing his boxers, and his button-up shirt was hanging open. Roxanne was wearing that red robe that barely tucked under her ass on the barstool and hung open in the front, and she was thinking he didn't seem the gym type but his stomach was flat and he had muscles.

"It was a long time ago. Back in the late seventies, '77, '78, I guess. I had just arrived in Calgary."

"What were you, fourteen years old?"

"Seventeen."

"So this is, 'I was a teenaged pimp'?"

"I'm trying to start at the beginning. You know, open up like you said."

She raised her eyebrows a little. She still had the mug in both hands, hiding behind it.

"I was working construction. That Gerry Rafferty song, 'Baker Street,' was huge that summer. Had that sax intro, I remember it came on like four, five times a day. The boom was on, you know, there were a couple thousand people a month moving to Alberta, and they weren't all bums like me. Some of them had jobs waiting for them, and so there was construction everywhere. Calgary will be great city when it's finished."

"It's pretty nice now."

"I'm sure it's a lot closer to finished. Back then there were ten, fifteen construction cranes downtown. The tallest building was the Husky Tower, the Calgary Tower. Now you can barely see it in all those buildings. You can't really imagine how fast that city went from a dot on the prairies, with practically dirt roads, to what it is now."

"As fast as you went from a pimply kid to a pimp."

"Ha ha, that's funny. Okay, so I was working construction way the hell out of town. And when you're way the hell out of town in Calgary, you know it, because you can see for a hundred miles. They were putting in all kinds of instant communities. Subdivisions. They were building the houses before they even had the roads. Some of them even have man-made lakes."

"Now that's added real estate value."

Vince looked her right in the eyes and she stared back. Then he said, "Not like this, of course," motioning to Lake Ontario, disappearing over the horizon. "Small lakes, but nice. Anyway, I was working this site, a new subdivision, the Woodlands. I don't know why they called it that, there weren't any woods for miles. Way out in the far southwest of the city, past Anderson Road. Anyway, it was just flat, dry land, all staked-out for roads, the foundations going in. That's what I was doing, cribbing."

He looked at her.

She slipped off the barstool and took a couple of steps into the kitchenette. "Okay, I admit it, I don't know what that is."

"Wooden frames for the foundations. Cement gets poured in and the wood comes off. I was banging the wood off, cleaning up."

"Not exactly skilled labour." She sat up on the stool, not even pulling the silk under her nice round ass, and dropped her cigarettes on the table. She already had one in her hand and her lighter went off first try.

"No. Bottom rung, that's for sure. But there was a boom on, they were hiring anyone. You showed up, you worked. We were wearing running shoes and shorts. I saw a guy step on a nail, went right through his shoe and his foot. The blood poured out like you turned on a tap. Anyway, we were out in the middle of nowhere, miles of nothing. Truck comes around twice a day selling sandwiches and coffee. And not like this."

He held up his mug and took a sip.

Roxanne motioned to the cigarettes and Vince said, "Ultra Lights?"

"I'm quitting."

He nodded, but picked up the pack. "So anyway, every Friday was payday — we actually got little brown envelopes with cash in them. At the end of the day, another truck comes by. A van really, one of those customized vans guys had in the seventies, the inside all covered in shag carpet, little window in the back shaped like a crescent moon or a star or something."

"Homer Simpson's Second Bassmobile." She exhaled a stream of smoke.

Vince lit an ultra light and sucked it deep into his lungs. He exhaled slowly. "Yeah, like that. Skinny Indian guy driving it."

"Indian like India, or like Native?"

"Native. There weren't really many guys from India in Calgary then."

"It really has changed."

"So this Indian guy, name of Travis Goodeagle, gets out and opens up the side door of the van. It's all made up inside, with a bed and a curtain down the middle. On each side of the curtain there's a girl. One's an Indian, a native, and the other one's blond, long straight hair."

"Oh come on," Roxanne said. "A whorehouse on wheels?"

"I swear, just like the coffee truck. Hey, Calgary's a service town."

"So you got in the van."

"I just told you, I was swamping, I was making maybe 200 a week. Those girls were fifty bucks."

"Fifty dollars. Shit. Okay, so how did you become a pimp?"

"I'm getting to that. All summer long, every Friday, Travis pulls up in his van. I swear, guys lined up just like they did for the coffee truck. Rank was strictly enforced. Foremen, department heads, seniority all the way. Very civilized. So one Friday, before Travis gets there, a white limo pulls up. Two guys get out. One's a huge bald guy, looks like a wrestler. He stands back by the trunk, arms folded over this huge barrel chest. The other guy's small, long hair. Looks like a biker. He's even got a handlebar moustache, leather vest, tattoos all over his arms. And this is 1977 remember. Tattoos are very rare."

Roxanne absently ran her finger over the butterfly tattoo on the top of her thigh.

"A woman with a tattoo was just out of the question."

She started, like she'd been caught at something. "Times change."

"So the little guy, he opens up the back door of the limo, and there's two chicks inside."

"Chicks?"

Vince smiled. "You got me thinking about the old days, I'm regressing."

"You're doing something all right."

"These chicks are younger and better-looking than the ones Travis has in the van. They don't look nearly as stoned. Two white chicks, a blond and a brunette. Guys start lining up, as usual."

"But you don't?"

"I didn't have enough money. And these were probably seventy-five bucks. No, I was scraping cement off the forms, the pieces of wood. Used to use the claw end of the hammer. My boss was always giving me shit for not getting them clean enough. Asshole, I forget his name. Garnet or Garth or Gavin or some G name. He's almost the first in line at the limo. He's done in about thirty seconds, and he comes over to his truck where I'm scraping away, big shit-eating grin on his face. Says he's getting right back in line, going again."

"Like the Wild Mouse at the Ex."

"A real wild something. So anyway, the little guy gets in the front seat of the limo and the line keeps moving. Moved pretty fast, too, those girls were pros. But no one seemed to complain getting out. Finally, Garth gets back in for his second round. Just then Travis pulls up in his van."

Roxanne took a long, deep drag on her smoke. "I'm either going to quit, or start smoking real cigarettes again."

"Go big or go home."

"Right. So Travis Great Eagle drives up."

"Goodeagle. He'd get a few drinks in him and start saying he was really only a fair-to-middling eagle. So yeah, he pulls up and gets out of the van. Smiling like a drunken Indian. Half-waving." Vince motioned with his hand. "He walks, he practically staggers, towards the limo. The big bald guy pushes himself off the fender, still has his arms crossed."

"You've got a good memory."

He looked right at her. "I haven't thought about this in years, but all of a sudden it feels like yesterday. Shit."

"You miss it."

"Being seventeen years old, my whole life ahead of me? Yeah, I miss that."

"The excitement."

"Yeah, some of that. So, Travis walks up to the big guy, like I said, looking drunk, and the guy barely looks at him, looks away like he's not worth shit. Travis says something like, 'Hey white man,' or something. Calls him 'sir,' I think, or 'boss.' The guy spits, just about hits Travis's cowboy boots, and suddenly, so fast you could barely see it, Travis has a knife in his hand sinks it right up to the hilt in the guy's arm. Right here." Vince tapped his finger on his arm between the shoulder and the elbow. "Right on the tattoo of the snake and the skull."

"Holy shit."

"Blood sprays all over the white limo. The big guy starts

screaming, grabs his arm, Travis pulls the knife out, stabs him again in the other arm, and kicks him full force in the nuts. The guy doubles over and Travis keeps kicking. Those cowboy boots come to a fine point and Travis just keeps kicking. Doors pop open on the car, and the little biker and Glenn both jump out. Glenn sees the blood everywhere, it's like two fountains now, the big guy on the ground and Travis still putting the boots to him, and Glenn runs. Runs right past me and jumps into his truck and takes off. I'm standing there with my hammer in my hand and the rest of his tools on the ground, and he doesn't even look at them, he just guns it."

"I guess so."

"The little guy, the biker, is swinging a chain, like a bicycle chain."

"Or a motorcycle chain?"

"Hey yeah, I hadn't even thought of that. Except instead of coming straight down the side of the limo closest to Travis and the big guy, he goes around the front of the car and all the way around, comes up behind him. I guess Travis is so into the boots he's laying into the big guy, he doesn't notice till the biker's already too close, and he gets a pretty good shot off with the chain. Practically wraps it around Travis's head."

"Ouch."

"Yeah. Knocks him over, but he grabs onto it and they both hit the ground rolling around, swinging, stabbing. The biker's got brass knuckles and he's hitting Travis everywhere he can. Gets him in the mouth once, but mostly he's hitting his back and shoulders. So anyway, they're rolling around and they're coming towards me, and as they get closer, I toss my hammer on the ground."

"For Flying Eagle?"

"I always liked the underdog, you know? So Travis got it and he smashed it into the biker's face. You could actually hear teeth cracking and his jaw coming off the hinge."

Roxanne shook her head a little, but she wasn't grossed out. Vince had been worried about that part of the story. He'd only told it a couple of times before, and only to guys. But Roxanne was cool with it.

"Didn't knock him out, though. The little guy got up and headed back to the limo. Travis followed him. The big guy was on his feet, the blood still pouring out of his arms, and they got into the car. Travis smashed it with the hammer as he drove away."

"And that's how you teamed up with the Indian pimp?"

"No, that didn't happen till a couple of years later. When I was in prison, I met Travis again."

"Prison?"

"Travis was pretty cool. Especially to a really naïve seventeen-year-old. He walked, kind of swaggered actually, over to me and tossed me the hammer, blood and hair and shit all over it. Probably said something cool like, 'Thanks, kid.' Then he got back in the van and drove off. I was standing there, miles from anything, with no way to get home. I walked about five miles to McCleod Trail and caught a bus."

"All right, so when exactly did you get into pimping with Screaming Eagle?"

"In Spyhill. I met up with Travis again. He remembered me. Called me the Hammer."

"An ex-con, I should have known."

"I was in the prison library. That's not like you imagine from the words, *prison library*, it's just a room with a few bookshelves and some tables. I figured I might as well finish up my high school."

"A high school dropout, ex-con, pimp, porno king. My mother will be so proud."

"Tell her I drive a Mercedes SUV."

"Don't worry, I'll open with that." Not like she really gave a shit what her mother thought, but Roxanne did imagine how it would go telling her. She liked that.

"Travis was getting his high school equivalency, too. Well, he was getting out of laundry duty, or something he didn't want to do, and we kind of did it together."

"You did it for him, didn't you?"

"He was pretty smart, he just didn't read or write that well. I had actually pretty much finished high school, a month or so to go when I took off for Calgary." That part Vince had thought about once in a while over the years. His girlfriend, Liz Downey, his high school sweetheart dumping him just before graduation. The first and last real girlfriend Vince ever had.

Roxanne said, "A month to go."

"He got out a couple of months before I did, said to look him up when I got out and I did. I tried to find a regular job for a while, but when you're looking at bottom rung kind of jobs, they can usually spot an ex-con. Travis was running an escort agency by then, and said he needed a white front."

Roxanne got up for more coffee, Vince watching her all the way and her knowing he was watching.

She came back to the table, sitting up on that bar stool, pouring them each some more coffee, the shortie robe falling open and her not making any move to pull it closed. She said, "White front?"

"Travis was smart. He knew he could deal with guys on construction sites and oil rigs, he could go out to the bars in Bragg Creek or Airdrie or wherever they were, talk to those guys. But in the go-go eighties it all changed, the business went upscale, downtown. Stockbrokers, lawyers, accountants, they all had lots of money."

"Right," Roxanne said. "This the 'for the first time in their lives' story?"

"They were coming in from the east, too, fresh out of McGill or U of T, away from home for the first time's more like it. First real chance they had. They hung out in nice places. Travis couldn't walk into the bar at the Palliser hotel, they'd throw him out."

"Just like that."

"Even dressed up, the guy was an Indian, dark-skinned, scars on his face. It worked for getting the girls, he looked like the bad guy in a Clint Eastwood movie, but he needed a clean-cut young white guy to be the front."

"And that was you." She watched Vince, nodding, like maybe he was a little proud of it.

"Yeah. Most of the guys coming into Alberta back then, high school dropouts from the Maritimes, you know? Small towns in Northern Ontario, they could work hard on the rigs, drive trucks, build whatever you want. But they couldn't sit in a fern bar and talk about what a genius Martin Scorsese was."

"But you could?"

"At the time I was more a Sam Peckinpah fan, *Pat Garrett and Billy the Kid*, you know. But it was before *Goodfellas*. But yeah, maybe I was the right mix of downtown guy in a nice suit, back then they were three-piece with vest, can you believe it? Big wide ties, shit. But also an ex-con, you know? Just dangerous enough for the young brokers to feel a little excitement."

"With some chicks for them to party with."

"We called it 'date.' I'd say I knew a girl they could

date, just for one night. We had apartments all around downtown. You could see how fast the place had grown, there were these nice residential streets, old houses with front lawns and gardens, and then right next door some fifteen-storey concrete apartment block looking like a bunker. We had a couple of girls working out of most of those buildings. That was another thing Travis needed the white front for: Indian guy couldn't rent in those places."

"And there was no, like, civil liberties cases against the landlords?"

"There were rental agencies in Calgary then, they did the screening out. If anyone got pissed off they just closed down the agency and opened another one."

Vince looked right at Roxanne, the way she listened to everything and didn't pretend to be shocked or outraged, the way the world worked. A while ago, Vince might have thought she was just trying to act cool in that Toronto way, that whole, I'm so world-class nothing shocks me, but she really seemed to think about it and accept it like business. Another thing he liked about her.

"It went great for a while," he said. "That was when I started advertising in newspapers and the Yellow Pages."

"Then what, you got your own franchise?"

"No, somebody killed Travis."

"Oh my God." After everything, she finally did looked shocked. "Another pimp?"

"No, he was back on the reserve and his girlfriend killed him."

"Girlfriend?"

"Gloria, yeah, mother of his kids. Travis gets home, three in the morning, and decides he wants hot dogs. Puts water on the stove and starts smashing around in the fridge, wakes her up. She tells him to sleep it off outside.

Travis, I don't know what he said exactly, probably something like, 'Go fuck yourself, you cow,' something nice like that. So she grabs the pot off the stove and throws the boiling water in his face."

"Ouch. And that killed him?"

"That and she stabbed him fifty-seven times."

"Fifty-seven?"

"She tried to plead self-defence. The judge asks why it was then, when the knife broke off in his chest after she stabbed him thirty times, she went to the sink and looked at three or four others before she found the one she took back to stab him the other twenty-seven times. And Gloria says, 'I had to find one with some decent heft to it.'" Vince shook his head, a little sadness and some admiration. "Yeah, Gloria, she was all right."

"Unless you want a hot dog in the middle of the night."

"I was, like, twenty-six then. I took over the women we had." Vince laughed quietly at the memory. "They really had to teach me. It went all right for a while, but with the boom fading it was tough. Picked up during the Olympics there in '88. You'd be amazed what sports reporters put on expense accounts."

"No I wouldn't."

"Later on, we started to advertise online and that led to the web pages and all this."

"When did you move to Toronto?"

"When I got out of Millhaven."

"Maximum security in Kingston? Oh my God. What did you do?"

"That's another story."

"It sure is." She stubbed out her cigarette. "Okay, well, you're the man all right. Let's go talk to the Russian strip club owner."

"Let's?"

She got up from the table and went to the kitchenette. The shortie completely untied now. Vince watched her, wondering how come, in his business where he saw naked chicks all day long, why was Roxanne, half covered up, so much sexier than all of them. He never really believed it, but maybe it's true. You sell the tease.

Maybe she was just a lot sexier.

She came back pushing buttons on the cordless phone, glancing at a pad in her other hand. "You think I'd go to a meeting with a Russian mobster and not bring my ex-con, pimp boyfriend?"

And Vince thought, boyfriend?

• • •

What Khozha did was, he got Olga to go for a walk, show him her neighbourhood. They walked along a boardwalk on a beach, looked just like a resort with people playing volleyball and getting suntans, except no one was in the water. They walked a while and there were the boards of a hockey rink, guys playing on rollerblades in shorts with no shirts. Middle of the afternoon, and this place was like a Saturday.

Olga saying, "Always so many people here — kids screaming, Pakis cooking their disgusting food on barbecues." They stopped at a little building, a snack bar selling ice cream and popcorn, and Olga looked at the park as it spread out from the boardwalk towards the street a long block away.

Khozha said, "You want to go have a drink?"

She said, "Let's go around," and started walking but Khozha didn't.

He said, "You want to walk through the park, walk through it." He'd never seen Olga Suliemanov scared before.

"No, it's fine." But Khozha didn't move.

She scowled at him, but walked into the park. They passed a lawn bowling green next to the hockey rink — only in Canada — and walked on the path next to the baseball diamond and the big oak trees where a half a dozen people stood drinking coffee. Khozha saw the leashes in their hands, the dogs running wild all over the park.

He said, "It's nice here," but Olga just tensed up. Khozha looked around and said, "Lot of dogs. Looks like they shit anywhere." Baiting her, but she didn't say anything. Fuck, not like her at all.

He said, "You have a problem with any of them?"

"All of them," she said, but wouldn't look at any of them.

Khozha did, saw a guy in the middle of the group, hair in a ponytail and a goatee. He said, "Do you know that one?"

Without even looking, Olga hunched over some more and said, "The rudest man I ever heard."

Khozha stared at him as they passed, the guy standing with a few other people, all drinking coffee, talking, none of them watching their dogs run around the outfield, pissing on the bleachers. The guy with the ponytail, he was short and thick, talked a lot, and waved his hands around. Khozha got a good look.

"Let's sit for a minute."

Olga shook her head and stared at her own feet as she walked. "That's his dog, stupid beast." It was some kind of small pit bull, like Khozha knew it would be. "So mean. Everyone scared of it."

Khozha hated to see her like this. He couldn't believe it, this woman who stood up to the KGB and the Chechen Mafia running scared through a park.

They came out of the park at the other end and they were on Queen Street, the main street in the neighbourhood. There were a lot of old businesses, a Chinese restaurant out of the fifties, a fruit and vegetable stand and a dry cleaner, but all the new places were upscale, trendy: coffee shops, expensive gardening stores, and sushi places. Every neighbourhood in this city always in the middle of change, always striving.

Khozha said, "Let's get something to drink," and they sat on the patio outside a coffee shop on Queen across from the park with their iced coffees.

"It's a miserable city, this Toronto," Olga said. "Everywhere to go you need a car."

"Boris will give you a car," Khozha said.

"Have you seen the way these people drive? Idiots, always in such a hurry with nowhere to go."

"He'll give you a driver, too."

"And where would I go? I can walk to temple."

Khozha saw the guy with the ponytail and the little pit bull come out of the park, the dog on a leash now, but straining at it, going for the hot dog stand in front of the dentist's. Khozha watched the guy pull the dog across the street, yanking it hard, calling it B.A., and not giving a shit that it was scaring little kids in strollers.

"And Boris, he never comes to temple, never comes to Seder."

Khozha looked at Olga for a second, thinking, Seder? Since when did she have a Seder?

The guy dragged B.A. up the street right past Khozha and Olga, not noticing them and Olga didn't notice him.

She was complaining about something else now, some people in her building and their garbage or something. Khozha watched the guy walk up past five or six houses and then turn in. A Range Rover in the driveway because, Khozha thought, this asshole spent so much time in the jungles of Toronto. All the houses on the street were a hundred years old and wooden, but they'd all been renovated — new windows, siding, rooms added, driveways in front where there used to be grass.

Khozha said, "I miss Moscow, too. But we have to keep busy, find something to do." He stood up to make sure he knew what house the ponytailed guy dragged the dog into, and then held out his arm for Olga. "We're the survivors, we can't sit still."

They walked around the neighbourhood some more, then had dinner at a nice place called Whitlocks, which served Pad Thai noodles and Swiss Steak even though the owner was a Greek guy. Khozha thought maybe someday, years from now, this Toronto could be a little like New York.

After a few glasses of wine and some ice wine with desert, Olga finally lightened up and laughed a little over some of the stories of the old days in Russia. Her Victor was quite the man, she agreed. He and Khozha, they had some times, always with Olga right there, knowing exactly what they were doing.

Khozha started to wonder if her real problem with Boris was that he was running his own show and not doing too badly, considering his brother screwed up so bad, and Boris had to start from scratch. Maybe she just wanted to be more involved.

It was getting dark when he walked her home, and he only stayed for one drink. Olga started to show her age a little, must have been a long day for her, and she didn't put up much of a complaint when Khozha said he had to leave.

At the door she said, "It was good to see you. Will you be in town long?"

"No, I'm leaving tomorrow."

"Can't wait to get away from here? I don't blame you."

He said, "No, it's not that," and then neither of them said anything for a moment. Then he said, "Well, good night." Awkward and formal. His best friend's wife. His best friend's widow.

He walked back along Queen Street, passing new buildings that had gone up where the racetrack had been, storefronts on Queen and four stories of condos above. Everything so new in this city, always so forward-looking. It used to be a working-class neighbourhood, he could tell, smelling of horseshit and gambling, and now a duplex cost over half a million dollars.

At the coffee shop, Khozha picked up an espresso and sat on the patio. The city was different than he expected, more going on, more assholes. More like a real city.

• • •

When *ER* ended, B.A. got up and came sniffing in the living room.

Rudy said, "You wanna go for a walk boy?" and the dog wagged his stubby tail and ran to the door. Rudy said, "Well, I'm too fucking tired to take you to the park." He looked at the leash hanging by the front door, the plastic bag tied to the end of it, on the hook his daughter had used to hang her coat on — or drop it in front of

— before Lee-Ann took her and moved to Vancouver. Bitch. Fucking actresses, the only jobs she ever got were in commercials he made. Now she was putting Ryley to work.

"Come on, boy, you go shit on Hasting's lawn." He opened the front door and stepped out on the porch. The dog ran down the stairs, between the cars, and disappeared into the neighbour's yard. Rudy thought, fucking pussy, let him pick up the dog shit, he'll never say anything. He went back inside to get his smokes and came back out a minute later.

He heard something in the shadows beside the house, an animal sound. He walked to the edge of his porch and said, "Fucking racoons." The garbage bag was ripped open, and old spaghetti was all over the porch. But the plastic garbage can was still standing, the lid still tied on with the bungie cords.

An old man stepped out from between the cars. Rudy said, "Yeah, what?"

The old man, standing in the shadows making Rudy think of Max Von Sydow in that spy movie with Robert Redford, said, "Shove it up *you* ass," and walked away.

Rudy said, "Fuckin' asshole," and turned back to his spilled garbage.

Except it wasn't his garbage. He got closer and saw the dog's face, glazed eyes looking up at him, belly sliced open, guts all over the place.

Rudy jumped down off the porch to the sidewalk, looking for the old man, yelling, "Hey motherfucker, come back here!" But the guy was gone.

CHAPTER EIGHT

ROXANNE SAID, "YOU THINK he'll come alone?" and Vince said sure, why not, he's just renting office space.

"Right?"

He was a little surprised she set it up so fast. Surprised Boris agreed so fast. A couple hours ago, they were sitting in her condo drinking coffee, thinking about going back to the bedroom before getting into the shower, and she'd called Boris. Now Vince was thinking about how quickly she seemed to move on everything.

Vince said, "So, he's got a peeler bar, I wonder what else he does."

Roxanne smoked her ultra light, tapped it in the little plastic ashtray and kept it between her fingers. "You mean for money?"

Vince said, yeah for money. Then he said, "Somebody told me that was the difference between Vancouver and Toronto. In Vancouver, when you ask someone what they do, they'll tell you, oh I snowboard or I go sailing or something like that and in Toronto when you ask, they tell you what their job is."

"You know what," Roxanne said. "Who gives a shit? I mean really, these overgrown teenagers, they think they're heroes because they climb a rock. Seriously? Grow up, already." She took another drag and blew smoke towards the ceiling.

Vince took a drink of his beer, Smithwicks in the big pint glass, and thought about that. She was right, really. He never thought about mountain climbing or heli-skiing or anything like that. Maybe he should.

Roxanne said, "What's the difference between a beginner snowboarder and an expert?"

"What?"

"A weekend."

Yeah, right. Maybe not.

Roxanne said, "Well, I guess if he has a strip club there must be drugs going through it."

"He might have had to make a deal with the bikers."

"You mean, like a concession? Like the hot dogs at SkyDome?"

Vince said, yeah, something like that. "Maybe. He's not going to tell us his business."

Roxanne looked around the place and said, "So this is the historic Wheatsheaf."

"Yeah, you've never been here before?"

"It says it's the oldest tavern in Toronto, and you know what? I believe it. Doesn't look like much has changed in a hundred years. Even the waiters."

There were a couple of pool tables that probably weren't there in 1812, and they sold chicken wings and nachos, but other than that, she was right. Wooden tables and chairs, cracked floor, and some serious drinkers in the afternoon.

"You didn't come here like all the other students in your college days?"

Roxanne stubbed out her cigarette and looked at Vince. "What makes you think I ever went to college?"

Well, he figured, she learned a few things somewhere. "Here's your boy."

Roxanne turned in her seat to see Boris coming in, by himself, and coming straight to the table.

He stood over her, looking down, recognizing her, and Vince knew it wasn't from trying to rent out space for a peeler bar three years ago. He watched as Boris tried to look casual and say something about how much Roxanne had changed, how her hair was different and how she was still so beautiful. But the guy was worried.

Why would this guy be worried about Roxanne Keyes?

Roxanne was saying, "This is Vince Fournier. He may be a neighbour of yours, he rents out the third floor of the Toy Works."

Boris, still trying to look casual and friendly, but Vince knew he had to be thinking, who the hell is this guy, held out his hand and they shook.

The guy sat down, and when the waiter came over, he looked at the taps and ordered a Keith's and then, finally, looked at Vince.

He said, "Neighbour."

Vince nodded.

Roxanne said, "You know, this place is something else. Imagine when the Toy Works really was a factory, guys finished work and came here for a beer. Just walked down the street."

Boris was still looking at Vince, still wondering who he was. It reminded Vince of the old days with Travis, when they brought a couple of cousins from the reserve to be the muscle. Big, dark-skinned Indian guys sitting in the bar with their bandanas and denim shirts with the sleeves cut off. Vince was never considered the muscle then, but now, now Boris was giving him some respect.

Vince really was getting nostalgic.

"What kind of business you have?" Boris said, looking at Vince.

"Online company."

"Oh yeah? Casino sites?"

Roxanne lit another cigarette and said, "Online porn."

Vince, still looking right at Boris said, "It works just as well."

"You looking for investors?"

Vince leaned back in the little wooden chair and shook his head. "I've got everything I need."

So now he could see Boris putting it together, seeing him as connected, the porn business, seeing him with Roxanne, who had some leverage. Vince still hadn't asked what kind of leverage she had on Boris. He figured maybe she'd slept with the guy and might threaten to tell his wife, though she didn't seem that stupid. Boris looked really clean-cut and businesslike in his Hugo Boss suit and diamond ring and 300 dollar leather shoes, but he owned a strip club out by the airport, so he had to be connected somehow. If he was married, his wife would know all about the strippers, she might have even been one. That's just a perk, it's not worth getting pissed about.

Unless she saw Roxanne as a threat because she was different. Not a stripper or an escort, but a business-woman in her own right, someone who could talk straight-up and make deals.

The way Vince saw her.

Boris asked her about the Toy Works, said something

about the bylaw against the peeler bars, and Roxanne was saying sure, that's right, but there's still some wiggle room.

Boris said, "If the price is right, there's always room."

Roxanne agreed and started talking about a nightclub with hostesses and private party rooms. Live jazz.

Vince sat back and watched Boris nod, looking interested, like he would be in any business deal, but wondering, really, about Roxanne.

Vince liked her, that's for sure.

Now Boris said, "You wouldn't mind a nightclub in your building?"

"It's not my building."

"Well, I don't know," Boris said.

Roxanne leaned a little closer. "There are a lot of other opportunities for the building."

"Yes," Boris said. "Opportunities."

Vince was waiting for her to make her play, use whatever leverage she had. He had no idea when would be the right time; this Boris guy was playing it very cool, but he was nervous. Vince said to him, "You married Boris?"

"No."

Roxanne said, "How's business out by the airport?"

"Good." He shrugged. Didn't look so good. "Lot of competition, you know. And, since 9/11, business trips are down, so the airport isn't as good a location as it was."

"Well then, if you could get around that bylaw downtown, there wouldn't be so much competition."

Vince saw Boris agree with that, but he had no enthusiasm. Vince said, "Classy place like that, takes a lot of capital up front."

Boris said, "That's no problem," and Vince knew what the problem was.

He said, "You looking to get out of the bar business?"

"Maybe. Someday."

"You want to open something else, not so much staff?"

"Maybe."

"Import, export?"

"Cigars, maybe. We have Cubans at the Club International."

"And you import yourself," Vince said. "So when Fidel kicks off, it'll open up, they'll be sold in the U.S., you'll be well-placed."

Boris said, "Like the Canadian boozemakers after Prohibition. Right place right time."

Vince nodded, sure, just like them. He could see Boris thinking about it. Roxanne was starting to slip, not really getting the story behind the story here, looking like she might jump in. Vince looked at her, willed her not to say anything. He could see Boris wasn't worried about her leverage or renting this space, he had something else on his mind. He was interested in this, in talking to them about something.

Boris said, "What about you? How long you going to run your porno business?"

"As long as I can make money."

Boris looked from Vince to Roxanne. He said to her, "Maybe I do need an office."

She said, "Then I think you'll find the Toy Works to be an excellent choice. The location is one of the most up-and-coming areas of the city."

Boris nodded, not very interested. "Yeah, okay. The thing is, maybe I pay cash for this office."

"I'm sure that would be fine," she said, glancing at Vince and looking back at Boris. "Money's money, right?"

And Vince knew exactly what Boris was thinking.

• • •

Vince said, "He seemed a lot more interested in doing business with you than with any particular kind of business."

"Or with you. He was pretty damned interested in your business."

They were walking back along King from the Wheatsheaf towards the Toy Works. A beautiful, sunny summer day.

Vince said, "Cash doesn't seem to be a problem."

Roxanne said, "How come people either have no money, or so much they don't know what to do with it?"

"There's a lot he wants to do with it," Vince said. "That's not his problem."

They walked into the lobby of the Toy Works, Roxanne thinking, then what is his problem?

Ella got off the elevator. She said, "That guy's back."

Vince said, "Hi, yourself."

Ella scowled at him. Roxanne noticed the pigtails and saw she was showing a lot of belly. Big pregnant belly. The gold ring in her now way-outy button looking huge.

"He's in your office. I think he has a gun."

Roxanne looked at Vince.

He said, "The girlfriend with him?"

"No."

"Okay." He looked at Roxanne and said, "Wait here," and she said, "As if," following him into the stairwell.

Roxanne said, "What are you going to do?"

"I don't know. I'll think of something."

And Roxanne followed, thinking, I've got to see this.

• • •

The black guy, Suss, was sitting in front of a bunch of monitors and a lot of other equipment Roxanne didn't recognize. Computers, sure, but the keyboards had bunches of bright coloured keys, yellow, orange, green, and there were wires hanging everywhere and speakers all over the place.

He was saying, "Smoking videos, shit. Biggest mover this week. Why do they want to watch them smoke?"

Roxanne was standing by the door of what Vince called the edit suite — but it was just another unfinished room packed with equipment — waiting for him. She really wanted to know what was going on with the guy in his office, but this time when Vince'd told her to wait down the hall, she went. He wasn't pissed off or scared, she could tell, but he was serious, and it just seemed natural to do what he said. She figured she'd have to watch out for that.

Garry said, "Straight guys, man, who knows."

Roxanne said, "Because men are pigs."

"I know why they want to watch them fuck and suck," Suss said. "And even diddle they own selves, but this, still?"

Roxanne was looking at the biggest monitor, a shot of two girls, early twenties, naked but with stockings and high heels, smoking cigarettes. The scene was in an office, one was sitting on the edge of the desk, the other one was leaning back in the chair, her feet on the desk and they both had their hair frizzed out in big eighties do's. The one sitting back in the chair had a white cast on one foot and crutches leaned against the desk.

Suss said, "Do fags like to watch the boys smoke?"

Garry said, no, he didn't think so.

Vince said, "That's my office."

Roxanne looked at him, just walked up and stood there all casual, looking at the monitor.

"Yup."

Roxanne said, "So, did he have a gun?"

Suss spun around on his chair, interested, but trying to be too cool to show it.

Garry said, "What?"

Vince waved it off. "No, of course not. Said he was going to get one."

Roxanne said, "Yeah?" She didn't believe him.

Garry said, "He's still pissed off he's not bringing in any cash."

Suss turned back to the keyboard, all the drama gone. "More like he's pissed off his girlfriend likes it."

Garry said, "Their site's just too vanilla to get any members."

"Yeah," Suss said, "but the girlfriend finds out she likes the kinky shit, then what's the boy gonna do? They start making easy money, he likes that, but he don't like her in the gang bangs."

"You see," Vince said, "there's no such thing as easy money."

He looked at Roxanne when he said it, and she shook her head. Look at him, making jokes about it. He's not the one needs the money.

Vince said, "And that's from, *Working Girl*, right?"

Garry, laughing, said, "Very good."

Roxanne said, "Which one's Sigourney?"

"The one in the chair, the boss. It's hard to find older women for this."

Suss said, "The sex was all right, they started out yelling at each other, slamming the door, then they tear each other's clothes off." He hit some keys and the shot on the monitor changed to the beginning of the scene, the two girls dressed, not exactly in the big shoulder-pad, *Working Girl* eighties look, but close. Just a lot more low-cut.

Garry said, "I'm calling it *Hard Working Girls*."

"You know none of the frat boys downloading this were born when *Working Girl* came out."

Garry watched his movie, nodding. "You wanted movie titles." He had his arms crossed over his chest. Proud of his work.

Suss said, "And then the smoking at the end, I say we cut it, but the numbers are up."

"It's the sucking." Garry said. "They like to watch girls take something long and round, and put it in their mouths and suck on it."

Suss was nodding. "Yeah, looks cool."

"I don't know," Vince said. "Sounds kind of gay."

"All sex is gay," Garry said.

Suss turned around in the chair. "What the fuck?"

A woman walked into the edit suite and Roxanne didn't recognize her until she said, "How'd it turn out?" Then she realized she was in the video, the secretary, Melanie Griffith.

Garry said, "Good."

Vince said, "I think it's because it's taboo. I think it's because everybody knows that all their lives these girls were told not to smoke, that it's really bad for them, and they do it anyway. Gives guys the idea that they might do other stuff people have told them not to."

"Okay," Melanie Griffith said, "why don't we have jaywalking videos or shoplifting?"

Vince said, "If they were naked and he shot it, it might work."

"You know it," Garry said. "You lost the evil fuhrer moustache, looks good."

Roxanne finally realized that Melanie was the same girl she'd seen the first time she came to VSF Online, the teenybopper in the jean shorts. Now she was wearing a denim miniskirt and a crop top with the word "groupie" in sparkling letters. Roxanne looked at the monitor — the sex had already started, no wasting time when you're downloading, and saw what Garry meant. She said, "Careful with that razor."

The teenybopper, real name Rosi, said, "No blades, I got a Brazilian."

Roxanne said, "Ouch."

"Naw, I smoked a big blunt before, it was nice. Relaxing."

Roxanne wasn't convinced, and Rosi said, "If you're gonna do something, you gotta go all the way, you know."

"I don't know."

"Take it all the way, once you start."

Roxanne said, "Go big or go home, right?" And looked at Vince.

Walking away Rosi said, "You know it, baby."

Garry said, "Six minutes exactly. I could make TV commercials."

"Not likc this," Suss said.

"You want to see what I got Monday?" Garry turned to Vince. "Blow job on the subway. It's great, the Bloor line, comes bursting out of the tunnel over the Don, there's sunlight, the boys look terrific." He started unpacking his camera, but Vince told him that it was fine, he'd take his word for it.

He led Roxanne out of the edit suite, Suss saying,

"Sure, you don't have to watch the fag action, what about me?"

"When you're the boss, Suss, you won't have to watch it, either."

Roxanne was looking closely at Vince, trying to see how much he was kidding, but he wasn't letting on. She could still hear Suss, saying, "Damned straight, when I'm boss this place will rock. You watch out."

Then Vince smiled a little.

Roxanne said, "You're not worried about him taking over?"

"When he's ready to go all the way."

And Roxanne thought, yeah, go big or go home.

CHAPTER NINE

"YEAH, OF COURSE," Price said, "you always remember your first one. She was sixty-seven years old."

Price driving the Crown Vic along Dundas, east out of Chinatown past the Art Gallery of Ontario, and the restaurants became more Vietnamese.

"The first homicide I ever worked, that I was the lead on, major case manager, was a guy broke into an apartment and raped a sixty-seven-year-old woman. Well, he didn't rape her, that's what he wanted everyone to know."

"He wanted everyone to know?"

"He wanted to tell his story, yeah."

Loewen said they all have stories, don't they, and Price said we just have to motivate them to tell.

"The place had been tossed, some jewellery stolen, rings, necklaces, and an antique watch. Looked like the old lady woke up while he was in there and he hit her with the jewellery box — big wooden thing."

"But he didn't rape her."

"Coroner tells us there was semen in her. A few days later, the guy tries to sell the watch in a pawn shop on Parliament. And we get him."

Price turned left onto Yonge, ignoring the no left or right turn sign. He drove slowly, like he was the only car on the road, saying, "But, of course, he doesn't say anything. He found the watch. We've got nothing else, no real way to connect him."

"Nothing?"

"I know, you watch TV, you think bad guys get caught by fingerprints and DNA and shit."

"But instead they tell you their stories?"

"Yeah. Well, not exactly. I mean, he wasn't a total amateur, he wore gloves. You can buy boxes of rubber gloves at every drugstore now, hookers are using them all the time."

"Nice."

Price nodded. "There really wasn't any physical evidence. Just the semen in the old lady. Didn't really make sense."

"How often do these guys make sense?"

"Right. We're just lucky the pawn shop owner got picked up in a massage parlour doing a fourteen-year-old Filipino girl a few weeks before."

"Lucky."

"Life is timing."

They crossed Bloor and the next block, Price turned left. They could already see the slow turning red lights at the other end of the block.

"So he owes us, and he calls about the watch. But the guy, he won't say a word. I keep telling him it's gonna be a circus when the TV gets hold of it. Still, he doesn't say anything. I say, I guess you had to hit her when she woke up, but why'd you have to rape her? Old lady like that, nearly seventy years old. He says, what the fuck? You know, it looks like he's gonna shit himself and he starts in with, 'You sick fucks, I never touched her.'"

"'Course not."

"Thing is, there's really no way we could ever get a warrant for his DNA, you know? All he has to do is keep his mouth shut and there's nothing we can do."

"But he wants to tell his story."

"Eventually, his side of it, yeah. See, other than her head caved in from the big wooden jewellery box, there's no other marks on her, no signs of struggle at all. So I tell him what he's gonna look like on TV, raping someone old enough to be his granny, and that *after* he killed her."

"Sixty-seven years old. That is pretty sick."

"Yeah, and that's what he doesn't want. He tells me, sure, he robbed the place and she woke up and he hit her. But he never touched her. Wants to make sure I write that down, never touched her."

Loewen said, "So, was that, like a deal you made with him? Get him to confess the murder and you won't charge him with the rape?"

"He didn't rape her." Price said. He stopped the car in front of a uniform cop and put it in park. "She was banging the guy upstairs, but he's married and doesn't want his wife to find out. I guess he left, the old lady fell asleep, and then our boy broke in."

"And you just let him talk."

"Wanted to tell his side."

Price got out of the car and showed his badge to the uniform.

The guy, well into his fifties, said, "Holy shit, we got every detective on the force out tonight."

"Better tie your shoes, the chief'll be here."

The guy actually looked down at his feet as Price and Loewen passed him.

Loewen said, "Shit."

"Yeah," Price said, "It's a little different when it's one of the beautiful people, eh? Not some gangbanger in Crackdale."

Loewen nodded. Yeah. Lots more cop cars, lots more techies, trucks from the TV stations, CityTV and the new one, SunTV right there. This being Toronto, though, there was also a TV van covered in Chinese writing.

"There he is." Price walked up to a guy in his late thirties, curly black hair, black overcoat, standing still all by himself in the middle of the busy crowd and said, "There a Chinese angle?"

The guy in the overcoat, Detective Theodore Levine said, "It's the bargain-basement duo."

Price said, "Teddy."

"Loewen and Price. Low in Price. You could work for my uncle selling *shmata*."

Price said, "Fuck," and Loewen thought he'd have to get a new partner.

Price and Levine started on the force about the same time, drove together in patrol cars out of 42 Division up at Jane and Finch, the worst division in the city, but they made detective about the same time. They were each partnered with someone older then, but now they're starting to flex in the squad, the new leadership emerging.

Price said, "The Chinese news van?"

"The victim, Isobel Cheung. This whole thing, it's *ferkokta*." He pointed to the crime scene, the restaurant. "Four guys come in, major dudes, line everybody up, kill a customer."

"Four?"

"Probably one in the car, look around."

Loewen saw the sidestreet lined with cars on both sides, leaving barely one lane for traffic. They couldn't very well have left a car idling out front — might have gotten blocked in. And they couldn't run very far to get one. Five guys to rob a place, doesn't even have a liquor license?

"Where's Louise?"

"The can. Everywhere we go, first thing she does, go to the can."

"Maybe she's pregnant again."

"Please." Levine held up his hand. "The last thing I need to do is babysit some kid while she's off on mat leave." He looked at Loewen and then back at Price. "So when's McKeon getting back? We might be below the Irish quota."

Louise O'Brien came walking out of the restaurant, a plate of cheesecake in one hand and a fork in the other. Mid-thirties with light brown hair and smooth skin and just a little makeup, stylish black-framed glasses, professional looking in her suit, like an office manager, except for the Glock on her hip and her swagger.

Price said, "Did you pay for that, Detective?"

"They wanted to give me one of those little plastic forks."

"So," Price said, "You knocked-up?"

"*Oy vey,*" Levine said. "Get to the point, why don't you?"

Louise looked at Levine and then at Price and shook her head. "It's 'cause I go to the bathroom a lot, right? That's all you genius detectives can come up with, I must be pregnant. Please."

"Are you?"

"No. Not that I'd tell you. So, how is Maureen? She ready to come back?"

"She's only been home a couple of weeks."

Yeah, Loewen thought, looking at the detectives, thinking, give me a chance here.

"It'll drive her nuts staying home. I was home with the twins six months, Jack had to take my gun away."

Price said, "So now it takes four guys to rob a place sells cheesecake? What's the split, fifty bucks apiece?"

Louise said, "It's not just cheesecake, Andre, it's *cheesecake*."

"Un-huh. They white guys, Chinese, what?"

"Black dudes," Levine said, and Price said, "Shit."

"Came in, lined everybody up, and started taking wallets and purses. A mass mugging."

Price said, "And shot Lucy Lui."

"Maybe she didn't understand English, though you'd think a big black guy with a gun in your face would get his point across. Maybe she just didn't want to hand over the Louis Vuitton."

Louise said, "I think it was Prada. But what about Ms. Musgrave?"

Loewen watched Levine not want to talk about it, try to wave it off, but Louise kept going, said to Price, "All the witnesses say the four guys come in, line everybody up, and start getting wallets. Except Ms. Musgrave, Mandy, says they come in, two of them go into the office in the back, come out shaking their heads, and *then* they start asking for wallets."

Levine said, "People were in shock, black guys with guns. This isn't Detroit or L.A. or something, it's Yorkville."

Yeah, Loewen thought, but it really wants to be L.A.

He said, "Place has a lot of security cameras. You know, even for a place the cheesecake is really good."

Levine said, "Andre, are you trying to teach this guy something?"

"Yeah, the security camera," Louise said. "Thing is, it broke down five minutes before our guys got here."

Price said, "Five minutes?" and let it hang there for a minute, no one saying anything. Then he said, "So, four guys drove probably ten miles across the city, passed two thousand other places and just had to come here?"

"Yeah," Levine said. "You got a problem with that?"

Loewen said, "They might," looking at all the TV news trucks.

Levine said, "No they won't. How you doing on that road rage?"

And Loewen thought, fuck, he's right, they'll believe anything we tell them. "But you got one witness, seems to know what she's talking about," and glanced at Price who didn't react at all.

Levine said, "And she's reliable. She's also a hooker."

"Escort, please." Louise dropped the china plate and the metal fork into a garbage can on the sidewalk. "She and her friend just finished double-teaming some visiting celebrity at the Four Seasons. Won't tell us who."

Price said, "We'll have to look at *Star Gazing* on Sunday."

"Maybe you detectives can figure it out. So Mandy, she says, 'Clarisse was just coming back from the powder room.' She actually said 'powder room,' and four black guys came in wearing ski masks."

Price said, "She say guys?"

"Might have been 'dudes.' She also said one black guy came in earlier, looked around and left."

"Did she say, 'casing the joint'?"

"She says she's not a bigot, of course, but there aren't many black guys in here, other than the busboys. Then she says he's definitely not one of the ones who came in later."

Levine said, "*Ferkokta*. The whole thing."

"Anything we can do to help," Price said.

"I'll remember you said that."

"So," Price said, "about our road rage."

"I knew it. I knew you didn't come out here in the middle of the night to talk to me about my troubles."

"Russian guy shot three times in the head. Shooter gets back into a Volvo and they drive away."

"You sure it was a Volvo?"

Loewen said, "Yeah, absolutely. s80, midnight blue," thinking about their one witness who wasn't a hooker, Roxanne Keyes, and about the reinterview coming up.

"The victim had an office on Bathurst," Price said. "Ran an agency bringing in dancers from eastern Europe. Made frequent trips."

Loewen said, "And dealt drugs. For both the bikers and other Russians."

"A lot of these Russian guys like European cars," Levine said. "Not that they have any registered in their own names."

Loewen knew that. They're mobsters, all mobsters work pretty much the same. Just a couple of months ago, an Italian guy was picked up for drunk driving in Montreal and his Escalade was registered to a concrete hauling company in Woodbridge he had no connection to. No connection anyone could prove.

"He might have been driving the Volvo a couple of months ago, too," Price said.

"A Russian guy who works with exotic dancers and drives a Volvo. You're not exactly narrowing it down."

Louise said, "What about that guy, took over the Galaxie Club out by the airport. He drove a Volvo."

"Louise did extensive interviews on the homicide of an exotic dancer," Levine said. "Her body was found in the trunk of a car in long-term-parking."

"Right," Price said. "Was the boyfriend, wasn't it?"

Louise said, "Isn't it always?"

"For some reason, I wasn't needed on those interviews. Can't figure it out."

Price said, "Louise didn't need you, or Rachel wouldn't let you?"

"Mrs. Levine does not interfere with official police business."

"That would make her the only lawyer who doesn't."

"Bite your tongue."

Louise said, "Club International, it's called now, since the Russian took over. Can't remember his name, he drove a Volvo."

Price said thanks, and Levine said, "So, when this thing blows up in our faces, all over the news, you'll be right there with us, right?"

Price just turned and walked back to the car, and now Loewen wasn't sure which detective would be the bigger pain in the ass to work with.

• • •

Henri had to carry her over his shoulder, naked and dripping wet, all the way through the club to Boris's office. Smacking his back with a high-heeled shoe and calling him a bastard the whole way.

Khozha was sitting behind the desk, lighting a Cohiba. He said, "What the fuck?" and Henri dropped Marie-Claire on the leather couch and told her to *"Ferme ta bouche, toi."*

She said, "That fucking cunt."

"Shut it."

Khozha was starting to smile. It was funny, the big frog all wet and the naked chick with the shoe in her hand, that streaked blond hair all wet and wild, yelling at him in French.

Then she looked at Khozha and said in English, "Do you know how much these cost? Do you? These are Jimmy Choo. Eh?"

He shrugged.

"Six hundred bucks."

"For that? It's a fucking sandal."

She was surprised he knew the word "sandal." "It's leather. Burnt orange," dragging out the word, saying it in French, *"o-range."* She calmed down a bit. "Always with the fucking jokes, that one."

Henri said, "Amelie, she threw her stuff in the shower."

"Not Amelie. Angie."

"So why you were bitch-slapping Amelie?"

"Because . . . she did it."

Khozha said, "What?"

Marie-Claire said, "Amelie, she put Angie's clothes in the shower."

Henri said, "So, what's that to you?"

"So then, Angie, she wants to know who did it. No one say anything, but she can tell, Amelie, she's laughing. So, Angie, she take all of Amelie's clothes and throws them in the shower."

"Okay," Henri said, "What the fuck is that to you? You Amelie's bitch?"

She gave him the finger. "Amelie, she switched her locker with me."

Khozha said, "So when the other one . . ."

"Angie."

"Yeah, when she went to Amelie's locker and threw her shit in the shower, it was really your shit."

"Jimmy Choo, 600 dollars, real leather." She was sitting back on the couch now, her legs crossed, twirling the sandal around by the thin orange strap.

Khozha couldn't help it, he thought it was funny. He said, "It's a good one. Why don't you throw Amelie's clothes in the shower?"

"Because she's wearing them."

Khozha stood up and said, oh well, if she's ready, he was leaving then.

Henri watched him stub out the cigar and put it in the breast pocket of his golf shirt. The guy dressed like an old man in Miami, which was what he should be. Henri couldn't believe Boris brought him in. He said, "You going to the airport?"

Khozha said, "When I need a driver, I let you know," and walked out of the office.

Henri said, "Fucking pig."

Marie-Claire said, "He the uncle, non?"

Henri spoke to her French. "Uncle, I don't know. Friend of the family. He and the father, they worked together for years in Russia."

"You like them?"

"Boris is okay."

Marie-Claire thought about it for a minute, still twirling the Jimmy Choo burnt-orange sandal. She said,

"Some things are okay since he bought the place."

"Yeah."

"More customers, different customers."

"Yeah." Henri was still looking at the door, still pissed at Khozha, just in general now. But it was true, he did like what Boris had done with the place. Pretty much what he'd wanted to do himself. When Henri was with the bikers, before Les Hells took over the whole fucking country, when he was almost a full patch with the Demons, he'd already started to get tired of them. Supposed to be tough guys, doing whatever they wanted but they had more rules than in fucking jail. Henri always thought there was a lot more potential in the strip clubs, the whole industry getting so close to going legit, legalizing prostitution, marijuana, but the Demons, just like the Hells, always looked so short term, took no chances. Drugs, hookers, cash businesses, and if they ever did try to turn it into something more, they had to go talk to the Italians. They always made him feel like a kid, asking permission.

Everybody always just assumed Henri was from Quebec, but he was Franco-Ontarian, from Sudbury. No way he was going to start over as a fucking hangaround with Les Hells, a step-and-fetchit, running shitty errands, taking all the risks, getting his own hands dirty, proving himself to fucking Mario "Mon Oncle" Bouchard for as long as the bastard wanted.

Not Henri Duguay. With Boris, he was a partner. Not fifty-fifty, but getting there. Boris had some deals he didn't know about, that's for sure, but he was finding out. He felt like he was on the right track, heading in the right direction. When the time was right, when the opportunity came, Henri knew he'd be ready.

Marie-Claire said, "Nicer place. Classier. It's better now."

"Yeah, better." But it really should be mine.

Marie-Claire uncrossed her legs and leaned forward on the couch, looking up at Henri. She said, "I'm glad you stay."

Henri said yeah, me too. And it was like he just noticed she was naked.

CHAPTER TEN

VINCE THOUGHT ABOUT telling Roxanne what happened, but decided not to. It was one thing, telling her his stories about Calgary, the Wild West in the wild seventies, but a guy in his office with a gun? What would he say, yeah he was threatening to kill me so I threw him off the fire escape into the dumpster?

She'd say, four stories, you could have killed him.

He'd say, the guy had a gun in my face, I was trying to kill him. I didn't know the dumpster was there. Sounds like that guy in the James Bond movie, threw the girl into the hotel pool.

No, he'd have to say he was just trying to get the gun away from him.

But his experience told him women didn't like to date guys who had guns pulled on them.

And all that happened was that he went into his office and Gord was there, and Vince could tell right away that he had a gun. He held it in his hand in his jacket pocket. Some jacket with a Labatt Blue logo on it, for Christ's sake. And he started in right away about how his girlfriend was on the computer all the time, chatting with other webchicks and getting advice and shit. They were all telling her she had to be wild, she had to get out. If she wanted to sign up members, she had to go to barmeets and invite them, and then sign them up.

Vince said, "Yeah?" and the boyfriend said, "Well for fuck's sake, she's gonna fuck them."

Vince said she could blow them and make out with the other chicks, lots of the amateur girls did that.

"Yeah, well, now we're driving to fucking Montreal to have a gang bang with Carla Cox."

That's when he pulled the gun.

Vince knew it was coming, so he pretended he didn't see it, or that it wasn't a big deal. He patted his chest and asked the guy if he had any smokes, then stepped out the door from his office onto the fire escape.

The guy followed him out, the gun still in his hand, and he started to get his smokes out of his pocket.

That's when Vince grabbed the gun and drove his shoulder into the guy, knocking him over the wrought-iron railing and four stories down.

Vince leaned over the railing and was surprised to see the guy climbing out of the dumpster. The guy looked up and said, "I think I broke my fucking arm."

Vince pointed the gun at him. A snub-nose .38, brand new. He said, "If I ever see you again, I'll kill you."

The guy scowled his best tough guy look, but he walked out of the parking lot.

Vince knew he couldn't tell any of that to Roxanne. She was getting a kick out of hanging around with him.

She liked rubbing up against the mobsters but he knew if it got too serious, she'd bail.

That was his biggest problem these days. He wanted to go out with women in the 'straight' world. He'd gone out with the woman who sold him his cell phone. She was sexy as hell and as wild in bed as any of the women he had working for him, but when she found out he was in the porno business, it was over.

So why had he told Roxanne anything about his past? He hadn't told anyone any of that since he'd been in Toronto.

Since he'd started using the name Vince Fournier.

• • •

When Roxanne told Vince what the leverage was she had on Boris, he said, "So you're going to rent him the office upstairs from me."

"It's the only listing I have." Now she was thinking, go big or go home. A commission on a few thousand square feet of office space just didn't seem like enough.

"You figured he needs the space anyway."

"But what is it he's really talking about?"

Garry knocked on the open door of Vince's office and handed Roxanne the plastic bag, tied at the top, with two round styrofoam bowls inside. She opened it up and handed one of the bowls to Vince, saying, "You know, you can get any kind of food in the world delivered in this city. Thai, African, Szechuan — stuff you've never heard of. It all comes in the same styrofoam bowls with the tinfoil lids."

Vince opened his Phad Thai and leaned back in his chair. "Why can't you get Chinese food in those cardboard boxes like in the movies?"

"Why?"

"I always saw them in the movies, but I've never seen them in real life."

Garry said, "The movies are real life."

"Yours might be."

Roxanne watched Garry leaning against the door, trying to look cool in his cargo pants and teal shirt. She might not have pegged him as gay right off, but it wouldn't take long. Not like he's trying to hide it.

"I've got to get the cast and the crutches back to Silverstein's. Don't want to pay an extra day's rental."

Vince said, "You work too hard."

"I work too hard? I'm just trying to keep up. Next to James Brown, you're the hardest-working man in show business."

Vince said, "Next to me, James Brown is a pussy."

Garry laughed. "I have to get some sunsets, looks great today. Something with the tower in the shot."

"For *Tunnel of Love*?"

Garry said, no, he wasn't sure what for, just to have, might come in handy. He was thinking about a whole gay-wedding-in-Toronto show. "Part documentary, and then some sex. Hot sex."

Vince looked at Roxanne. "Garry has a whole theory about porno movies. Thinks they're too, what was it? Restricting?"

"Whatever."

"No, really, what's your theory?"

Roxanne looked at Garry, but she was more interested in Vince, the way he tried to be so casual about everything, but was actually interested in this.

Garry said, "I don't think porn is really movie material, I don't think it should be."

Roxanne said, "What should it be?"

"It's like books, you know? Some books have stories, plots, characters, and some books are just big coffee-table books of pretty pictures." He looked at Vince's bookshelves. "What have you got there? Look, a whole book about bridges. You never complain it has no story, right?"

"Right."

Roxanne could see Vince had heard this all before, but he liked to hear it. He liked the theory. Roxanne was never much interested in theory.

"So, when people complain about porno movies having no plot, or no story line, I think they're on the wrong track. Of course they're lousy. The morons making them think conflict means people fighting, but they can't have people fighting because they can only see that as action-movie fighting, and you can't have sex and violence. Without violence, these idiots don't see how they can have any conflict, and all they know about story is that there needs to be conflict."

"But you don't think there does?" Roxanne didn't really care about Garry's theory, but she watched Vince, who did.

"Sometimes. Not always. Sometimes a movie is great if it's a real character study. But, you know, feature films? Ninety minutes long? Who wants to sit down and watch ninety minutes of porn?"

Roxanne looked at Vince and said, "I thought this whole industry turned over billions a year."

Vince nodded. Looked like he really enjoyed watching Garry get worked up.

Which he was doing. Garry said, "Yeah, sure, ten minutes at a time. You notice how the videos have all been fast-forwarded over anything but the sex?"

Roxanne said she'd take his word for it.

"And on the computer, you surf. No one watches one thing on the computer for more than a couple of minutes. That's why the computer is perfect for porn. My kind of porn."

"The kind with no story?"

"The kind that doesn't need a story. It's a coffee-table book, it's a travelogue. Here's ten minutes of beautiful people having great sex in the Grand Canyon."

Roxanne said, "But you just made a *Working Girl* spoof."

"That's exactly what I'm talking about."

Roxanne looked at Vince. Bastard was smiling. He really did like to watch Garry get all worked up.

Vince said, "We have a lot of customers we have to serve. They aren't as . . . forward-thinking as Garry."

"Short-sighted morons."

"I believe in you, Garry."

"Thanks."

Roxanne couldn't tell if Vince was being serious, but Garry sure thought he was. This'd been going on a while.

"We sneak in a few of Garry's beautiful sex movies when we can. They're selling all right."

Garry said, "This is just tip-of-the-iceberg stuff. There are a million amateur sites. Everyone can shoot video now, but they all look like shit. Street Blowjobs and the Bang Bus, and that guy who was here complaining he's not making any money. Well no kidding he's not making any, he's shooting the video himself, it's all crap. Just because every idiot can afford a camera and you can edit on your home computer doesn't mean you know what you're doing."

Vince said, "Garry knows what he's doing, though. He went to the Film Centre."

Roxanne said, "The Norman Jewison school? Does he know what you're doing?"

Garry was on a roll. "We can put eight or nine really good ten-minute pieces together, sell it to a distributor."

"When we're ready."

"We could distribute ourselves. Suss could put together the web page, we're handling all the credit card stuff for the amateur pages we host already."

"Yeah, maybe."

"Sell it as another line along with the stuff we have, just a little bit more expensive. Classier."

Vince said, "And there's the problem."

That knocked him off his roll. "It's always money, isn't it?"

"It sure is," Vince said. Roxanne watched him, still easygoing, but ready to finish up now.

Garry got it, too. He said, "Well, I better get the crutches back."

Roxanne watched him go and then turned to Vince. "You like getting him worked up."

"He's an artist."

"Why do you do it?"

"It's funny to watch him rant."

"No, I mean, why do you let him make his movies, his beautiful-settings movies. They're expensive?"

"Always the bottom line. I don't know. I like movies, you know? It's my generation. The sixties had rock'n'roll, and the seventies had movies. I spent my teen years in movie theatres. *Taxi Driver*, *Pat Garrett and Billy the Kid*, that Gene Hackman one with the car chases."

"So you want to make movies?"

"I don't know."

She watched him think about it, looking like he'd

thought about it for a long time. Before, she saw him as a guy running the show, taking charge, putting on the easy-going act, but now she wasn't so sure. Now she could see him as a guy who was just moving from one thing to the next.

"Well," she said. "What's Boris really talking about?"

"Money-laundering. He's got all this cash. Drugs, probably, prostitution for sure, and probably some other stuff, too. Who knows? Anyway, he can only pass so much through his club. That's why he asked about online gambling, it's a big way to money-launder."

"And you told him this worked just the same."

"Right. Any time money changes hands online. It's Al Capone's furniture store."

"What?"

Vince finished off his Phad Thai. Roxanne watched him getting ready to explain. Another theory.

"A front. It's where these guys usually screw up. You start having all this money and no way to account for it. The FBI was after Al Capone for years, all that *Untouchables* stuff. Sean Connery was good, so was Charles Martin Smith, I don't know about Kevin Costner. But it was really the IRS that got him. How could such a little furniture store do so much business, no one ever going in or out?"

"But online, who can tell how many people go in and out?"

"Right. Say you've got an online gambling company. Your drug dealers just get accounts and lose the money. You get paid by Visa and MasterCard."

"That goes on?"

"Every day."

"So, Boris was thinking he could maybe use this place to launder money."

"Getting it into the system is usually the hardest part of crime these days."

"Right." She liked this. This is no theory, this is real. "How come you don't have gambling on this site?"

"I can kind of fly below the radar here, do my thing. You start gambling, you need an office somewhere it's legal: Antigua, Costa Rica, that kind of thing. Usually you need a bigger operation, because a lot of it's betting on football and soccer. You need some real connections."

"So why doesn't Boris just start his own?"

"He probably will. It gets a little tougher every day, though. FINTRAC, stuff like that."

She looked at him.

"New computer system. I don't understand it myself, uses some complicated math stuff. You'll have to ask Suss for the details. Used to be, only deposits over ten thousand dollars had to be reported. You could send out Smurfs depositing nine grand at a time."

"Little blue guys from the cartoon show?"

"Because they're everywhere. They'd take a million bucks in cash, fly to Calgary. Have accounts in every bank in town, spend a week driving around depositing 9900 dollars at a time. Then they'd drive to Edmonton, do the same thing, drive to Banff, all the way to Vancouver, till the money was gone."

"How can they keep track?"

"They can keep track. But it's a hassle, you know? These guys, they'd get caught because the money-counting machines were so loud they'd wake the neighbours. It was the same in the escort business, until they started taking credit cards and Interac."

"More convenient for everyone."

"Cash is always the problem. All those 9000 dollar

deposits in thousands of banks get transferred to hundreds of accounts offshore, then to a few accounts, then to one account. So now they're looking for patterns. A brand new company suddenly getting a lot of customers, even at a thousand bucks a pop, shows up on somebody's computer."

Yeah, Roxanne thought, everybody likes new stuff. But the old stuff? Who gives a shit? "So, if the company's been up and running for years, no one would notice."

"In theory."

Yeah, Roxanne thought, in theory.

• • •

In the passenger seat of the Jag, Marie-Claire said, "That would be a great place for a club," looking at the sailboats in the bay.

Henri said, "There's a club there, the Docks."

"I mean a dancer club. Could really make some money."

"It's downtown, you can't open a new club downtown." Stupid city council, like they're ashamed of it. They take the money, though, taxes and kickbacks.

"Too bad, lot of business."

The big car turned off Lake Shore, rolled over the bridge onto Cherry Street quiet and smooth. Henri thinking, now this is a car, man, brand new Jaguar X2, British Racing Green, less then 10,000 clicks on it, Alpine sound system. They passed the Docks, a huge place right on the water, has a driving range during the day and a drive-in at night. It's got rock climbing and bungee jumping and beach volleyball, and about five bars — indoors and patios — all over the complex. Henri smiled, knowing how badly the bikers wanted to run the whole show. But even they weren't going to muscle the Italians out.

"Maybe private rooms," Marie-Claire said. "With hostesses."

"That what you want?" Henri said, "Be a hostess?"

"I want to make some money."

The Jag rolled over another bridge over another narrow shipping lane, and Henri hung a left, thinking everybody wants to make some money, you just have to pick your spot. Like this place. The politicians and developers were always coming up with new waterfront plans. Get rid of these old broken-down warehouses and abandoned factories and put up office towers or condos, some kind of huge "world class" development. But the amount of fingers in that pie, shit. The payoffs and kickbacks and no-show jobs and overruns and you name it. Only the Olympics would be a big enough scam to grease all those wheels.

"You want to get into management?"

"You think I'm too old?"

Shit, these chicks, always so fucking testy.

"Here." He pulled into the gravel lot in front of a warehouse building. Behind it was a small shipping lane, in from the lake.

Marie-Claire pulled her sunglasses down and said, "Eh? You said it was a sailboat."

"You want to know what it is, ask Nugs."

Marie-Claire stared at the huge boat, must have been fifty feet long, the mast rising as high as the warehouse. Wood trim, shiny railings, the whole thing looked brand new. "How come it's not at the marina?"

"They own all this. It's like a private marina."

She pushed her glasses back up and opened the door.

"I thought you said they were bikers."

"They were," Henri said. "Now they're a corporation."

• • •

Henri hated looking at Nugs's legs, all covered in scar tissue, white blobs and blue lines everywhere. It looked painful, but Nugs never said anything and he always wore shorts or a bathing suit, like he was showing off. You put a bomb in his fucking car, it better take him out. And then the fucking rampage he went on, killing the three guys who did it, or he thought did it. Henri was pretty sure Nugs threw the bodies off this very boat. Body parts, was the rumour.

Nugs said, "So, Anzor had a little traffic accident."

They were just sitting down with their Caesars, actual celery sticks in them, and Henri said, yeah, he saw something on the news.

Nugs laughed. He liked that. "He was a bad driver."

"Yeah," Henri said, "and slow."

"Yeah, slow. Hey honey," Nugs leaned over to look into the other stateroom of the boat and a girl came out, older than Henri expected, maybe even thirty, but tall, tanned all over, even under the tiny strings of her bikini, you could tell, sunglasses on and curly dark hair. "Get me another pen, would you?"

Henri watched her go back into the room — probably a bedroom, but the place was so big he couldn't see a bed through the doorway — and come out again with a dry erase. Henri watched her, and thought she moved with the confidence of someone who grew up with money, like the daughters of the big-shot mining company executives he knew up north. Girls who all went to private schools and came home to raise hell, and then disappeared when charges started to get laid.

Nugs told her to go up on deck and get some sun, and she left. She'd hang around as long as it was different and exciting and pissed off her father enough, and then one day she'd start an art history degree somewhere, go work in a museum, wear designer dresses to fundraisers.

Henri wondered what she'd have to say to Marie-Claire.

Nugs wrote, "How many cars," on a white board with the marker.

Henri said, "Eleven and one truck."

Nugs made a face, held up his hand.

Henri said yeah, yeah, okay, and motioned for the board. He wrote, "FedEx Mercedes delivery van," and showed it to Nugs.

"We got an order." He erased the board and wrote, "Saturday." Hated this fucking shit. The cops were all over the bikers, he knew, with task forces and combined units and big budgets. But come on, sitting on his own boat tied to his own ten acres of waterfront?

Nugs told him once how the bikers were going after the cops. They had better surveillance equipment, more up-to-date computers, better access. In fact, they bought so much they actually took over a chain of stores, SpyWare, that sells the stuff. They even sent chicks into the cop bars to pick them up and get information. Nugs laughed then about how cops would brag, tell a chick anything for a blow job in the parking lot before going home to the wife.

Henri figured it was good to be safe, but shit, it took them an hour to go over everything on the white board. Then Nugs turned up the DVD, playing a porn movie on the built-in flat screen so the moaning on the nice Bose audio system would drown them out. Gave Henri a headache. But they settled it, twelve containers, one oversize for the Mercedes delivery truck, midnight Saturday at the dockyard off Cherry Street. Henri would deliver the cars; Nugs's guys would load them into the containers and onto the ship. Like Halifax, Vancouver, all the big ports, the bikers ran Toronto's docks.

As they were getting up, Nugs said, "Who's taking over for Anzor?"

"We're working on it."

"Anything we can do, you know, reasonable rates."

Henri said, "Thanks, I'll think about it," and Nugs said, don't you mean Boris will think about it?

Henri said, "I'll let you know."

Nugs was all innocent smiles as they went up on deck, saying, of course you will, digging at him like he was Boris's go-boy.

• • •

Marie-Claire's burnt orange 600 dollar Jimmy Choo sandals had wobbled on the gravel of the lot, but were perfect for the deck of the boat. A Hunter Marine 44 Deck Salon, Amber had explained, brand new, could sleep twelve, "if you're close."

Marie-Claire sat in a lounge chair sipping her Long Island Iced Tea, from a mix she could tell, looking at the view. Except there was no view. There was a power plant and the old warehouse and the raised expressway and underneath it, Lake Shore Boulevard. But she was right about Henri. He was more than just a bouncer or club manager. He seemed to know what he was doing.

Amber was on the lounge next to her, on her back, wearing sunglasses and a ballcap. She'd come up from below, untied her bikini, top and bottom, and spread suntan lotion all over herself. She called to one of the guys, there were three or four that Marie-Claire had seen, and told him to bring her a Long Island Iced Tea. Then she looked at Marie-Claire and asked her what she wanted.

She was quite at home being in charge, this Amber. And, Marie-Claire noticed, not a single tat.

CHAPTER ELEVEN

Roxanne looked at the five pictures spread across the building's directory, Boris Suliemanov second from the left, and said, no, she didn't recognize anyone. She thought she was getting pretty good at this lying to the cops. She didn't like the look the black one gave her, though, nodding okay but not believing her at all, pretty much just dismissing her. Pissed her off.

Vince was standing behind him, looking at Roxanne. They were in the lobby of the Toy Works, she and Vince were just coming out when the cops showed up, saying someone in her office said she might be here.

Loewen said, "Are you sure?" and Roxanne said, pretty sure.

The black one, Price, said, "But not positive," and that was enough for Roxanne.

"Positive. I've never seen any of these guys before in my life."

The cops thanked her, shook hands again like they did

when she introduced them to Vince, and they left.

Vince said, "You're getting pretty good at this."

"I don't know why," Roxanne said. "I should have told them, but that bald one pissed me off."

They walked out onto King Street. Roxanne said, "You want to come back to my place? Order some food?"

Vince said, no, they had that Thai for lunch, he didn't want to have restaurant food twice a day. "Why don't we go to my place, I'll cook."

Roxanne said okay, sure, surprised. He really was opening up, more than she expected. Looked like they were going to another level and she was thinking, good, she didn't even have to push that hard.

Then, as they walked into the parking lot, she wondered who was doing the pushing.

• • •

Loewen said, "Why is she lying to us?"

"Who knows? Usually I'd say she's scared to get involved, but that doesn't seem the case here."

"No."

They were sitting on the patio in front of the Starbucks on King, Loewen taking a bite of a spinach and feta croissant, and Price sipping a latte.

"What was that guy's name again?"

Loewen said, "Vince something, hang on," and got his notebook out. "Why?"

"'Cause he's driving your girl home."

At the light, a Mercedes SUV was waiting, Roxanne in the passenger seat and Vince behind the wheel.

"Fournier," Loewen said. He wrote down the license number. "She said he rented space in the building."

"Didn't mention the carpool."
"No."

• • •

The offices of the homicide squad at 40 College Street look like any other office in downtown Toronto in any other new office building: reception area, a big open area with wall dividers, which even the cops call a cube farm, and a few offices around the outside walls for inspectors. The jargon also tries to make the place seem like any other office, calling the lead investigator on a homicide the Major Case Manager, and the suspect a Person of Interest.

Then a guy like Ray Dhaliwal walks in, wearing a wrinkled light-blue suit and even though his parents had an arranged marriage in Bombay forty-five years ago, he grew up on a street in Toronto called Hiawatha and could only be a cop. Actually had a moustache and wore sunglasses all the time. He was saying, "These fucking wannabe gangbangers are pissing me off," and pushing a clothes rack on wheels out of his way to get to his desk.

Loewen was sitting on the edge of Maureen's chair, using her computer and trying not to touch anything. Especially not the pink mouse, that looked like a mouse with whiskers and eyes and a tail. He was looking up at the white board on the back wall, ten feet long with lines up and down making boxes, filled in with the names of homicide victims, dates, and the major case managers. He was thrilled to see his name right there beside Price's, even if it was in red, meaning ongoing investigation, but he tried to be cool, to pretend it was no big deal. He said, "This that guy in the boozecan?"

"That you fucking dumped on me."

Loewen didn't know if he should apologize, or offer to help, or what the fuck to say.

Price hung up the phone and said, "You opening up a Danier Leather outlet in here?"

Dhaliwal said, "You ever heard of the Nealon brothers?"

"They those guys make the expensive salsa and blue chips?"

Mastriano had walked up behind Ray and he said, "That's the Neal Brothers. That corn salsa's good."

Dhaliwal said, "The vic's a guy named Javier Vasquez, from El Salvador. Snow Dawgs. Maybe somebody'll want their coat back, come in and claim it."

Loewen said, "The papers say they're too scared."

"You know what? They're right. Except they're all Snow Dawgs, or hangarounds, so we figure they're just gonna settle the score themselves, you know? But no, they really are scared."

Price was standing by the rack now, picking out a grey leather jacket with a little red on it, not too flashy but a little something. "What size you think this is?"

Dhaliwal said, "Too small for you."

"Why, you think it'll fit you?"

"Got a couple there could be good for my wife. See the blue one?"

"Are these pants?" Price said, holding up a pair of black leather pants.

"People left in a hurry."

"You got some pagers here, any cell phones?"

"Plenty, none with service. That's what happens, you get twenty-four hour customer support."

Loewen said, "Who are the Nealon brothers?"

Dhaliwal said, "Couple of Indians."

"Nealon? What kind of Indian is that?"

Dhaliwal tapped his hand against his mouth and made "whooh-ooh" sounds. "Indian Indian. Native."

Loewen said, "That's who they're scared of?"

"Two guys. Not a gang, not connected at all. We went after the Christie Boys, hard. They're scared of them, too. Vasquez was in the Don last year, and so were the brothers. They move a little weed they grow on the reserve, but mostly they sell guns."

"Great. How you gonna find them?"

Another detective walked into the offices and said, "Indians? You dig a big hole and put a couple cases of two-four in it. When they fall in, you got 'em."

The others looked at him, a big guy with a big gut, used to being the big man in the room. "Just like they did with watermelons in the Old South, looking for niggers." He winked at Price and said, "No offence."

Price said, "What you want, Burroughs?"

"Where's Mo?"

"Mat leave."

"No shit, she having a baby?"

"That's usually what they do on maternity."

Loewen sat back and watched. He'd hadn't seen Price defensive before. Well, not really defensive, more like pissed off but not showing it.

The other guy, Burroughs, looked around the homicide office and said, "You guys could be salesmen in here, calling people up, asking them how much toner they need for the photocopier."

"Yeah," Price said. "That's what we do."

"So, let me know when Mo has the baby."

"Couple of weeks ago."

"No shit. Hey, that's great."

Loewen watched the guy looking around the office, thinking, come on, man, you came here for something, what is it? He noticed now that Price had relaxed, sat back down at his desk and was looking up at Burroughs waiting, not going to ask him.

Burroughs said, "You know this Levine guy? Working the Great Rewards thing? I might have something for him."

"Yeah? Narcotics interested in that?"

Burroughs never looked directly at Price. "I think I got an ID off the security tape."

"The one from the broken camera."

"On the guy came in before, looking around. If it's the guy I think it is, then he probably knows the guys came in later."

"'Cause we all know each other?"

Loewen almost laughed out loud. There was Price, straight face, looking at Burroughs.

"Because they're known associates. We keep files in narcotics, you know, we don't just clean up the mess after everybody's gone."

Price said, "Levine's working it with Louise O'Brien. They're down checking ballistics now."

Burroughs said, "Okay," and started to walk out. He stopped and said, "You guys looking for wagon burners, where's Armstrong? More sensitivity-training bullshit?"

No one said anything till he was gone and then Dhaliwal said, "Wow, there goes a real cop."

Behind him Mastriano said, "Come on, let's go talk to the Brothers."

Loewen watched them go, thinking, yeah, there's a Native guy in homicide, Armstrong. He was working some extradition thing with cops from Michigan, been in Detroit a couple of weeks. Then Loewen wondered, city this diverse, criminals from all over the world, what chance did a white guy have getting into homicide?

Price said, "Who'd you run through CPIC?"

"Everyone," Loewen said. "Suliemanov, his bouncer, Henri Duguay, guy who got shot, Anzor Vladmirski, the bikers who sold the place to Suliemanov. I even ran that Fournier guy our witness is seeing."

"Did you run the witness."

"Yeah."

"Somebody got a hit. The Mounties want to talk to us."

"Yeah?" Loewen was a little excited, like he was getting closer to the big time.

Price waved him off. "It's a friend of mine. Wants to give us the heads-up, that's all."

• • •

"You're not my first, you know," Roxanne said.

"Really," Vince said. "I had you figured for a virgin."

She was still naked, sitting cross-legged on Vince's bed, a small plate beside her. "I went out with an ex-con once. Well, I guess he wasn't really an ex, because I dumped him while he was in jail."

Vince was stretched out on the bed, his hands behind his head. He said, "You dumped a guy in jail?"

"Yeah, I did. Is that some kind of big no-no for cons?"

"Well, it's just a lot of women like guys in jail. They can't cheat, they always know where they are."

Roxanne twirled her cigarette on the plate and said, "I was nineteen years old. He was my high school sweetheart. We didn't meet in school, I don't know when he dropped out. He was twenty-four. Sammy."

"Drove a Trans Am."

"Camaro. He was a dealer. Well, a delivery guy, really, but I didn't know that. Anyway, he got busted, and he was in the Don Jail for about a year waiting for his trial. I used to visit him on Saturdays."

"They have those cubicles with the phones and the plexiglass?"

"I thought they would, I thought it would be like a movie, but it was just a big room. Full of little kids running around and guys getting hand jobs under the tables. I hated it."

"Kids can be noisy."

She smirked at him and took a drag on the cigarette, blowing smoke up towards the ceiling. "It just hit me one day, standing on that ramp outside, a whole lineup of white trash chicks. All wearing the same acid-washed miniskirts, black stockings, and halter tops, bleached blond with pink lip gloss. I just though, shit, this isn't me."

"I can do better."

"Well, I never figured I'd stay with my high school sweetie forever."

No, Vince thought, but he did. He wondered again what Liz Downey was up to. Driving a couple of kids around in a minivan, probably, out on the West Island, Dorval, or Pierrefonds or the South Shore, something like that. He just knew she was still hot, though. He could picture her pulling on a pair of tight Levis, tossing back her hair, and giving him that look. That could be a nice life, out in the burbs.

Roxanne said, "So that's why I wasn't all that shocked to be with an ex-con."

Vince said, yeah.

"What about you? You have a high school sweetheart?" Like she could read his mind.

"Yeah, I guess. The only real girlfriend I ever had."

Roxanne said, "Please."

"Really. It was my last year of high school. My Dad died the year before, and my brother Danny was in the Golan Heights with the peacekeepers. My Mom and I moved to this little apartment in the Bronx."

"The Bronx?"

"It's a part of LaSalle. Montreal, just past Verdun, out by the Seagram's plant and the Labatt brewery."

"Right in the heart of the tourist part of Montreal."

"Yeah." But he smiled. He did like her attitude.

Roxanne stubbed out her cigarette on the plate and put it on the little table beside the bed.

"I met some kids, you know, hanging out in the park smoking up, and one of them was this girl, Elizabeth. Liz. People drifted away, you know, till I ended up walking her home." Vince smiled at the memory.

"Just you and her." She stretched out beside him, her feet up by his head, and pulled the sheet over herself.

"Yeah. We got to her house and we just stood there. I didn't know what to say. I knew what I wanted to do, but I didn't know how. How to go about it, you know? Then she kind of leaned her head to one side, like she was deciding, and she reached out and grabbed my arm and pulled me close and kissed me. Wow."

"Wow."

"I just felt so, I don't know, normal, like a real person. I was so happy. I don't know if I was ever so happy."

"Ever?"

"She went up onto the balcony of her house, the kind they have in LaSalle, two stories, four units. They all look the same. I was still standing on the sidewalk. I couldn't move. Finally she went inside, and I realized I had no idea where I was. I walked around all those streets that look the same till I found the park."

He shook his head, "Liz Downey. Man, I haven't thought about her in years." Didn't know why he said that, just felt like he should. Roxanne was looking at him, interested, and she wasn't going to say anything, so he said, "She had these big ugly glasses, and braces and zits on her cheeks, and I thought she was the most gorgeous girl in the world." He didn't like all this talking about his past with anyone, but Roxanne was really getting to him. "Till she dumped me."

"Sounds like a self-esteem problem."

"What?"

Roxanne shook her head. "Yeah, look, you don't know what it's like to be the dorky girl in school."

"And you do?"

She gave him a look. "Then you come along, all big eyes and puppy love and giving her all kinds of attention and making her feel good, but that makes her feel weird and she doesn't know what to do."

"I thought when the braces came off, and she got contacts and started spending money on her hair, she realized she could do a lot better than me."

"You give her gifts?"

He thought about it. "Yeah, stuffed animal. You know, they used sell those two monkeys with their arms around each other? Kissing? Velcro on their hands, holding them together."

"There you go."

"Come on, we used to go to movies. We saw *The Man Who Fell to Earth* and *The Song Remains the Same*. We saw *Gone with the Wind* on the big screen at the old York Theatre on Ste. Catherine."

"You smothered the poor girl."

"I remember sitting in her mother's kitchen. Sunday afternoon, and she's breaking up with me. I didn't get what she was talking about. I couldn't figure out why is she so nervous? We're not doing anything, it's not like her mother will catch us. Then I finally got it, and I felt like I had to throw up. She walked me halfway home, we stopped by that park I met her in and she kissed me again. Broke my heart."

Roxanne said, "Awwww," and put her hand on his leg. She moved it up and down.

"A couple weeks later I just couldn't take it anymore. I had a cousin working construction in Calgary so I blew off the last two months of school and hopped on the old grey dog."

"The what?"

"The bus. The Greyhound. Anyway, then you know what happened. I went to jail and started working for Travis, and since then pretty much all the women I've been with have been pros."

"Of one sort or another."

"Pretty much the same sort." He stood up, stretched. "Elizabeth Downey, wow. She's probably married, living in some suburb."

Roxanne stood up, too. She pressed her naked body against his. "Now may not be the time to find out."

"No."

Vince leaned back a bit, looked her over and smiled. She said what, and he said, all this going way back, old times. He looked down between her legs and said, "Haven't seen one like that in a long time, reminds me of Danny's *Penthouse* magazines."

Roxanne ran her fingers over herself, her soft hair,

almost no curl in it, fairly long, just the slightest trim around the edges. She was thinking it wasn't really bikini weather yet, but she was also thinking about how far she was willing to go.

Vince said, "What are we gonna do now?"

"Let's take a shower. See where we go from there."

Of course, they went to see Boris.

CHAPTER TWELVE

THEY WERE SITTING IN ONE of those Fiddle and Firkin, or Faken and Beaver, one of those places that are supposed to look like Ye Olde English Pub but are all brand new franchises, part of a chain, serving Coors Light and chicken wings.

Price said, "You ever deal with the Mounties?"

"Never had the pleasure," Loewen said. "Filled out my application, though."

Price was surprised. "What happened?"

Loewen figured he wanted to hear the story, so he said, "I was doing fine, passed everything, looked good. Right up to the interview."

"Then what?"

"I don't know. I mean, I don't want to say, you know? But the old fucker interviewing me? Still had his British accent."

"You think he had a problem with a nice white boy from Brampton."

"Kitchener. Used to be called Berlin, you know. That's the thing with . . ." He almost said "you people," thinking WASP, but caught himself. "The Brits. Live in the past. He kept asking me when my father came over from Germany. I told him my *grand*father came over in the twenties. I don't know, maybe this guy was in the fucking war. Anyway," Loewen shook his head, "there's no affirmative action for Germans."

Price considered it, then said, "Sometimes you just not white enough in this country."

Loewen laughed. "You got that right."

"So anyway," Price said, "I guess you know the Mounties coming on like they're smarter than everyone else and doing us the biggest favour of our lives, since Traci-Anne Ellis's hand job in her father's Pontiac 6000."

"Man, you knew Traci-Anne, too."

Price said, "I know this one, we did a little something together last year. Still a Mountie, but not so bad. Here," Price looked at the door. "Brought a date."

Loewen watched the two Mounties cross the bar, the guy looking exactly like he expected, Dudley Do-Right clean-cut, but the woman was younger and looking good — skirt, kind of loose hair but styled, a little too stylish for Scarborough.

But it turned out good-looking women Mounties are still Mounties.

• • •

After they sat down and ordered pints of Smithwicks, Dudley Do-Right, actual name of Martin Greggs, said, "You ever deal with the Russian mob?"

Loewen said, "When I was up in North York, they had a GST scam. We got a couple of them."

"GST, shit. How long you been in homicide?"

Loewen said, "Long enough."

Greggs looked at Price and said, "He busting his fucking cherry on *this* one?"

"Don't worry yourself."

Greggs said okay, sure. "A Russian guy said how come it is that my country is so fucked up, but the crime is so organized?"

The woman Mountie said, "The thing is, it's not that organized."

Loewen had been ready to make nice to this lady Mountie, Sergeant Jennifer Sagar. Not to flirt or come on strong, just to be polite, a little respectful. He figured with this partner it'd be something she wasn't used to, but by the way she was looking at Price, Loewen figured she was the one he'd done a little something with last year.

She was saying, "There are really about 150 gangs in Moscow. It's hard to keep track. A lot of them are Chechen, and they went home to fight in the war. Or they got distracted by the war right in Moscow. You may have heard about a theatre being taken over? Sometimes we call them terrorists, sometimes we call them mafia. It's usually the same guys."

"So that was just for ransom?"

Greggs looked at Loewen like he was an idiot.

Sergeant Sagar said, "Who knows? That's the thing, their motives get mixed up. Usually it's just crime, but politics is more involved over there."

Right, Loewen thought, involved. At least our crooks don't give a shit about politics.

Greggs said, "You guys want some wings?" He was waving over the waitress. "City of Toronto have any budget these days?"

Price said, "We came all the way out here, didn't we?"

Sagar was still talking to Loewen, the only guy who seemed interested. "There are three main Chechen organizations and two main Slav organizations. They're enemies, they fought a war in the mid-nineties that killed more people than the real Russian–Chechen war."

"Well," Loewen said, "I bet they are better armed."

"They sure are. And a lot better funded. They operate in the UK, Poland, Turkey, Jordan, the Netherlands, Yugoslavia, Hungary."

"And Canada."

Sagar leaned back and took the first drink from her pint. Loewen noticed she took a nice long drink. "To be honest, we don't know how directly tied the local ones are to Moscow. Your victim, Anzor Vladmirski, ran an agency that brought over strippers and hookers."

"We saw the pictures in his office," Loewen said.

"Some great looking chicks." Greggs said, "Good attitude."

"Hockey players and hookers," Price said, "our main import from Russia."

Sagar said, "Well, don't forget about all the hash and heroin."

"And the cars we send them," Loewen said. "It's a great economy."

"Yeah, the black market one. Anyway," Sagar said, "Anzor had a lot of people's life and death in his hands. He picks a girl from some slum in eastern Europe, brings her to Toronto. She can make more in two years than she can in the rest of her life back home."

"She get to keep any of it?"

Greggs put down his beer and said, "Probably not, but a lot of it ends up back home. Pays off someone."

"And if Anzor doesn't pick a girl, she can't exactly come over on her own."

Loewen liked the way Sagar talked. Matter of fact, but knowing the implications. He figured she was good at her job, smart. She just couldn't completely shake that Mountie indoctrination that they're the best.

She said, "Immigration used to give them one-year visas. They were on the list."

"The list?"

"The jobs that need to be filled. Whatever there's a shortage, immigration allows businesses to bring people in from other countries. Exotic dancers, they were on the list. Under the busker category."

Price said, "You wouldn't think we'd have a shortage of jugglers and mimes."

Greggs said, "Don't forget those one-man-band guys, they have a drum on their back and cymbals strapped to their knees."

"I guess you need to import those, yeah."

Sagar said, "For a while immigration was just letting in as many strippers as these guys could bring over. The girls were desperate, they were all from Romania, or the Czech Republic or Slovakia or Russia. The club owners — it was mostly bikers in those days — they got contracts with Russian guys like Anzor to bring in the girls. The girls would do just about anything in the VIP rooms. But then the Russian guys wanted a bigger piece of the action, so they started taking over the clubs."

"Which brings us to Boris Suliemanov."

Sagar looked at Price and then at Loewen. "You sure

he's the shooter?"

"He was driving, older guy did the shooting. We've got a witness."

"This witness have any idea who they're identifying?"

Price said, "The witness is reluctant."

Greggs snorted. "Have you talked witness protection? Relocating them to Redneck City, Alberta?"

Loewen thought, shit, this guy. He said, "Don't worry about our witness."

Greggs shrugged. Loewen figured he didn't worry about anything because he didn't really give a shit about anything.

"Anyway," Sagar said, "Boris Suliemanov doesn't show up in any Interpol database."

"We know."

"His father was arrested a few times in the old Soviet Union, and also in Romania and the Czech Republic after the wall fell."

Loewen said to Price, "Older guy, that could be the shooter."

Sagar said, "Unlikely. He died five years ago. Lung cancer. From what we can tell, he wasn't a full member of any gang. He was a smuggler and did a lot of dealing on the black market. His first son, Mikhail, was starting to make some moves in the Tsentralnaya Gang."

Loewen said "Do they call them 'made guys' in Russia?" He was just trying to be funny, but Sagar ignored it.

"Apparently the gang knew him, but they really started talking after he killed the virus guy."

"Computers?"

"Some of these Russian programmers write a virus to show how good they are at infiltrating security systems."

"Bastards."

Greggs laughed. "You looking at a lot of online porn, there, Price?"

Sagar said, "The story goes, Mikhail and a bunch of other smugglers lost a lot of important data, contacts and such, when a virus wiped their hard drives. He found out who wrote the virus and set up a meeting in a bar. Place actually owned by a Canadian, guy from Halifax. The programmer shows up because he thinks Mikhail wants to hire him to break into security systems. He thinks his little audition piece worked."

"Yeah, but what happens," Greggs said, "is that Mikhail picks up the guy's laptop and beats him to death with it."

"Holy shit."

Price said, "He got killed for that?"

"Didn't even get arrested," Sagar said. "It actually worked, and the Tsentralnaya liked him. We're not sure how he was killed. Probably another gang, or another Tsentralnaya. He was moving up pretty fast."

"So," Greggs said, "it looks like Boris is the idiot son, sent to the colonies."

The waitress brought the wings to the table and Greggs was the only one to order another beer.

Then he said, "Maybe even T.O.'s finest can pin a murder in broad daylight on the idiot son."

Sagar did a pretty good job ignoring her partner. She said to Price, "I guess you know all about his club out by the airport."

Price said, "Yeah, Club International. He classed the place up a lot."

"Maybe you can tell us how he managed to get the bikers to sell out."

"Imagine he made them an offer they couldn't refuse.

With no army behind him, he probably just gave them a lot of cash."

"Cash may be his biggest problem these days. Once he gets it in the system he can move it around pretty easily. But it's getting tougher — or really, more expensive — to get it in. This guy doesn't seem to have the best connections in the world. He doesn't really have a motive to take out his own courier. You sure it was him?"

"Yeah, we're sure," Price said, the first time Loewen heard him admit it. "So you got a CI working him?"

She said, "Now, Andre, you know I can't tell you that."

Loewen watched her react to the idea of the "confidential informant," someone inside paid very well, that being how the Mounties do it. It's all about budgets.

"But the hit came up when we ran Boris."

"Why do you keep asking these questions you know I can't answer."

"Never know till you try."

Loewen thought he saw Price wink, but he wasn't sure.

• • •

Roxanne waited till they got out of the shower to mention it, but she'd done everything she could to put Vince in a good mood.

Then, drying herself off with a towel, she put a foot on the edge of the tub and rubbed her leg, saying, "Have you got any more razors?" and tugged on her soft hair.

Vince said, "You don't want to take it all the way," and she said, no, she didn't. But she was sure thinking about it.

Then she said, "So, what are we going to do about Boris Suliemanov and his dirty money?"

Vince was standing in front of the mirror and she caught his eyes, glancing at her as he lathered his face. He didn't look surprised that she'd brought it up. "What do you want to do about it?"

"I thought maybe we could help him clean it."

He kept looking at the mirror, taking out his disposable razor and starting to shave. "I had a feeling you might say that."

She'd been thinking about telling him her idea since at least yesterday, but she wanted to be sure he'd go for it. Or pretty sure. "The way I see it, he's got all this cash and he needs a way to get it into the system. And you collect money from all over the world and deposit it into your account here."

"You're saying his drug dealers all open accounts with VSF Online? Get memberships on the porno pages?" The way he said it made it sound like a crazy idea, but he just kept shaving.

"Why not? You have customers everywhere. They can pay by credit card."

"They can also pay by Digicash and Internet cheque, and a few other ways." He was casual about it, but she could tell he really was interested. "Like Western Union, but places set up especially for Internet transactions. Some credit card companies won't handle porn sites anymore. Looks bad, I guess, but they all have subsidiaries that do. We work with a few different ones."

"So you're already doing it. You have a reputation, you pay taxes, you're legit."

"If I suddenly get a lot more customers, it's just because I've got good product."

"So Boris's guys can just be new customers. Once the money gets to Canada, you can pay it out to all kinds of companies. Boris can be a consultant, it even looks good. He can pay a few taxes, start going legit like he wants."

Vince nodded. "You've got this all figured out."

"I just see the opportunities."

Vince turned from the mirror and looked at her. "What's in it for you?"

Roxanne said, "Well, I would expect some kind of finder's fee, some brokerage fee." Not phony coy at all, standing there naked in his bathroom.

"Every month?"

"If that's the way you think it would work."

"It could. It sure could."

"Okay," Roxanne said, "let's go see Boris."

She walked out of the bathroom while Vince finished up. She was really starting to like this. The money would be good, pay off Angus, get some breathing room. But there was more to it. Her heart was pounding, feeling that rush, way better than driving around with Sammy. She wasn't just some kid following anymore.

She could take this far.

CHAPTER THIRTEEN

Marie-Claire was thinking lots of people get paid to use their bodies. There was a guy in her confirmation class back in Lac St. Jean. He was a hockey player now in California, San Jose or Anaheim last she heard. He got paid to use his body. Got paid a lot, and really, just to hit people. He was an enforcer, a fighter, not even much of a player. And the bouncers here, or even her father, working construction, he got paid to carry shit.

So fuck her, that Amber and her attitude. Like she was so much better. You have a nice body, she said, for your age.

Henri said, "You going to work today?"

"Or what?"

"Nothing. Shit."

They were pulling into the parking lot of the club, Henri parking the Jag in front of the garbage bin by the side door. Next to Boris's new yellow convertible Saab.

"I don't know if I want to."

"Then don't."

Yeah, and don't get paid. Thirty-four years old and starting to feel it. Dancing for nineteen years, and what do I have to show for it? All those years in the biker bars in Quebec not paid shit. Then, when they started taking over Ontario, they brought a lot of the French girls with them. At first. Till they started bringing in the Russians. Now what? Make a grand a week, 1500 sometimes, and spend it all. Where does it all go? Cabs and restaurants and clothes and makeup, and trips south and eighteen-fifty a month for the condo in Etobicoke, and there's nothing left.

Just her body.

Henri said, "You want, come in the lounge, have a drink, I have to talk to Boris and then we can go."

"Yeah? Go where?"

He looked at her. She realized he'd been looking at her different. Like he was really looking at her. "Go out, someplace. Nice. Have dinner."

She said, yeah okay, that sounds good.

They walked into the club, and Marie-Claire thought again about how much nicer the place was since Boris took over. Big renovation, new lights, new tables and chairs, new carpets, even put in new hardwood on the stage so their spike heels didn't get caught. Like the time that Hungarian chick broke her ankle. Shipped her home in a hurry.

Henri nodded at a few people as they walked through the main floor and back to the VIP rooms. He asked a bouncer, big English guy with a spiderweb tattoo on his neck, if Boris was in and the guy said, yeah, in his office.

Marie-Claire liked the way Henri was in charge, like a boss, but a good boss, the way her father explained the difference to her when she was ten, and used to take him his lunch at the building site.

Henri told the English bouncer not to let anyone in the private VIP room, and then opened the door for Marie-Claire.

A real gentleman.

• • •

Boris told his mother, no, he didn't know where Khozha was, but he was sure he was still in Toronto. He knew that because he still couldn't get the old fucker on a plane. That part he mumbled under his breath, and when his mother asked him what was that, he said he had to go.

Henri was coming in from the private VIP room, that French girl in there on the couch but not working, she was watching TV.

Boris said, "She working today?"

"We're going out."

"Now you, too."

Henri sat down on the couch facing the desk. "What the fuck that mean?"

Boris waved him off, these guys always looking for a fight. He couldn't let it look like he was backing down, but he really didn't give a shit. He said, "Take it easy. We're short today. Khozha is still out with Amelie, now she's not working."

"I'll call in some freelancers."

Boris said good. Then he said, "Fucking Anzor," and regretted it right away. He looked up quick at Henri, but he didn't seem to care.

"There are lots of other agencies. And plenty of dancers who don't even have visas. They just stayed here, work straight cash."

"Yeah," Boris said, "but they all worked with Anzor, too."

Henri waved him off and Boris thought, yeah, he's right, there's always a way. It was just all happening at the same time.

"Everything's set with Nugs."

"How many more we need?"

"Just the special order. Working on it now."

Boris leaned back in his chair and relaxed a bit. Twelve cars at forty grand apiece. Four hundred and eighty grand. "When?"

"Sunday. Well, after we close Saturday."

Boris would pick up half the cash then, and get the other half when the boat got to Riga in two weeks. Shit, he still had the last payment from the last delivery in cash in the change room. He would have given the money to Anzor and he would have taken it to Bosnia, deposited it in a bank he knew, and then transferred the money over the month, nine grand at a time, to Boris's account. Even that was getting riskier with the new European Union and the banking laws, computers looking for patterns and finding plenty.

If only his brother hadn't gotten himself fucking killed, he never would have needed Anzor in the first place. Boris knew Anzor had only ever been a short-term solution, but he still didn't have anything else in place. And now he'd be holding a half-million in cash.

Henri said, "Nugs made an offer."

"I bet he did."

"I told him I'd think about it."

"What's his rate?"

"We didn't get into it."

"Do you want to?"

"Hell no. They'll want some huge fucking piece of it, for sure, but they're still too public, still too many task forces after them."

"They're the ones out shaking hands with the mayor."

"I fucking know that," Henri said.

Always so tense, this guy, Boris thought. Sometimes he could see the spot Henri was in, stuck between him and the bikers. Couldn't be so sure he'd really left them behind, what he'd do if he had to make a choice. He said, "You still think like them."

"Fuck that."

So which was he, really, Boris wondered. He knew that Henri and the bikers who owned the club in the nineties, the Demon Keepers, were a small gang from up north. They stayed out of the way of the Italians and the Para-Dice Riders downtown. They didn't have much ambition and didn't see too far into the future. Boris thought the cops called them "mumblies," what they called "losers and users," but when he came along and made them an offer for the club, only Henri seemed to know what he was doing.

They'd been bringing girls in from Quebec for years, but that was drying up and the Filipino and Thai chicks were totally controlled by Triads. Guys like Anzor started bringing in the eastern European girls from the "white Third World." Henri saw right away that the Russians were going to take over, but the rest of the bikers didn't. At least the mumblies out here.

Boris made them a couple of offers and they turned him down, so he had to pay off a few cops to get the place raided over and over — amazing how cheap that was — and they got fed up. Most of the bikers in that gang were losers and users. Henri told him later that they really didn't know what to do, the whole thing was up in the air. There was lots of talk of war, of takeovers. One day it was Les Hells or the Rock Machine from Quebec, the next day it was the Banditos from the States. Some of them set up in Kingston or Niagara Falls, but then figured it would be easier to just patch-over the guys already here. There was going to be a one-year probation — Henri said they talked just like bullshit managers at any fucking job — and they'd all have to start over as hangarounds.

Henri hadn't said anything, but there was no way he was going to do that. Nugs thought it might be okay. Nugs was the only other Keeper could think of anything past lunch, and Henri could tell he was starting to see the future. Nugs was going to some of the meetings, mostly the Para-Dice Riders and the Outlaws meeting with Les Hells.

When they did it, they hand-picked the guys they wanted and patched them — made them full members right away. Henri said he didn't want to, it looked like a corporate takeover. Nugs told him no hard feelings, and they made a deal for the club.

Then when Boris came around again, he made a deal with Henri and they really started to change the place. Now they were almost making legit money as a bar, and they had the weed and speed and some ecstasy and some girls set up in condo hotels around the airport the customers could charge to the bar bill, make it look like they took some clients out for dinner.

And the stolen cars they shipped to Russia.

Boris said, "I might have something else."

"Yeah?"

"You remember the real estate lady?"

Henri said, yeah, he did.

"She's got someone else in the building, runs a bunch of porno websites."

Henri said, "Yeah? . . ."

Boris knew from the very beginning that Henri could

see a little of the future. He didn't always react fast, sometimes he actually waited to hear the deal.

"They're coming up today." Boris said, "We'll talk."

Henri said, "Good. Keep our options open."

Right, Boris thought, all of us.

• • •

Roxanne said, "You listen to the Mighty Q?"

"So?" He looked at her as he sped up the ramp to the Gardiner and cut across three lanes of traffic, T Rex, "Bang a Gong" coming from the stereo.

"It's just so . . . old."

"I'm old."

She rolled her eyes.

"For a while there, I tried jazz. Fusion stuff: Herbie Hancock, Chick Corea, Jean-Luc Ponty. I bought the first Wynton Marsalis album. It just wasn't me."

"But this is?"

"Yeah, it is."

Roxanne looked through her bag and brought out her cigarettes. She held out the pack for him, but he shook his head. She said, "You were ten when the sixties ended. You don't remember any of this psychedelic shit."

"I like the psychedelic shit. But you're right, it's not really mine. I had an older brother, I used to listen to his records: The Doors, C.C.R., Led Zeppelin, Bowie, Uriah Heep. Even this one here, T Rex."

"You've got a brother?"

Vince nodded, looking straight ahead, but not, Roxanne noticed, at the road. "Yeah, Danny. Joined the army when I was like ten. Got himself killed."

"I didn't think the Canadian army ever went to war."

"Oh he went," Vince said. "With the peacekeepers in the Golan Heights, '74, '75. That's not where he was killed though."

Roxanne watched Vince thinking about it. Then he smiled, shook his head — she could tell he was just shaking it out. She wondered how he could do that. She could never let things go.

He said, "They say this psychedelic stuff is from '65 to '75, so yeah, it's more Danny's, it ends pretty much where I start. I like the Super Seventies Sundays on the Hamilton station, Y108. That's really my music."

They were in the outside lane, topping 120 clicks, Vince holding the wheel of his Mercedes SUV, the G500 that looked square like a Land Rover, with one hand, one finger. The wheel was made out of wood, the same kind as the shift knob. She wondered if he was always so relaxed. She sure hadn't seen him stressed out yet. Well, this meeting with Boris might change things.

"Isn't seventies all disco?"

"Are you kidding? Alice Cooper, Aerosmith, 'Back in the Saddle,' back when they were good. That *Frampton Comes Alive*, man everyone had that. Rush. And yeah, disco, and disco sucks, right? It wasn't all bad, you know. There was some decent funk in there. Here." He pushed a button on the CD player and the music changed. "You know Donna Summer had a lot to do with Madonna."

Roxanne smirked. She was thinking, no way, but didn't say anything. She watched Vince cut across three lanes of bumper to bumper and take the Islington exit, heading for the 427 north.

"What's this?"

"Donna Summer. You've only ever heard 'Love to Love You,' right?"

"I don't even know if I've heard that." She was starting to get into it, the beat was pretty good, but then the song changed. Another disco song, a woman singing about wanting more, more, more. Roxanne said, "Did she just say that if you want to know how she feels you have to get the cameras rolling?"

"*More, More, More*. Andrea True Connection. She was a soft-porn star in the seventies. Had a disco hit."

"They all think they're singers. Not just Traci Lords."

The expressways always made Roxanne nervous. On her first trip to L.A. she rented a car at the airport and was completely psyched up for the incredible driving experience the movies always talked about. But really, after the expressways in Toronto, it just wasn't so bad. Vince weaved in and out, bumper to bumper at 120, 130 clicks, the big Mercedes so smooth, him not even looking. Roxanne just knew no matter how much she drove, she'd never be able to do it like that.

"Why don't you have one whole song on here?"

"Because Suss made the disc. I asked him to put together some late-seventies music and this is what he gave me."

"Are those rockets?"

"'Afternoon Delight.' Suss only liked the rockets. Now he's on to Boston, 'Peace of Mind.' Just wait for the Peter Frampton."

"You go see these guys at Casino Rama?"

"He did a great job mixing it with Cheap Trick, the two live albums, it sounds like the same concert."

"Where did you get that guy?"

"Fred D.S. Mills."

"That's his real name? What's the D.S. for?"

"He'll never tell. I met him years ago when he was still

in high school." Roxanne watched Vince settle into his storytelling pose, left arm on the edge of the window, one finger on the wheel, turned half-sideways, looking at her more than the road. "I was working for the escort king, Mickey Kennedy. He had about fifty agencies listed in the Yellow Pages, but they were all one place, really."

"I remember that. He got busted last year. He ran all those companies out of a house on Coxwell. Him and his wife."

"Yeah, Carole." Roxanne watched Vince smile a little, the way he did thinking about his past life. His life of crime, like he missed it so much. Or maybe not, she couldn't really tell. Like the Hip say, "My baby she don't know me when I'm thinking 'bout those years."

"Carole really ran the business. She took out all the ads, came up with all the names: Classy Ladies, T.O.'s Best, Top of the Tower. Very patriotic. I took a few computer courses in Kingston."

"Millhaven."

"I like to say Kingston. People might think I went to Queen's."

"Sure, yeah, that could happen."

"And the Internet was just starting to take off. The browser was called Mosaic, before Netscape, before Explorer."

"Prehistoric."

"It was. So Carole figured they should get in on it. She's a very smart lady."

Roxanne couldn't remember from the news accounts if the wife had been an escort before she started running the companies, but she was pretty sure she was.

"I went out to register the domain names, but every time I tried, they were taken. Torontosbest.com — taken.

Classyladiesofto.com — taken. Everyone of the Yellow Pages company names was taken, and all the websites had nothing on them but an email address."

"Suss@aol.com?"

"I forget what he called himself back then. Yahmon, something like that. Always trying to sound Jamaican, our Trinidadian Suss."

"He's not Jamaican?"

Vince cut across a couple of lanes of traffic to the 401. "That's why he's Suss. It was how the Jamaicans insulted people, said they were suspect. Suss. I started calling him that, man he hated it. But that's the thing. All the black kids in town, what do they say? Jamaican by birth, American by choice, Canadian by default. All the other island kids want to be Jamaican."

"God, why?"

"Toughest on the block, don't take no shit from no one, mon. So finally I sent the email. He offers to sell me the names for a thousand bucks each. Twenty thousand bucks. People were doing it all the time, registering anything they thought they could sell. It was called domain mining or something. I've heard that some big companies really did pay out millions for site names, but it sounds like an urban myth to me."

"So you didn't pay?"

"Carole said we should give him a hundred bucks and a half hour with one of the escorts. We didn't know he was fifteen years old. Mickey used one of his favourite lines, said, 'Hey, we're crime, everybody knows, crime don't pay.'"

"I've heard that before."

"You think? I email him, tell him sure, I'll pay. We set up a meeting at a donut shop on Jane. I knew right then."

"You knew what?"

"I knew he was a kid. I mean, a donut shop? Sure enough, I walk in, there's these two black guys sitting in a booth. Well, the place is in the jungle, so everyone in there was black, but I could see the two I was meeting. Kid with wire-rimmed glasses and a guy in his twenties trying so hard to look tough. They wanted to meet in the afternoon. I made it ten at night and *they* were scared to be in there."

Right, Roxanne thought, looking at Vince, but you weren't.

"I sat down and said I'd give him a hundred bucks and a half-hour with an escort. The older guy said, 'A half-hour each?'" Vince laughed at the memory, shaking his head. He barely moved as he pulled off the 401 onto Airport Road and then south on Dixon. "Suss was so pissed, he tried to act so tough. Turns out the guy was his cousin, a student at York, brought along to look legit. They were wearing leather jackets and hats and bandanas and shit, but they were such students. I almost offered them a ride home. But I was impressed that Suss was thinking ahead so much. Turns out he used his high school's online account to pay for the domain names and they never knew. I told him to stay in touch and stay in school, learn programming. I didn't know it would be so big. When I was ready to leave the Kennedys, I called up Suss and we started VSF together."

"He's a partner?"

"He's got an interest. So does Garry." They pulled into the parking lot of the Club International. "Here we are. Someday I'll tell you how I met Garry. That's a story."

Roxanne watched Vince get out of the SUV and walk towards the club. She got out herself and closed the door, never taking her eyes off him. Here he was, going to meet a Russian mobster about a money-laundering scam that could make them all rich or send them all to prison for fucking ever, and he acted like it was nothing. Like he did it every day.

Maybe it was nothing to him. Maybe he wasn't kidding when he said he was only ever in the right place at the right time. She just couldn't tell if he was a guy who carefully planned things, or if things just fell in his lap and he landed on his feet.

Shit.

• • •

Loewen said, "I told you there was something about that woman."

"You liked her legs."

"I liked her attitude."

They watched her drop her cigarette and follow the guy she was with yesterday into the strip club.

"What do you like about her now?"

"Everything."

"And Mr. Fournier. He have a record?"

"Nothing."

Price opened the door of the Crown Vic and said, "Let's go see."

CHAPTER FOURTEEN

Vince told Roxanne and Boris he'd wait outside while they went over the details of the lease. He was going to sit at the bar, have a drink, work out this plan they'd come up with for Boris to go on the payroll as a consultant to VSF, but when he came out of the office, he saw a bald black guy sitting at a table by himself and thought he knew him from somewhere. He just didn't know where.

Then the guy waved him over and Vince realized he was one of the cops who showed the pictures to Roxanne in the lobby of the Toy Works. Vince sat down and said he was sorry, he couldn't remember the guy's name.

"Andre Price."

"I'm Vince Fournier."

"You just here checking out talent, looking for another All Nude Sports Report babe?" Letting him know they checked him out.

Vince said, no, he's got more girls coming in to see him

than he could use in 100 years. "Everybody wants to be a star."

"I guess." Price watched the woman on stage for a bit. She turned on the pole, way up high, both bare feet on the pole. Like she worked out dance routines. He looked at Vince again and said, "You have any trouble finding ones that speak English?"

"A little. Can be hard in this city. But we use some French girls for Quebec and France, and a few Indians — India Indians I mean. Some others speaking Farsi, Arabic, places where they can't make the stuff themselves but sure love to chat."

"Great thing about Toronto, so multicultural."

Vince looked at him and couldn't tell if he was being sarcastic. He looked at the office for Roxanne, hoping she didn't just walk out into the bar, be tough to explain what she was doing here, meeting a guy she said yesterday she didn't know.

Vince said, "Yeah, well, Toronto's okay."

"You're not from here?"

"No."

"No one is." Price said, "Where you from?"

"Montreal."

"Yeah? Me too. Whereabouts?"

"LaSalle."

"No shit. I grew up in the Heights."

Vince said, "Twelfth Avenue," but he knew the Heights. A lot of apartment buildings and fourplexes, not quite a housing project or slums, but that's the idea. "I was only there my last year of high school, though." That year Vince was thinking about so much lately. Going out with Liz Downey, thinking about going to CEGEP, community college, having a normal life. Wondering what she was doing now. He said, "Before that I lived on the South Shore, Greenfield Park."

"We used to play ball against you, the Greenfield Park Packers."

"I was a wide receiver. You a LaSalle Warrior?"

"Used to get the shit kicked out of us by you guys."

"Take their ball pretty seriously in the Park."

"We used to sit on the bench, have a smoke between plays. You guys, all business, man. We lost once, sixty-three zip. What brought you to Toronto?"

"It's the centre of the universe."

"Yeah," Price said. "And you don't speak French."

"Not a fucking word. You?"

"After LaSalle High I went to Dawson, took Law and Security. Applied to the RCMP but I couldn't see myself in Buttfuck, Yukon."

"Be the only black guy for a thousand miles."

"You really stand out against the tundra. I got offers from police forces all across the country, but not my own hometown."

"You did all right."

"See a chance, you take it."

Vince knew he was watching, checking out his reaction. All he said was, "Isn't that a Steve Winwood song?" He saw the office door open and looked over. Shit, there was Roxanne, just standing there.

• • •

What could she do? They saw her. They both did, Vince and the black detective, sitting together. Roxanne watched the waitress stop at their table and put down two bottles of light beer, so she walked right up to the table and said, "When you showed me the pictures, I thought there was something familiar, you know? But you were talking about that thing that happened on King Street and I knew that wasn't it, so I couldn't really place it." She sat down at the table and said to the waitress, who was still standing there, "Rye and ginger," then looking right back at them, said, "You guys look like old friends."

Price said, "Turns out we used to play football against each other in Montreal. Mr. Fournier here was a Greenfield Park Packer."

Vince was nodding. "We had the same green and gold uniforms as Green Bay."

"Yeah," Price said, "with the G on the helmet. LaSalle Warriors, we were black and red. You go to LaSalle Protestant?" Looking at Vince.

Roxanne watched him, Vince, casual like he always was, like nothing ever bothered him. Sitting here in Boris Suliemanov's strip club having a beer with the cop investigating a murder everyone knew Boris paid for.

Vince said, "Just one year."

"You said that, right. Your last year. Then where'd you go? You come straight to Toronto?"

The cop trying to get Vince to say something. Roxanne watched him take a drink of his beer. If he was stalling, trying to think of something to say — to avoid letting him know he had a record, that he'd done time — you couldn't tell. Roxanne was impressed at how casual he was.

And maybe a little worried, if she really thought about it.

Vince said, "I went out west, like you do when you're eighteen. Calgary, Edmonton. Even went up to Buttfuck, Yukon." He smiled a little at the cop, and Roxanne saw Price smile back. Shit, now they had inside jokes, they really were buds. "Worked construction. Stole some construction equipment."

What the hell was he telling him that for? Roxanne looked from Vince to Price and back. What was he doing? He had to know Price was trying to get this kind of information out of him, but he just kept talking, saying how he worked with some Indians, not India Indians, Blackfoot guys from Southern Alberta. They stole heavy equipment, Price interrupting to ask, like bulldozers? And Vince saying, yeah bulldozers, backhoes, loaders. They drove them across the border into Montana on back roads on the reserve. He told him the whole thing and Price just laughed.

He said, "The Wild West."

"You know it."

The waitress came to the table and gave Roxanne her rye and ginger. Roxanne took a drink, too fast and too much she thought right away, but she needed it. Shit, these two old friends. She wanted to know where the other cop, the younger good-looking one was, but she didn't want to ask.

She said, "You know, now that I think of it, the guy with the gun might not have even gotten out of a Volvo."

Price looked at her. She could tell he didn't believe her for a second and she just wanted to shut up, but she couldn't help it. She said, "Yeah, I know I saw a Volvo, but I guess that was just because Boris was down looking at the Toy Works, the building I'm leasing on King."

Price nodded along like everything was fine with him, like all that made perfect sense, but even as she said it, Roxanne knew it didn't. She looked at Vince for help, but he was just sitting there.

"I didn't actually see Boris that day, I guess he was just checking out the building, but then when that happened, well, like you said, I must have been in shock and got it mixed up."

"Sure," Price said. "That must have been it."

Roxanne told herself, keep quiet, just stop talking, shut up.

But the two guys, the old friends Price and Vince, weren't about to say anything. She thought Vince was just hanging her out to dry and she didn't know why. The longer it went on, no one at the table talking, the more she wanted to just say something.

Then Price saved her. Sort of. He finally said something, but what he said was, "You know, Boris doesn't drive a Volvo. He drives a Saab. Yellow one. A convertible."

Roxanne said, "Really?" And she started to think of an explanation, some reason why she thought she saw Boris in a Volvo, but not while some other guy got out and shot a guy sitting in a Navigator.

That guy right there, walking in with the other cop.

She couldn't believe it. It was definitely the guy who'd pulled the trigger, three times, exploded that guy's head all over the window and all over the bike courier. He was coming out of the VIP room with a huge guy in a suit, who must be the bouncer, and the other cop, the younger white one, Loewen.

Price said, "Something wrong?"

Roxanne said, no, of course not, she just had to go to the washroom, and left before anyone got to the table.

• • •

Coming out of the bathroom, which was way nicer than she'd expected, Roxanne saw Vince standing by the small stage. He was as casual as always, leaning against the bar looking around, not watching the toned chick with the crew cut do the splits. Hell, even Roxanne noticed another Brazilian wax.

Vince said, "They've got business, we might as well take off."

Might as well. Like, as if the cops didn't have business with the Russian mobster they'd stick around, check out the strippers, maybe have a drink in the VIP room.

In the SUV Roxanne said, "You guys really seemed like old friends."

"So you said."

She watched him drive, one hand on the wheel, shifting through the gears, changing lanes on the 427. Usually she had some idea what guys were thinking, especially when they walked out of a peeler bar, but not with this guy.

"You were telling him a lot of stories."

"Yeah, my misspent youth."

"Aren't you worried he's going to look you up?"

"He already did."

"So, you don't think that's a problem? That you've done time?"

Vince didn't react at all. He just tapped the wheel in time with "Sweet City Woman." After the chorus he said, "Look at that, we're talking about the old days in Calgary and they play the Stampeders. You think that's a coincidence?"

He looked at her and she looked back, staring at him till she thought he was going to drive right off the fucking road, and she said, "Okay, so you're not worried, nothing to be worried about."

He said, "Not a thing," and it was really starting to piss her off, this couldn't-give-a-shit attitude of his. This deal with Boris could really work, the guy told them how many cars he was stealing and shipping to Lithuania, the biggest used-car lot in the world, and the money could all go through Vince's company, and he still won't take it seriously.

Roxanne lit a cigarette and blew smoke at the windshield. She said, "So, what did you go to jail for, anyway?"

"Theft over 5000 dollars."

"What'd you steal, a car?"

"Bunch of tools, stereos, barbecues."

"What'd you rob?"

"Sears."

"Shoplifting? How do you shoplift a barbecue?"

"I was a night janitor in the Sears in the Chinook Centre. There were twelve of us. They'd lock us in the store at eleven, let us out at seven in the morning."

"They locked you in?"

"There were some fire exits, but if you opened one, the alarm went off and cops were all over the place."

"So how'd you get the barbecues out?" She was still pissed off, but now she really wanted to know.

"Yeah, that was me. Well, it wasn't my idea or anything, I was barely eighteen, I'd only been in Calgary a couple of months."

"Right, after the love of your life dumped you."

She thought maybe she shouldn't have said it, it seemed to slow him down, and she could tell what he was thinking about then.

But he said, "Yeah." And then, "After I got fired from the construction site, my cousin got me the job, working the night shift. He was working there, too. Couple of years older than me. I was just a scared kid, spent most of the night vacuuming the carpets in ladies wear and the men's department. How come it's ladies wear, but the men's department?"

Roxanne inhaled and blew smoke all over the SUV. "I have no idea."

"Most of the other guys were older, and looking back on it now, I realize they were tough guys. Had tattoos, you know?"

Roxanne nodded and kept looking at him.

"They all claimed to be construction workers, heavy equipment operators, and I believed them, I was such a kid. Some of the other guys, clean-cut looking guys, actually wanted to work in the Sears. I couldn't understand that. Who would actually want to spend their days sucking up to housewives, trying to sell them Lady Kenmores?"

"I can't imagine." She wanted him to get on with it, but she was also calming down and listening to his story. She had a tough time picturing him as a scared kid, but everybody comes from somewhere. It wasn't that long ago she was hanging out at Fairview Mall wishing she could get a job at the Le Chateau.

"So one night, my cousin and I took a couple of gloves and a ball and went down to the loading dock to throw a little. Later on, in the lunchroom, I said something about there being a door down there and the alarm being incredibly lame and easy to get around."

"Mr. Professional."

"Mr. Naïve. I never thought anything about it, really. I was back vacuuming, Eddie Money blasting through the store, 'Two Tickets to Paradise,' or it could have been Meatloaf, *Bat Out of Hell* was huge that summer."

"Either one." She couldn't be patient forever. Then she said, "Shit."

Vince said, "What?" and she just motioned to the solid line of cars stopped in the two lanes of the ramp to the QEW heading towards downtown.

"You in a hurry?"

And she said, "No," but she couldn't understand anyone who wouldn't be pissed off in traffic. Could this guy really just inch along on an expressway and not get worked up about it?

He said, "So, one of these guys, some guy from northern New Brunswick, comes up to me and says, 'Show me the door.' He was so serious, I just about dumped a load in my pants, so I took him down to the loading dock and showed him the door. I thought he'd get it right away, but he didn't."

Roxanne said, "You had to explain it to him," thinking how Vince was no scared kid now, forced into showing people the crime. Now he showed it to them and let them decide.

Or did he?

"It was one of those deals where there was a magnet on the door and another one on the door frame, so if you opened the door, they came apart and the alarm went off. I told him you could just tape the two magnets together and take the screws out of the one on the door and open it."

He shook his head. "So the guy, his name was Roger, said to me, 'Do it.' Just like that. Man, I was so fucking scared."

Roxanne watched him and thought, yeah, maybe back then, when he was eighteen years old in the middle of the night in some Sears 2000 miles from home with a real tough guy he was scared, but she knew if he saw a guy like that Roger now, he wouldn't even notice him.

"So you did it."

"Damned right. And it worked. They started moving stuff out that night."

"But you got caught."

"It's the greed. That's what always gets them."

Stuck in the line of cars, probably three miles long, he looked at her and nodded. She nodded back.

"If they had just taken a little, you know, from a few different departments, it could have gone on for months. But those idiots, they backed a van up to the loading dock every night and filled it."

"Idiots."

"One night I'm cleaning the change rooms in ladies wear. And I have to say, a lot of those ladies were real slobs. The shit I had to clean out of there . . ."

"Right."

"Right. So, I think I see someone hiding. I just catch a shadow of someone going past, ducking out. I think I must be losing it, you know, the night shift getting to me, and these tough guys. I'd thought about quitting but they told me not to. I didn't even understand why till that morning, when we were getting ready to leave, and instead of our boss there to open the door there were five cop cars."

"Wow."

"Turns out there were half a dozen cops in the store with us, taking notes. Thing is, it was always my job to undo the lock."

"Because you thought of it."

They were at the top of the ramp now, the Tower and the big bank buildings up ahead. Roxanne loved driving this road in the middle of the night with no traffic, coming off the turn at 120 clicks and heading for the Gardiner Expressway, but she hated inching along in a jam.

Vince really didn't seem to mind, though. He said, "Turns out most of those construction workers had records halfway across the country, been in and out of jail a dozen times. That's what it was like in Calgary back then, they were so desperate to fill the jobs they'd hire anyone."

"Even you."

"Even me. Some of the guys tried to claim the whole thing was my idea, but the cops could tell how scared I was. They made me an offer and I took it, two years less a day for my testimony. The worst guys got federal time and got sent back home to Dorchester. My cousin pleaded to theft under two hundred bucks for some headphones they found in his car, even though the suit he wore to court cost four hundred and he wore it out of the Sears two weeks before."

"And when you were in jail you met up with Soaring Eagle again."

"Travis Goodeagle. Sometimes I wonder, you know, what would have happened if I hadn't gone to jail. Be a whole different life, you know?"

Roxanne said, "Might not be as good."

She watched Vince think about that, maybe like he'd never thought about it before. A real turning point.

Just like this one with Boris.

She said, "Well, that's the past. What are we gonna do about the future?" and Vince said they should get a drink, talk about it.

CHAPTER FIFTEEN

After the real estate lady left, and the cops — shit, the cops, at least these ones didn't have their hands out, yet — the bikers showed up.

Boris, sitting in his office starting to work out the plan, thinking it could work if they could get the details right, looked up and saw two guys just standing there. Henri nowhere in sight.

One of them, the taller one, they both had huge stomachs hanging over their belts, said, "Hey Boris."

Boris said, "Do I know you?"

They were wearing pleated pants and golf shirts, they had short hair and the shorter one was clean-shaven, but anyone could tell what they were.

"Sure you do, we have a deal here."

Boris said, "I deal with Frantisek." He saw the short one had no idea who he was talking about.

The taller guy said, "Frank, yeah. Well, you know, Nugs is like a branch office. We're head office."

Boris said, "So fucking what," and they started the stare down, like tough guys.

Uncle Khozha came into the office. He walked around the two bikers, but it didn't break the tension and he sat on the couch.

The tall one said, "We're having a meeting here."

Khozha said, "That's what it is. I thought you were looking for a place to jerk off."

"Who the fuck are you?"

"Who the fuck are you?"

Boris could see this wouldn't go anywhere and he wanted to stop it. He said, "Okay, that's enough. Get out of my club."

The tall one said, "Look, we both know you have a problem, you have something needs to be cleaned and we can clean it for you. Let's be businessmen about it."

Boris said, "You don't have anything I need."

The biker said, "We both know we do. We're making changes to the whole territory. Get on board while you have the chance."

Khozha stood up and said, "Let me ask you something."

The bikers both looked at him and Khozha said, "How come you're so fucking fat? Can't you take care of yourselves, don't you have any self-respect?"

The short one said, "Get the fuck out of here."

"You all red in the face. You're going to have a heart attack."

The short one still, he was the one with the temper, said, "Look old man, don't fuck with us."

Boris was still behind his desk, still trying to find a way out of this so everyone could just walk away. He was thinking how he was the only businessman in the place, the only one who knew this bullshit would just hurt them all but he couldn't see a way to stop them. He thought about Khozha's Tokarev in the desk drawer and thought, yeah, take it out and point it at them, show them they fucked with the wrong guy, but that would just dig him in further. These assholes would get stuck on the gun and forget about business.

Then Khozha was pointing a gun at them, looked like a .45, and saying, "My nephew says to get out of his club."

The tall one said, "You're fucking crazy you think you can point that at me."

Boris felt his stomach tighten up. He wondered how Khozha, two days in the country, had a gun.

Boris said, "This is over. Out."

The tall biker said, "We came here in good faith. You fucked it up." He gave his best evil stare and they walked out.

Khozha didn't say anything right away. He sat down on the couch. Then he said, "Fucking punks."

Boris said, "Where'd you get that? You don't know anyone in this country."

"What, this?" Khozha looked at the .45 in his hand like it was the first time he'd seen it and put it back in his sports-coat pocket. "I thought you had a deal with those slobs?"

Boris could feel his stomach still churning, sweat all over his back, his neck knotting up and said, "They just like to act tough."

"So? You let them?"

"They're just learning how to run this kind of big business. They think they're in charge, I let them think it."

Khozha stood up and took a step closer to the desk, looking down at Boris. He said, "I'm here in this fucked-up city because you looked weak, everyone thinks they can have a bigger piece of you. It looks like you're letting them."

Boris shook his head, but he was having trouble calming down. He had to take a breath so he wouldn't yell at Khozha. Fuck this shit. He said, "You think you can deal with them. You think they'll react the way they should, what's in their best interest, but they won't. They're still fucked up about who has the biggest dick, who's the meanest motherfucker. They'll slit their own throats, they'll take everyone down with them to prove some fucking bullshit, small-time, I'm-so-fucking-tough point. Well, I'm not going down with them, you understand, Khozha?"

"Don't get pissed at me."

"Don't think because I don't play like them I'm going to lose. I'm going to win."

Khozha stared at him for a second and then said, "I don't give a shit, Boris. Do whatever the fuck you want."

Yeah, Boris thought, watching Khozha walk out, keep going, go all the way back to New York, back to Moscow. This is a new city, a new country, and it's so fucking ripe. People been coming in here and taking what they want since the fucking fur traders. They took it all, every damned beaver, they took all the fish, they're going to cut down all the trees, drain all the water, this country so fucking stupid they're just going to let it all go.

Yeah, Boris thought, and I just need my piece.

And this real estate lady and the Internet porn guy have a pretty good plan.

• • •

Loewen said she was a good liar, and Price said she was getting better.

"She still talks too much."

"Don't they all."

"He doesn't." Price was driving the Crown Vic, and saw the line of cars backed up on the ramp to the QEW, so he went west and took the first exit. "He talks, but he doesn't really give anything up."

Loewen said, "Where are you going?"

"Where you think?"

"So why'd you get off here?"

"Look at that traffic, might as well take the Queensway."

"All the way through town, have to stop at a hundred lights."

Price said he'd rather feel like he was getting somewhere than sit in a damned traffic jam on the expressway in the middle of the day.

Loewen said, "If you want."

The Crown Vic came around the big, wide off-ramp and stopped at the red light. A big Home Depot on one side of the street and a line of fast food places on the other. Up ahead, the Queensway was lined with stores all the way to Parkdale. On the north there were houses, getting nicer all the way up to Bloor, and on the south, where there used to be trucking warehouses, and where the Ontario Foods Terminal still was, there were new condos going up.

Loewen said, "So, the guy doesn't have a record."

"Anything show up on him at all?"

"I'll tell you what was weird," Loewen said. "Guy didn't get a driver's license till he was thirty years old."

Price said it wasn't all that weird, no driver's license, guy from the avenues in LaSalle. His parents might not have had a car, lots of those guys working in the Seagram plant or the big General Foods plant took the bus. "But he said he went out west when he was still a teenager, and in Calgary the high school lots have more cars in student parking than in the teachers'."

"There was nothing," Loewen said, "from out west."

"We should check this guy out some more."

"You know what?" Loewen said. "This guy didn't have much of anything before he was thirty. Maybe he's who got the hit."

Price said, "Guys usually turn informant because they need the money, even the Mounties couldn't be paying that guy's bills."

Loewen said, "You sure?" and Price had to admit, when it came to the Mounties, you never really knew anything.

He said, "All their task force money is for the bikers these days."

"Yeah?"

"The Mounties are all image. Remember they signed a deal with Disney to market themselves? If the bikers are in the news every day, that's who they're going after."

"This Fournier guy doesn't seem to have any connection with any bikers, though."

Price said, "But Boris does."

"He bought the club from some."

"And he kept one around. What did he have to say?"

"Henri? You know he's not from Quebec."

"New Brunswick?"

"No," Loewen said. "Right here in beautiful Ontario. Sudbury. Says he never was a real biker, said they had more rules and sucking up than anyone he knew. They spend years as gophers, doing all the shit work. He said they never saw the big picture till the guys from Quebec came and showed them."

"Took them over."

"Yeah, and who's pulling their strings? So, he says he met Boris, and they see a lot of things the same way. Classier clubs, going more mainstream. He says guys actually bring dates to their club."

Price said, "I bet."

"Henri thinks the laws are going to change soon. Table dancing turned into lap dancing, into couch dancing. He tells me in Montreal they have something they call contact dancing. Pretty soon, they'll just have rooms in the back."

"Or give blow jobs right there at the table. Meantime they have rooms at hotels nearby."

Loewen said, "I guess."

It wasn't like Boris told them anything. Said he knew Anzor, called him, "My good friend Anzor." Price said, "You guys were close?" And Boris said, "Not close like, you know, close, but we have a working relationship. We're both from Russia. Anzor had an agency, he brought over the dancers. To be honest, this really fucks me up."

"Yeah," Price said, "how's that?"

Loewen had watched Boris, looking for him to squirm or something. Maybe stall, like he was giving himself time to think something up, and he was willing Price to push him more, really get in his face, but the guy seemed sympathetic for Christ's sake.

And Boris had looked stressed. He said, "The dancers are on work visas, six months at a time. Most of the girls here are about to go back, Anzor was going to bring in some more."

"A new batch," Price said. "Fresh meat."

Yeah, and then Loewen watched Boris react, like he was going to get pissed off, but then he just looked hurt and he said, "A lot of these are good girls. Our country, other countries, got fucked up bad by the communists, takes a long time to recover. You don't understand."

And Price said, "Who understands communism? But I see a guy taking advantage of a situation, could piss people off."

"You think one of the dancers killed Anzor?"

Loewen watched then, seeing Price look all innocent, seeing how he'd let Boris think he wasn't too bright.

And Boris shook his head and said, "I don't think it's something one of these dancers could do, in the middle of the day like that. Would take a lot of balls, probably someone did that kind of thing before."

And Price said, "Yeah, I guess you're right," and he looked at Loewen like he was finished asking questions, like that was it. But then he looked back at Boris and said, "But maybe one of them has a boyfriend."

"Boyfriend? I don't know, they're not in Canada that long."

"Maybe Anzor's taking too big a cut. Maybe it's just business. How are you going to get the girls now?"

"I don't know."

"You can't use Canadian girls. Can you? They don't really bring in the customers, that attitude they've got."

"Some Canadian girls are okay."

"So you're not going to close down. You're a professional, right? You're not really going to miss Anzor all that much."

"Not that much."

"So you don't really give a shit, one way or the other, somebody kills this guy?"

"Guy gets shot in the street, it's bad for business. Lot of tourists come in here; if tourism is down, it's bad."

But he showed them something, and Loewen had to

admit Price got it out of him. Now, in the car on Spadina heading into downtown, Loewen said, "So Boris and the old guy go and kill Anzor, because who knows why, but it's business, and the real estate lady sees it. But she won't tell us, and now she's doing something with Boris."

"Seems a pretty big risk to take to lease out some office space."

"It's a tough market in this town."

"But she was there with the porno king."

"Yeah, we've got to find out more about these people."

But really, Loewen knew, they only needed to find out more about Roxanne Keyes.

• • •

Roxanne lit another cigarette and looked around, sitting on the patio of the Lion on the Beach under the trees, feeling protected even out on Queen East, and said, "So, it's more like an ongoing thing, every month or every couple of months."

Vince said, yeah, why, what'd you expect?

She pushed her D&G's further up on her nose and said she didn't know, she thought maybe it would be like a movie, you know, one big score.

Vince said, "The formula, like Garry tells it. Somebody who's already retired and they have to come back, one last job."

Roxanne said, "Yeah," getting into it, "because the score is so big. Or no — wait, better — for revenge. But there's a double-cross."

"Or two or three. And in the end, the greed gets them."

"It's always the greed that gets them."

The middle of the afternoon, and there were only a couple of other people on the patio, young guys in their twenties, looking like salesmen. Trying not to. Everybody drinking pints or Coronas with the lime wedge sticking out the neck of the bottle. "I don't know," Vince said. "These days, they always get away with it. Remember at the end of the original *Ocean's Eleven*, they're all walking away from the funeral home, Sinatra, Dean Martin, Sammy Davis. I think even Joey Bishop. They just watched all the money get burned up in the crematorium."

Roxanne said, "George Clooney and Matt Damon get the money."

"Same thing with *The Italian Job*."

"You don't really know in the original, they're hanging off a cliff."

Vince was surprised Roxanne even knew *The Italian Job* was a remake. He said, "Yeah, what a lame ending. What does he say? 'I'll think of something.'"

"I've got an idea. It was an okay ending. If you like him, you think he'll find a way. It's these new endings you don't even have to think about, they always get the money."

"One of those big directors, Sidney Lumet or somebody, said he was tired of these yuppie happy endings."

Roxanne looked at Vince and said, "I like them."

And Vince thought, yeah, I bet you do. He looked over the fence at the people passing on the sidewalk. Queen East, area known as the Beaches. Or the Beach — the locals, they couldn't make up their minds, a real battle between the old-timers and the new ones flooding in. Hippies with money. That's what Garry called them when Vince first bought the condo. When VSF Online first bought the condo. All those people in the media, ad companies, TV and movies — CBC types all moving in and renovating the old clapboard cottages.

Across from the Lion, the original pub in the area, there was a new one, one of those chain places, the Gull and Firkin, and a framing store with trendy prints in the window, and another discount clothing store selling low-ride jeans and crop tops.

A couple of women in workout clothes pushing baby strollers with huge bicycle wheels, jogging strollers, walked by. Identical. The same brand of bottled water in their hands, the same ball caps, the same shoes. The kids probably looked the same. Yummy Mummies, Suss called them, even put up a site, yummymummie.com. Did okay for a while, but memberships were down. They were down across the board.

Vince said, "So it's not one big score."

Roxanne took a deep drag and exhaled the smoke towards the blue sky. "Does that ever really happen?"

"I doubt it. Would it even work? I mean, what would you do, go to some South Sea island?"

"Sounds okay."

"Talk to the same three people every day who don't speak English. You gonna learn whatever they speak in Tahiti? May rolls around, I like to see a few hockey games, see who's gonna win the cup."

"I'm sure you could get a satellite dish." She wasn't going to let it go, it was inside her head now.

"You see the last shot in *Body Heat*, she's on the beach all alone."

"That's the yuppie happy ending," Roxanne said. "She looked pretty happy to me."

Vince said, "You'd miss it. You like the action."

He thought she might try and deny it, say she had no choice, justify it the way people always seem to feel they have to in this town, but she just said, "Yeah." And she kept going with it. "But you'd have to go somewhere."

"I've been to Costa Rica a few times, it's nice. A lot like here, but without the snow and ice. Same kind of economy except prostitution and gambling are legal. Offshore gambling. That's why I went the first time, me and Mickey Kennedy checking it out."

"I thought his wife was the brains." Showing him she paid attention and remembered everything. Which impressed Vince, but he didn't let on.

"Yeah, Carole. Anyway, it was nice there. Great beaches, great food. Even felt like home. We were in a little place called Jaco, they had a Pizza Pizza."

"Costa Rica it is then."

"Except this isn't one big score."

Roxanne nodded, right.

Vince watched her thinking, he could see her working out a the plan. He figured at this moment, she could go either way. It'd be a lot of work, ongoing, but there could be a great payoff.

But it meant real bad guys.

Vince was thinking she's a big girl, she knows what she's doing. He figured he could push her into it, but on her own she'd walk away. Good enough for him, he didn't really need it.

But it did look good.

Roxanne said, "It could really work, though."

"It's possible."

"What did you call it, Al Capone's furniture store?"

"The front."

"You have the one thing Boris can't get himself. You have history."

"Almost ten years, doesn't seem so long."

"You're a dinosaur."

"That's what Garry called me when I said I wanted movies with real characters instead of explosions."

She gave a little smile, just enough to crinkle her red lips, show him she thought he was cute, for an older guy. Made him realize he'd been at this longer than anything else in his life. Making him wonder if this was what he was, if he could hang in there forever doing this.

She looked around at the sales guys flirting with the waitress, talking about her cute tattoos, saying stuff like, "The ones we can see," and laughing, and she said to Vince, "So Boris gets a half a million bucks in cash and he needs to get it into the legit system. It's too much to make it look like his club brings it in, on top of what else he's not declaring there. But if it goes to buy memberships on your sites, then you can just pay him a regular salary, like an employee."

"Or as a consultant."

She liked that. "Yeah, they bill out at 200 bucks an hour, no one bats an eye."

"And we can spread out the membership purchases over time, so it's not like there's a bubble for FINTRAC."

She asked him what that was, and he explained about the federal government's Financial and Reports Analysis Centre to track large or suspicious transfers of money. In theory, they're looking for terrorist money, but as Vince said, it's just another excuse to invade your privacy.

"But you can get around it?"

"You can get around anything if you have enough money."

She really liked that.

She said, "I'll call Boris, set it up."
Vince watched her.
And he realized he couldn't have pushed her into it.
He couldn't have held her back.

CHAPTER SIXTEEN

Up on the board, Loewen was still happy to see his name next to Price's on the list of homicide detectives but now the date was getting old and Anzor Vladmirski's name was still in red.

Price said to Dhaliwal, "I heard you talked to the Nealon brothers."

"They have a loft on Liberty Street, like the whole floor of an old factory." Dhaliwal was walking through the office with an armload of folded-up cardboard boxes. "Got these Indian rugs all over it and paintings and sculptures. Looks like a museum."

Mastriano was coming in behind him, saying, "So we talk to them, you know, through the door 'cause they won't let us in. One of them, Carl, did five years in the U.S. Marines and three in Millhaven, he's wearing a T-shirt says, 'Fighting Terrorism Since 1492.'"

"I've seen the bumper sticker," Price said. "Says, 'Custer Got Siouxed.'"

Dhaliwal said, "Tells us they're scared of the gangs in Toronto."

Price said, "*They're* scared?"

"That's what he said. His brother, did five in Millhaven, they look like twins, says they don't like the big city."

Dhaliwal said, "Carl says they were in the boozecan when Vasquez came in. They were going to buy some weed from him."

"They were going to buy from him?"

"That's their story. Nice eh? Admit to the small crime, then bullshit all the way."

Mastriano said, "They said they were scared of Vasquez."

"They were scared of him?"

"Said they had a disagreement, he threatened them, threatened their family."

Price said, "They were scared Javiar Vasquez from El Salvador was going to drive 600 miles in the bush up to the reserve and kill their Momma?"

"What they said."

Dhaliwal said, "Carl says this Vasquez was really a nutcase — dangerous, could go off on anyone for no reason."

"First true thing he said."

Dhaliwal said, "So I told them, I said I didn't think big tough guys like them would be afraid little Javiar. Guy looked queer to me."

Loewen laughed.

Mastriano said, "So Carl says, 'We're just lazy Indians.' Asshole."

"Yeah," Price said, "but he's making it work."

"They had a disagreement all right. We figure the

brothers set him up. Javiar had a guy was supposed to be his bodyguard, and a girlfriend, they're both missing."

"You'll have to check every outhouse on the reserve."

Dhaliwal said, "Ha ha."

Price said, "You know, on TV you'd pull them into an interrogation room and go at them. Separate them, say the one was giving the other up."

"Or even better," Mastriano said, "you'd trip him up, outsmart him in the interview, get him to confess."

"That would be great," Dhaliwal said. "And it would be totally admissible."

They all thought it was funny, but no one laughed.

Dhaliwal said, "Yeah, TV."

Price said, "A fantasy world with no lawyers."

Dhaliwal said, "A fantasy world." He was packing the leather coats into the cardboard boxes. "But what really happens is, these two Indians, afraid of the big city, have Mitchell Fucking Morrison number one on their speed dial."

They all rolled their eyes, even Loewen knew the mob lawyer.

Price said, "Nice to have money."

Dhaliwal said, "So now we got nothing. No witness, no way to get a warrant, no wiretap, nothing."

"They'll keep fucking up, though." Price said, "One of these days we will get them."

"Yeah, too bad you can't just say, 'Look I know this prick did it, he's living downtown in a loft with fifty handguns, some grenades, and a couple of machine guns. Let me pick him up.'"

Mastriano said, "Or wait, don't they usually have to say they need twenty-four hours on the case?"

"A fantasy world."

• • •

Nugs said to them he could handle it, and the short one, Denis, said yeah, yeah, they knew that, this was just about maximizing profits.

Nugs said to him, "Profits? We're taking twenty grand a week out of that club."

They were on the deck of Nugs's boat, the *Four Stroke*, forty-four feet long, the sail up but the motor moving it slowly out past the Toronto Islands. They could see the top of the roller coaster at the Centerville amusement park and a couple of other rides, the skyline of the city getting smaller. Denis and the tall one, Claude, were drinking Molson Ex out of the bottles and Nugs had what he said was a Caesar, but Denis wasn't sure, he was thinking maybe Nugs was back in AA and it was virgin.

Denis looked down at the deck of the boat, at Amber lying naked, face down on the towel. Her skin was shiny from all the sunscreen she'd spread on so slowly, pretending she didn't see them staring at her, so smooth and light brown. No tattoos, no piercing. So different from anything Denis had ever seen.

He stuck his chin out at Nugs and then at Amber.

Nugs said she was okay.

Claude said she sure was.

Denis said, fuck that. "This fucking Russian is moving twelve luxury cars a month."

"And a delivery van," Claude said.

Denis said, "And he goes out and shoots his cleaner in the head."

Nugs said the guy was skimming too much, and telling anyone who would listen that there was nothing Boris could do about it.

"Well," Claude said, "I guess he got that wrong."

"But we know he's got nobody else. We know his uncle came in to do it, and there's nobody else."

"We know that for sure?" Nugs said, looking right at Denis.

"Yeah. We know."

Amber rolled over. No tattoos on the front, either. No piercing. Denis looked at her and wondered when was the last time he saw a chick without nipple rings, or a belly-button ring. Or a tat. Shit, must have been when he was ten, sneaking in the girls change rooms at the Hogan's Bath pool in the Point.

Then he thought it looked like she had a hairstylist working down below, too.

He said, "We should be getting a lot more out of this Russian prick. When do the cars leave?"

Nugs said, "We load up Saturday night, Cherry Street docks."

"Somebody's going to give him the cash, and he's going to do something with it. Let's find out."

Nugs said he could put a guy on him.

"Put two guys, twenty-four hours."

Nugs said okay, sure, relax, man. "You're so tense, look, it's a beautiful day." He spread his arms out to show him Lake Ontario, so blue, the sky, the skyline now tiny in the distance.

Denis said, "We have to ride to Hamilton tomorrow, show the colours."

"So?"

"I haven't been on a fucking bike in six months. Hurts my back."

"How'd you get here?"

"How do you think?" He finished his beer and held

out the bottle. One of the hangarounds, a young guy covered in tats, appeared out of nowhere and took it away, handing him a fresh one. Denis scowled and twisted off the cap and dropped it over the side. "We flew. You think I'm spending six hours on a hardtail, no cruise? Couple of Coyotes are bringing in the bikes."

Claude said, "If they don't crash them."

"We got so many guys in the slam, fuck. These kids are useless, stoned, or drunk. Always wanting to shoot someone."

Nugs said, "They don't understand business."

"Fucking right," Denis said. "No shit it's business. Look at that city, four million people? Two years ago we had nothing here. Now we own the fucking place. You think that was easy?"

"I was here," Nugs said. "All along."

"You think it's going to be easy to keep? I never seen anything like this place, this Russian? There's a couple dozen more like him, and Pakis and Chinks, you fucking name it, Africans, they're in this town and they're moving shit like crazy."

Nugs said, "There's some cops here, too."

Denis said, "Least of my worries. But you keep your fucking eye on these hangarounds, and whoever you put on the Russian, you make him good."

Nugs said, "Don't worry, I know my guys."

Amber sat up a little, leaning on an elbow and said, "Remember, I've got to be at the spa by two."

Nugs said, yeah okay, I know, don't worry about it. Then he said, "How about another drink."

Amber put her head back down on the deck and said, "No, that's okay, I'm good," and closed her eyes.

Denis laughed. Then he got serious and said to Nugs,

"Watch your fucking ass."

• • •

Sitting in her Jeep on the roof of the parkade at Yonge and Wellesley, Roxanne smoked another joint and talked herself into it. The dope was Blueberry, which didn't keep getting her higher and higher, but let her float on a nice steady buzz. She could do this, she knew it.

Madonna on the stereo, the *American Life* CD, Roxanne relating to all that stuff about the American dream, about how nothing is what it seems. But that doesn't mean it can't work, if you're willing to take a chance. Then Madonna was singing about she's so stupid because she just wants to be like all the pretty people. I'm so stupid, I'm so stupid, I'm so stupid.

No you're not, you're a fucking genius.

Like in the movie, when Madonna was playing right here in Toronto and the cops were going to arrest her on morality charges — this city just can't get over being Toronto the Good — and she just wouldn't back down. Roxanne was thrilled by that.

But then she found out that before she refused to back down, Madonna made sure that all she could get out of it was a fine she could pay. No jail time, no lost time on the tour, she could still make the next gig and get tons of free publicity.

She weighed the risks.

Roxanne took another hit on the joint and weighed the risks.

If she stayed close to Vince, there probably weren't very many. He seemed smart enough to distance himself.

At least he seemed to learn from his mistakes, his

"youthful indiscretions" as he called them, sounding like that black guy from the sitcom with all the southern women, his "unfortunate incarceration."

Or he was getting better at picking the right opportunities.

"I Deserve It," on the stereo. Great CD, Roxanne thought. *I deserve it.* She knew that if she didn't do this, if she didn't make this move, she'd have gone as far as she could. Angus would want something — money for sure, but something else, too — probably work for him, he'd hinted around at that. There'd be no money in it; she'd lose the Jeep, she'd lose the condo, everything. Right back where she was almost ten years ago, glorified receptionist showing off her tits for customers.

But a little older and a little more desperate.

Another hit and she leaned back, closed her eyes, and saw the whole thing in her head. Like a lousy porno movie, one even Garry would hate. Every time digging herself a deeper hole to crawl out of.

Shit, like her mother, end up drinking forty-ouncers in public housing.

Or, she could just do it. Just get up and walk out and do it.

Now Madonna was singing about an easy ride. How she doesn't want an easy ride, how she wants to feel the blood and the sweat on her fingertips.

All right. Roxanne took one last hit from the joint and stubbed out the roach in the Jeep ashtray. Fuck it.

• • •

She stripped from the waist down, hung her jeans and boy-cut white cotton panties over the back of a chair, and climbed up on the gurney. It was covered with paper, not like her regular visits at all.

Mirjana came back in and went straight between her legs. "Is very long."

Roxanne said, yeah, well, she figured it would be better that way, get a better grip.

"Oh no, is better short. This more painful."

Great. Feel the blood and the sweat.

This place bragged it used pine resin instead of wax, all natural, except for the green colour. Roxanne realized that was it, what looked like a quart paint can of goo sitting on top of a hotplate. She leaned back, tried to ride the nice buzz from the Blueberry.

Mirjana, who was probably twenty-one and might have even been from Brazil, but more likely Portugal by way of College Street, dipped some wax with a tongue depressor and smeared it in the crease of Roxanne's leg. "Here we go."

And holy shit, did it hurt. No buzz could soften it.

Dip. Smear. Pull.

Roxanne breathed in and out fast, thinking, okay, I can feel this, this is real.

Dip. Smear. Pull.

Holy fuck.

Mirjana worked her way around to the tip of the pubis, and the wax felt extra hot on barer skin. "Is a lot of hair."

Roxanne's eyes were closed and she thought, no shit, Sherlock. Should have trimmed. This wasn't anything like a bikini wax.

"You're going to have to help me. Hold here to pull the skin."

Great, doing it to herself.

But then, getting involved helped. Roxanne was starting to feel like she'd had lovers who didn't spend this much time down there, and really, she'd hardly ever had any who seemed so interested. Mirjana had tiny hands and nails that Roxanne figured would be too long for this kind of work, but she was quick; dipping, smearing, and tossing away the inch-square knots of hair stuck to the linen strips. She was even quick about wiping away the blood.

Feel the blood and sweat on her fingertips.

A few deep breaths and it was okay. Roxanne was thinking about making some real money. She still couldn't tell about Vince — what he wanted, what he was willing to do — but she was ready to take it all the way. And Boris, it was his life, he didn't even think about it. Moving a dozen cars a month overseas and who knows what else. Yeah, taking a piece of that every time.

Thinking like that, she was relaxed, getting into it. That guy saying she reminded him of his brother's twenty-five-year-old *Penthouse* magazines. Shit.

"Okay, now the legs," Mirjana said and Roxanne was used to that. Leg waxing, shit it was so easy after the Brazilian she nearly fell asleep. Dreaming about the kind of money, the kind of independence she could get dealing with these guys. No more running like a fucking hamster on a wheel getting nowhere, taking all the risks, freaking out every time interest rates go up, or the condo market gets flooded, or some fucking terrorists destroy the economy. Nothing hurts the economy Boris plays. She even thought if Angus got too anxious, Boris could have Uncle Khozha take care of him.

"Okay, over." Mirjana did the back of her legs fast, there wasn't much hair, and then spread the crack of her ass, smeared the wax, and finished her off.

Roxanne looked up over her shoulder at Mirjana and said, “That’s it?”

Mirjana said, “You did great. For first time, amazing. From now on, it just get easier, better and better.”

Roxanne thought, yeah, this is it. Better and better.

• • •

Khozha walked into the Club International with Amelie and saw Boris standing at the bar talking to Henri. He said to her, “Wait here.”

She made a face behind his back as he walked away, but then she smiled at the Canadian waitress and sat at a table near the small stage. She ordered a gin and tonic and watched the dancer. Not bad, really, for a girl probably nineteen years old, thought she was coming to Canada to be a nanny. Great tits, but no hips and no ass.

Khozha said to Boris, “There’s some asshole in a car outside taking pictures.”

Boris said he didn’t know who it was and looked at Henri.

Henri said, “Could be a cop.”

“Why,” Boris said, “would it be a cop?”

Henri said, “Don’t fucking ask me, they been all over asking about Anzor.”

Boris looked at Khozha but didn’t say anything.

Khozha said, “He’s not a cop.”

“How do you know?”

“Because,” Khozha said to Henri, “I offered him a thousand dollars to get the fuck out of here and he said no. A thousand American.”

Boris said to Henri, go see who it is, and then he

chewed on an ice cube and looked around his club. Almost empty on Friday afternoon, looking like another half empty night. Business still wasn't back from fucking 9/11 and it might never be. He saw a woman at a table by herself watching the new girl, the kid from Bulgaria, and thought that would be okay, if women started coming on their own, but then he realized it was Amelie and she was supposed to be working.

He looked at Khozha again, thinking when the hell are you going back to New York? He was going to say something, tell him to pack his bag or something, when Khozha said, "Your mother's condo, Biba, how much you pay for that?"

Boris said, "Three-fifty."

"Three-hundred-and-fifty thousand for that?"

"Canadian."

Khozha said, "Oh, okay. They have any more?"

Boris said, "Why?"

Khozha said he liked the area, the neighbourhood. Walk on the beach, eat a nice meal. He said there was a butcher on Queen Street that looked good and an Austrian pastry place.

"But nothing like you have in New York," Boris said, thinking what a disaster it would be if the old man stayed in Toronto any longer.

"No, of course."

Boris said, "You ready? I can get you on a flight tonight."

But the old man said no. "I don't want to fly on the weekend. Maybe next week."

"I'll book you for Monday."

Henri came back in and said, "I don't think he's a cop."

Khozha said, "I told you."

"He a biker?"

Henri said he didn't know him.

"But he's fat," Khozha said. "Like you."

"Fuck you."

Boris said, "Okay, okay, quiet, both of you." He looked at the bartender in her white shirt and black vest, and told her to bring some drinks into the office. The girl asked him what kind and how many, and Boris said, "Bring me a fucking bottle of vodka and some ice and three glasses," and he turned and walked away. "Shit."

In the office, Khozha sat down on the couch, settled in.

Boris sat down behind his desk and got out the cigars.

Henri stood by the door, and when the girl came in with the tray, he took it and put it on the desk. There was an unopened bottle of Smirnoff vodka, an ice bucket, three glasses, a small dish full of peanuts, and another one full of olives.

Boris poured them drinks and said, "I have a plan to replace Anzor."

Henri said that was good, because he'd been dead for three days.

Boris said, "We're getting into the Internet business."

Henri said, "Finally."

And Khozha said, "You sure?"

"Yeah, I'm sure."

Khozha said, "Boris, he had a brother was in the Internet business."

Boris sat back and waited. Khozha was going to tell the story, there was no way to stop him. Might as well just let him, get it over with. The story of Saint Mikhail, the anointed one.

Khozha looked at Henri and said, "Did you know Boris had a brother?"

"I heard, yeah."

Khozha downed his vodka and motioned Boris for a refill. "In Moscow, Mikhail was taking over the family business, expanding it, modernizing it."

Boris walked around the desk and filled the old man's glass, but then he stayed standing there because he thought he heard something a little less than reverence in his voice.

"Went to Budapest, Vienna, all over. Started to make transactions online. The money, all the money, goes in one friendly bank. Then Mikhail transfers it all over." Khozha waved his fingers in the air. "Like magic."

Boris thought, right, like magic. Get to the good part.

Khozha said, "But sometimes what goes through the air gets dirty."

"He got a virus," Henri said.

Boris said, "A bad one. Wiped out everything."

Khozha sat on the couch nodding like he was talking about Peter the Great. "Everyone who did business at that bank lost money."

"But Mikhail lost the most," Boris said.

"That we know. But Mikhail, he didn't go to bed and cry. He went to find out who did it."

Henri said, "Who made the virus?"

"Yes," Khozha said. "They infiltrate financial systems to prove they can, prove they are better than the security. Mikhail, he said he wanted to find who did it so he could pay him to get past other security."

Come on, Boris thought, get to the point. He said, "A lot of these viruses are started by guys to be like auditions, to show what they can do, how far ahead of everybody they can be. When Mikhail put out the word he wanted to meet the guy, he figured they were on the same side."

Henri said, "Because the cops were after both of them."

Khozha said, "So Mikhail sets up a meeting. The guy, the virus guy, wants to do it somewhere public so they meet at a café in Moscow. Nice place. Tourists."

Boris said to Henri, "You ever have a computer virus?"

"Hate those fucking things."

Khozha said, "So Mikhail meets with the guy. Says he's very impressed with him, The guy says he can break into any system in the world."

"And Mikhail picks up the little prick's laptop," Boris said, "and right there in the middle of the fucking Hungry Duck, beats him to death with it."

Khozha finished off another drink and said, "Mikhail dropped the pieces of the laptop on the floor, looked at the tourists, and said, 'Guy makes computer virus.' They all said, 'Oh, okay then,' and Mikhail walked out."

Henri said, "He killed the guy?"

"With his laptop."

Boris said, "He sees the irony."

Khozha said, "All I'm saying is, be careful when you do business online."

And Boris said he was always careful.

"So what are you going to do with the fat slob outside with the camera?"

Boris said he'd have to think about it. Be careful, do it right.

Do it when Khozha was long gone back to New York.

CHAPTER SEVENTEEN

Suss said, "So this a real Homer Simpson crisitoonity."

Roxanne watched Vince shrug and said to him, "What he called it when Lisa told him the Chinese have one word for crisis and opportunity."

And Vince said that's what it is all right. A crisis. And an opportunity.

"What's the crisis?" Suss said, "We can just say no."

And Roxanne thought, yeah, what's the crisis, and she watched Vince, seeing the way he set it up so that Suss would go for it. Pushing him into it easily, telling him these aren't the kind of guys they can say no to, now that the ice has been broken — that would be the crisis. Boris is in a tight spot, it's a good time to make a deal with him, he's vulnerable — that would be the opportunity.

Suss was way ahead, nodding, liking the idea right away, saying something about how they could really use it because memberships were down across the board, but what Roxanne wondered was how much had Vince pushed her into it?

Vince said, "Basically what we'd need is a program that could generate thousands of new memberships every month, spread out over the whole month, all recurring."

"Okay, no problem."

Vince said, "Just like that?"

Suss nodded. "Two kinds of math problems, still. The kind you can solve and the kind you can't."

"So for most of us," Roxanne said, "there's only one kind."

"It's called computational complexity." None of his Toronto patois accent now.

Roxanne looked at Vince and he shrugged.

Suss said, "Like when you pay online with a credit card? What happens is the card number is multiplied by two random prime numbers. They both, like, a couple hundred digits each. Then they use the answer to code your transaction and send it off to never-never land."

"And you're telling me," Roxanne said, "that no one can crack that code?"

Suss shook his head. "Take every computer in the world a few hundred years to find the first two primes."

"So how does this help us?"

Vince said, "We can use the same technology, the same coding, to create thousands of membership sales on the websites. Turn a single 250,000 dollar transaction into 5000 fifty-dollar ones."

"Or," Suss said, "Twelve thousand five hundred at nineteen ninety-five."

Roxanne said, "Twelve thousand five hundred?"

"And change."

"Any amount, really," Vince said.

"Yeah," Roxanne said, "as long as it's less than ten grand."

Suss said, "Well, you know, FINTRAC's looking for more than just ten grand at a time. My boy's looking for patterns, spikes, structuring, all kinds of shit, still. We can randomize the amounts, so many at forty-nine ninety-five, so many at ninety-nine fifty, some preemo ones at 500."

"But like you said," Vince said, looking at Roxanne. "We've got history. A few more memberships sold won't tip off anybody."

"And you know someone who can write this program?"

"Program's already been written," Suss said. "Just need to fine-tune it, some." He looked at Vince. "Eccentric Arts."

Now Vince looked at Roxanne and said, "You think Boris will go for it?"

And Roxanne said, "If it'll get him his money, I don't see why not."

• • •

Louise said, "He looks just like you," and Maureen said thanks.

She was walking around the homicide office, looking at the names on the board, the desks and computers and where the leather coats were. Price was holding the baby, still wrapped up in the sling Maureen used to carry him in, the straps hanging down.

Loewen thought Price actually looked comfortable holding the baby, something like that would have freaked him out, and then he thought Maureen really did look like she wanted to come back to work.

She said, "I heard you really caught a break on that Great Rewards thing?" and Louise just said, yeah, I guess. "Imagine Burroughs picking out Alston Jones on that video."

Louise said, "Yeah."

"And him giving up his running buddies."

"The whole force out looking for them now."

"Are we looking in Jamaica?"

Loewen watched the two detectives, Maureen and Louise, kind of circle around each other. More what he would have expected out of Price, but man, he was making goo-goo eyes at the baby, which was awake but not crying. From what little he knew about babies, Loewen figured that wouldn't last too long.

"Where's Levine?"

"Riding with your friend, Burroughs."

Maureen said, please, and sat down at her desk. The one Loewen was using.

Price said, "He looks a little like MoGib, got the vacant stare."

"Dazed and confused. It's how I feel."

Price said, "It's spring now, you must be getting out a lot, having a great time with the little guy."

"Honestly," Maureen said, talking to her partner now, "I hate it. I mean, I like the other Moms, but we're going crazy. All of us. We sit in the park, all these women used to be executives, nurses, professionals. Now we talk about how to get spit-up stains out of cotton. We talk about the fucking Wiggles. I'm going nuts."

Price said, "Beep beep, chugga chugga, big red car," and Loewen realized he had no idea if Price was married, if he had kids, or what. He must, the way he held the baby, so easy.

Price said, "Enjoy it, Mo, it goes by so fast."

"Everyone says that. Then how come every day drags on so much? I keep looking at the clock: three o'clock, four o'clock, I can't wait for the day to be over."

"Five o'clock, the arsenic hour."

"Who'm I supposed to poison, me or him?"

"Just wait till you're getting regular sleep again," Price said.

"When will that be?"

"I don't know, my kids are only eight and six. I'll let you know when it happens."

"Great."

"What about MoGib, what's he doing?"

Maureen leaned back in the swivel chair, looking at the computer and all of Loewen's Post-its. "He's on something called *SkyBlast* now, it'll take him through the summer. Of course, he hates it."

Louise said to Loewen, "Maureen's husband works in the movies."

Price said, more to the baby than anyone else, "He the head gopher now?"

"Location manager."

Loewen said, "This the one with Keanu Reeves?"

"That's the one. And that girl from the sitcom about the doctors, used to be Roseanne's daughter."

"Oh yeah," Loewen said, "Sarah somebody. She's Canadian, right?"

"From Vancouver."

Loewen said, "Yeah, she's good."

"She's the spunky SkyDome attendant the cop hooks up with to thwart the terrorists."

Price said, "MoGib say that, 'thwart'?"

Loewen said, "Arab guys going to blow up the Dome?"

"No," Maureen said. "Not Arabs. Cubans. Well they

don't call them Cubans, it's just some Latin American country on an island ninety miles off Florida that's been run by a communist dictator for forty years."

"Oh, that one."

"And the dictator, he's a big baseball fan. Before he was a revolutionary, he was in the Tigers system, but he hated Detroit."

"I thought Castro's problem was he didn't like the farm system, wanted to be a free agent."

"Maybe the real one. This one hates our freedom."

Loewen said oh, right, that's what they hate these days.

"And the Americans, they've had sanctions against his country, no contact since he took over. But now he's getting old, and he's broke, and he wants to maybe open things up to the Yanks. So he comes close, he comes to Canada instead."

"Wait a minute," Loewen said. "This movie actually takes place in Toronto, it's not dressed up to be New York or something?"

"We're all shocked. Morton said this was the first time he ever scouted locations in Toronto that are actually supposed to be Toronto. The director kept telling him the places didn't look right, they were all too New York or too Chicago."

Price never took his eyes off the baby. "That's funny isn't it little guy, that's funny, yes it is."

"It's the All-Star Game, so everyone's there, and the dictator and his guys are all there, and a bunch of terrorists have planted bombs all over the Dome, threaten to collapse the place."

"Wouldn't take much," Loewen said.

"Holding 50,000 people hostage and they don't even know it. The bad guys claim they're going to kidnap the dictator. His private plane's at Pearson, and so is every cop and soldier in the province. Keanu is one of our guys, just happens to be in the Dome with his kids. His kids he never sees, because he's always working and they don't get along. Don't worry, they bond."

Louise said, "Homicide guy?"

"Organized Crime. Sexier these days."

"Surprised he's not Crime Scene."

"Well, Morton tells me there's still rewrites coming in, you never know. They can do that, change the whole character after they've started. Anyway, our guy figures out it's a scam, the dictator planned it all himself, just trying to get his hands on the frozen U.S. assets. There's a big ending. They blow up the Dome — that's mostly special effects — there's pandemonium, the dictator gets to Island Airport, but our guy's on him and takes off in a Cessna. Big chase scene through downtown, just missing the Tower, all the buildings."

"Sounds all right."

"They're going to close the Gardiner for twenty-four hours, all of Sunday, and a whole pile of streets downtown. So it's actually a nightmare for locations."

"But there'll be a million hours of overtime for paid-duty officers."

Maureen said, yeah, there sure would be. "These days, I'd even take that, just to get out again."

Price said, "You'll be back before you know it, and you'll spend all day thinking about this little guy."

"You can't win."

Louise said, "It's not that bad. You get out and do something you like, something you're good at. Then when you get home, you're a better parent. Are you going to get a nanny or look at daycare?"

"*SkyBlast* should be over when my mat leave is, so for a while, Morton will stay home."

Price said, "Watch out, he might like it."

"He says he's had a lot of practice dealing with tantrums and whining all day, so just one baby will be a breeze."

Price smiled at the baby, waving his finger in front of his face, the little guy giggling, and Levine came in.

He said, "Oh. Oh, oh, oh, is this him? He looks great. Even with that guy holding him."

Maureen said, yeah, he's a great-looking kid, and really, at the end of the day, a great kid.

"Yes, he's a great kid," Levine said. "He's a fantastic kid. Look at him. And he looks nothing like MoGib, for which we're all thankful."

Loewen noticed Maureen was making no move to get up from her old chair. In fact, she seemed to be settling in. She was okay, he liked her and he'd like to hang out with her some time, but right now, he wanted her to leave. He was getting territorial.

He said to Levine, "How'd it go?"

"Oh, we got one. I don't get it, I've been to Jamaica a few times, it's great. Why don't these guys want to go back? We always find them hiding out in Scarberia."

"Call it Scarlem now," Price said, and Levine made an exaggerated look, like he had no idea. "Like Harlem."

"Yeah, sure, that's what it's like there. This city, man, if New York has it, we want it."

Loewen could feel them getting off track again and he said, "That's great, though, you got one."

"And you'll never guess what he said."

Loewen said, "What did he say?" before he saw it was a straight line, and Levine said, "Not a fucking thing, except to tell Mitchell Fucking Morrison where he was."

They all shook their heads. Loewen said, "Wow, him, too," and Levine stared at him expecting more and Loewen said, "Oh, the guys from the boozecan, killed the Snow Dawg, couple of Indians, they hired him, too."

"They don't hire him," Levine said, "they have him on retainer."

Loewen said, "Still, it's funny four guys with a mob lawyer on retainer would drive all the way across the city to rob a place sells cheesecake," and he looked at Louise.

She didn't take it this time, she looked at Maureen and said, "What do you think?"

Maureen stood up and reached out to Price for the baby. He stood up, still making googly eyes and twirling his finger around slowly in front of the kid's face till he poked him in the nose. Maureen said, "I think you're going to get your guys." She took hold of her son and looked at Louise and said, "And if some asshole newspaper reporter does some digging, he might find the name of the guy who owns Great Rewards in some previous narcotics investigations. Might find out he's been in debt in the past to someone other than a bank." She started to put the straps of the baby sling over her shoulder, and Price helped her out till she could click them into place herself. "Maybe he even used to work out at an all-night gym where some of the guys you're picking up used to work out."

Loewen said, "Holy shit."

Maureen said, "But it doesn't matter, because your guys pulled the trigger."

Levine said, "You got that right."

Price walked Maureen to the elevators, telling her what a great-looking kid she had, how good she looked, and even how much fun MoGib was gonna have when he finishes the movie and stays home.

Loewen said to Levine, "Is there anything you can do about that?"

"About what?"

"What she said, that connection between the cheesecake place owner and the shooters."

"What connection?"

Loewen said, "Come on, owing the money? The gym, where'd this guy get the new start, must have been drugs, probably still in debt. Drug squad guys show up out of nowhere, recognize the guy. There's a lot more here."

"Here's the thing." Levine said, "There really aren't that many guys who can walk up to another human being and shoot them in the head."

Loewen said he knew that.

"If it's for money," Levine said, "or revenge, or to try and be the biggest dick on the block, whatever puts them up to it, it's just not that many that can actually do it. And we're getting these four assholes off the street. That's what's here."

Loewen said yeah, okay, that's what's here. He thought about explaining how he was just anxious to be in homicide and a bit of a keener, but he knew trying that would just dig him in deeper, make him look like more of what he didn't want to look like.

Then Levine said, "Hey, you know that real estate lady you're talking to, Roxanne someone?"

"Keyes."

"Yeah, I saw her name, I thought of that song, you don't have to put on the red dress, sell your body for money."

"I know it."

Levine said, "I bet she does, too. She had a boyfriend years ago, was a bit of an up-and-comer, did a year and a half in the Don. That's where her name came up, she used to visit him. I saw her name in the file."

"Why'd you have that file?"

"Because he just turned up. Finally ID'd the body. Looks like he's been dead a while, couple of years anyway. He was in a building that was reno'd a couple of years ago. Plumbers doing some work found him."

"And it's a homicide?"

"Could be. Coroner doesn't want to go out on a limb yet just 'cause the guy was naked and shot in the back of the head. He'll have a full report next week."

Louise said, "We haven't ruled out suicide."

Loewen said, "What's his name?"

"Samuel Dawkins. Sammy Boy."

Loewen said thanks and went looking for Price, who was still standing by the elevators with Maureen.

• • •

Boris was starting to feel in control again. This real estate lady, her plan was even better than what he'd had going with Anzor. He'd get the cash from the cars into the system in Canada, he'd get himself on the payroll of a legit company with almost ten years of history, and he might even get into the Internet business for real.

If only Khozha hadn't killed the biker.

Guy was sitting in his car, taking pictures with a night-vision lens. Some flunky doing what he was told, and Khozha had to go up to him, tell him to get the fuck off the property. Of course the guy had to be a tough guy, had to get out of the car, had to tell Khozha to go fuck himself.

Then the old man comes into the office, says to Boris, that fat biker's still there. Boris told him, yeah, I know, I told you I'd take care of it.

"I took care of it," Khozha said. "I shot him."

Boris said, "He dead?" and Khozha said what do you think? I shot him in the head three times. A regular fucking MO this guy's got.

The last fucking thing Boris needed, but he made himself take a breath before he said, "You the one telling me to be careful?"

"You let these punks think they can walk all over you."

"And what you do is so much better?"

Boris took another breath and grabbed the desk, telling himself don't lose it, it's so close.

"Come on, Boris, big shot like you, you can take care of it."

And he did. He got Henri to get rid of the body and got the car to the Jamaicans. They'd get rid of it clean.

Now, back in his office, he was calming down again. But fucking Khozha just wouldn't go away. He'd have to do it.

Boris reached into the drawer and touched the steel of the gun, the Tokarev. Khozha sat on the couch across the desk, flopped back on it, and Boris was thinking the old man finally relaxes and it's too late for him.

"Your father never left a mess." Khozha was still going on about the old days, drunk now. One of those guys who missed the communists and the Cold War, it was so good for business. "That's what your father knew, never leave a mess."

Yeah, yeah. Boris wrapped his fingers around the gun, feeling his way to the grip, the trigger. Would he point it at the old man and take him out into the alley? Right there by the dumpster where Khozha killed the biker? Yeah. Point it at him, watch the old bastard's face, see the fear.

"And he was always one step ahead. After I knew him, I didn't even ask. He said we doing something, we did it. Why wait for a reason, he knew what he was doing all the time."

Boris could see them, his father telling Khozha what to do, telling everyone what to do. The only memories he had of his father were giving orders, do this, do that, and "Uncle" Khozha doing it. Or Mikhail, twelve years old acting like a big shot, always right there thinking he knew everything. The gun felt good in his hand. Raise it up, point at Khozha, and tell him to get up.

But what if he didn't? Boris looked at him, almost lying down on the couch, lost in memories. What if the old fucker just said no or laughed at him? Would he shoot him right here in his office?

"Your brother," Khozha said and stopped.

That's it, that decided it for Boris. He starts going on about how Mikhail would have taken over, would have kept up the family name, would have been as great a man as —

"I never liked your brother," Khozha said.

Boris held the gun steady, still in the drawer. "No?"

"No, little shit always sucking up, always in the way. Then he went to fucking Diplomatic School, thought he was better than everyone else. Where's my drink?"

Boris picked up the phone and said to send in a couple of straight vodkas on ice. Doubles. Then he said to Khozha, "Yeah, Mikhail, he thought he was something."

"Took over a business your father and I spent our whole lives building. Had it handed to him on a fucking plate. What do you call it?"

"A silver platter."

"A silver platter. Little shit, always acted like it should have been more. Like we did nothing. He was going to make it a fortune, like we did nothing. We had to deal with the fucking communists, the KGB. When he took over, Mikhail, the bourgeoisie were falling over themselves to give him business."

One of the waitresses came into the office in her skimpy outfit carrying a tray. She put a glass on the desk and looked around for a place to set down Khozha's, but he just held out his hand and said, "Here, honey."

He sat up a little and took the drink. The waitress left.

Khozha took a drink and shook his head. "Timing. It's all timing. Your brother was in the right place at the right time. The whole fucking country was on its knees begging to be raped." Khozha downed the rest of the vodka and shrugged. "He did the least he could and made it look like it was something."

Finally. Boris couldn't believe it. Finally someone was admitting what Saint Mikhail really was.

"I'm surprised it took one of his hookers so long to kill him."

There. Right there. Not a heroic gun battle with one of the big gangs from Moscow. Not a gallant fight to keep the family's territory. A pissed-off hooker.

Boris let go of the gun and picked up his drink.

"You know, you little pisher, you've done a lot more here than he did there. You did it all on your own. I never thought you could. You always seemed worse than him, but here you are. You can never tell."

"No you can't."

"It's all timing."

"No," Boris said, "it's not timing. It's opportunity.

There's always opportunity, you just have to see it, know what to do with it."

Khozha shrugged. "That was your father. He always made something. If he had the chances Mikhail had, I can't even imagine the money he would have made."

That's my legacy. Boris sipped his vodka and realized that was his legacy. I'm running the show now. Two more years, with this Internet business, he'd be totally legit. Get married, have some kids, get them into business. One more generation and they'd be the establishment, just like those bootleggers in Prohibition, have buildings and hospitals named after him.

He just had to get through the weekend. Pick up the first payment for the cars, get them on the boat, and make sure this membership deal works.

And talk to the real estate lady some more. She could look pretty damned legit in a big house up at Bathurst and Lawrence, and he could talk to her.

CHAPTER EIGHTEEN

ROXANNE SAID SHE HADN'T thought about Sammy Dawkins in years and Loewen wondered how she could be such a bad liar.

She drank her iced latte, back on the patio at the Starbucks where Loewen and Price first interviewed her. Now it was just Loewen and it was just a "chat," nothing formal like an official interview. She'd asked him that, "Is this official business?" and Loewen had said, no, why would you think it was?

Roxanne had said, "Well, you don't know who killed that guy," looking at the spot on King where the guy had his head blown off.

"We haven't made an arrest. There are some persons of interest."

"Some?"

"Well, there's the one who pulled the trigger and the one who hired him. We'd like to get them both."

Roxanne looked at him like she was impressed. A

little. But not that interested. She said, "When I was in high school, Sammy Dawkins was so cool. Drove a Camaro, had lots of money."

"Then he went to jail."

The straw made a gurgling sound in the ice at the bottom of the cup, and Roxanne kept it in her mouth a little longer, looking up at Loewen. It was a moment, for sure, then she put the cup down and said, "He was going to be a tough guy, do his time and not rat on anyone. Get out and be a hero."

"That what he told you?"

"At first. When he first got picked up I was his loyal chick, you know? God, that was a long time ago. The first few months he talked so tough. Told me the day he got there, a guard told him he was starting his life sentence, punched him in the face."

Loewen said it happened sometimes.

"Then pretty soon all he did was complain. They put the cuffs too tight, they put him in with psychos screaming all night, he couldn't sleep, there were five guys in a cell made for two. He was scared, didn't want to admit it. They made him a server, sent him around with breakfast trays. He said he'd never eat the stuff, he saw how they spit in it when they made it."

Loewen said, "Hey, if you can't do the time."

"He said they beat him up a lot. He used to ask me to bring him in extra shampoo and deodorant. I wanted to know who he wanted to look good for in jail. He said it was to wash his cell with, get the stench out." She sucked a little more on the straw, getting a few drops of melted ice. "Said he couldn't go to the bathroom in the open like that, hung up a shitsheet, he called it. Said they took it away, he had to sleep on the bare mattress, covered in stains, germs, who knows what."

"But he never testified against anyone."

"He was way more scared of them."

Loewen said, "I guess he was right."

Roxanne said, yeah, I guess so. She looked a little sad. She said, "I stopped going to visit him."

"Couldn't stand to see cool Sammy like that?"

"Couldn't stand to see myself like that. You know, the white trash line in front of the Don on Saturday mornings?"

"Hey, it's Toronto, that lineup is pretty multicultural these days."

Roxanne said, "I guess so. It just wasn't me, I just couldn't believe this was my life. I saw women in that line, in the visiting room, I thought they were forty-five years old, they weren't even thirty."

"You moved on."

"Felt like I was getting back on track. Poor Sammy."

"You didn't miss him?"

"I bought my own car."

Loewen said, "But it wasn't a Camaro, was it? It was a Cavalier."

Roxanne said, "You look it up?"

"I guessed. It was either that or a Sunbird. You look like the Cavalier type."

Roxanne said maybe she was back then. "When I didn't know any better. I walked onto the lot, salesman saw me coming. I learned since then."

Loewen thought, yeah, I bet you did. But he still wasn't sure. He wondered about her leaving Sammy behind, making sure. "And you never saw Sammy again?"

"The last time I saw him he was in the visitors room of the Don, begging me to put my jean jacket over his lap."

"Never thought about him again?"

"Once in a while, you know, I think how lucky I was he got arrested. I mean, if he hadn't, I would have stayed with him, till . . . well, I don't know till when. Forever, I guess."

"Till something else came along."

She stared at him for a second and then said, "I wasn't looking for anything else."

"No," Loewen said, "but sometimes you can't help but see it."

He watched her, but she didn't show him anything.

Then they went over Sammy again, quick, just the facts ma'am, and Roxanne said she was sorry but Sammy was such a kid trying so hard to be tough, it was probably bound to happen.

She was getting up to leave and Loewen asked her about the condo building where they found Sammy's body. "Naked, shot in the back of the head."

"That place was an office building and then it went residential condo. I never deal in residential, strictly commercial."

"You ever heard of Alfred Whitmore?"

"The developer? Sure, I've heard of him." She walked around the iron railing out onto the wide King Street sidewalk. "I've never met him."

"You know if Sammy ever did?"

"Sammy and Alfred Whitmore? Not in a million years."

Loewen watched her walk back to the Toy Works, not even noticing the guys in the cars on King looking at her. Well, he figured, she noticed but she just didn't care. She was getting better, not talking too much. He stood up and saw her get to the front of the building and wait. A minute later, the Russian strip club guy, Boris, walked up and they looked like old friends.

Loewen watched the guy introduce Roxanne to the two strippers with him and wondered what kind of real estate they were interested in.

• • •

Marissa said, "Arthur's an aardvark, right?"

Linda said, "Yeah, in the books he has a much longer face, looks more like an anteater."

"An aardvark's an anteater?"

Marissa looked at Rosi in her cropped T, barefoot, a ballcap on backwards, grey sweats rolled down at the waist so far she could almost see where her tattoo ended, and she wondered how low low-riders could get. She thought soon women'll be getting their hip bones shaved, or some other whacked out surgery, now that they have another feature to show off. She said to Linda, "His friend's a rabbit, right?"

"Buster Baxter, yeah."

Linda lit another cigarette and Rosi asked if she could bum one. Linda said, "You can't smoke O.P. your whole life."

Rosi said there was nothing wrong with other people's, the two or three she smoked a day.

Marissa asked her if she wanted one of hers. "Gitanes. They're French." They were in the lounge, taking a break. Actually, they'd been taking a lot of breaks lately, the hits on the live "interactive, talk to a sexy chick" sites were way down. Marissa had stopped wearing the lingerie and was in the same cropped T as Rosi — "Get Me Off Good," in gold script on the front.

Linda never bothered getting dressed after a session and was flopped on the couch, naked.

Rosi took Linda's Belmont Milds and said thanks anyway to Marissa. She fired up and sucked it deep into her lungs, enjoying it, looking like she smoked a lot more than two or three a day.

Marissa watched, thinking how easy it looked for Rosi, kid with no one to look after, her whole life ahead of her. Course she knew it wasn't easy for anyone. She said, "This was the only one I could find big enough. The show's on five times a day, you'd think there'd be more."

Linda said, "It's old now. You gotta get Spongebob Squarepants."

"He likes Arthur. But I don't know, this has D.W. on it, too."

"So?"

"I hope he doesn't mind, that's all. A girl on his backpack."

Linda blew smoke at the ceiling and said he better not.

Rosi said, "Why does it have to be so big?"

"Senior kindergarten, they have something called borrow-a-book. They bring a book home every day, you have to read it to them. Some of them are big picture books."

"Be glad," Linda said, "that's your biggest problem. Josh needs more physio and I don't think it's covered by OHIP anymore."

"That's shitty."

"One of the moms in my group, her son's autistic. They only get treatment till they're six."

Marissa said, "Then they're cured right?"

Linda smoked and started to look pissed off, and Marissa got worried. She wanted to say something, anything, but she didn't know what.

Then Rosi said, "Okay, so what's the big one? The one held back a grade?"

"Binky Barnes? I think he's a dog, you know, like one of those British bulldogs."

Rosi said, "But they have dogs and cats as pets and they can't talk."

Marissa said, "I didn't know you had kids."

And Rosi said, "I don't."

"Oh." Then Marissa said, "I think he's a hippo." She looked at Linda, saw her nod like she was making a decision.

"He's a hippo."

Marissa laughed. "Can you get any more shifts here?"

Rosi said, "You want to be in Garry's new movie?"

"Are there women in it?"

"Yeah, it's sorority lesbians."

Linda said, "I think my school days are over."

"If you need the work, Garry will find you something. You can be the mean landlady, or a professor. You know, and I have to *please* you to get a better grade."

Linda was going to say something, but she stopped and motioned to the hallway.

Marissa watched the real estate lady walking by with the Russian guy, like she was giving him a tour. Two girls followed, looked like strippers, probably couldn't speak a word of English.

Rosi said, "Shit, now they're coming in here."

Linda said, "I wonder what they want?"

"Business is down," Rosi said. "Maybe new partners."

"You think Vince needs partners?"

They didn't know. They didn't like the look of it, though.

Rosi said maybe she'd talk to Vince and Linda, said, oh, is it Friday already and they laughed.

Then Marissa said, "I'll tell you one thing about Arthur, though. They're all kinds of different animals, but they never breed with each other. Both of Arthur's parents are aardvarks. Both of Muffy's parents are monkeys."

Rosi said, "If Muffy's a monkey, what's Francine?"

• • •

The first thing Boris said was, "Why make your own content? There's so much porn online, why not just steal it from other sites?"

Roxanne looked at Vince to see his reaction. He looked like he was thinking about it. Which she realized she should have expected, because now that she thought about it, she'd never seen the guy overreact, or give anything away.

He just said, "We could, but we compete with the big guys, you know, so we have to be more of a niche marketer. They can get away with stuff because of the volume. They're like McDonald's and we're like a small French restaurant."

Boris said he got that, yeah, "but the guy owns that little restaurant, he's there twenty-four hours a day, he's got no life."

Roxanne looked at Vince again. This time he said, "It can be like owning a club, they're all different. You can't buy a franchise strip club."

Boris said, "Someday. It could be like McDonalds. You think Vegas will stay in Vegas forever? Someday there'll be a Chicken Ranch at every casino."

Vince said, "The chicks all wear the same colour golf

shirts? Take the training course in Reno?"

"That's right," Boris said. "It's like any other service."

The two girls who had come in with Boris, he hadn't even introduced them, were watching one of Garry's movies on Vince's monitor. One of them sat in Vince's chair and the other sat on the arm. Roxanne looked at them every once in a while. They always looked bored.

Roxanne and Boris sat on the soft leather couch, and Vince sat in a wooden chair facing them. He did lean back, though, with his feet up on the coffee table.

He said, "I think you're right, the business will go legit."

"Everything does," Boris said. "If there's money in it."

"But then it'll be corporate," Vince said. "Those guys, stockbrokers, lawyers, bankers. I'd rather deal with the mafia."

Boris laughed and said, "I didn't know the mafia was real."

Roxanne stared at him, thinking, shit, these guys, joking around. Feeling each other out. She was enjoying it. These two guys had a lot in common, she realized. They both liked to work alone, but they knew the way the world worked. They could make a deal if they needed to, but they'd never have real partners.

Thinking the way she did.

"You know," Boris said, "ten years ago, everyone in Moscow was broke. Now, you look at Abramovich, playing with his football team in London."

Roxanne said, "What?"

Vince said, "He may be the richest man in the world. Controlled the oil and gas in Russia. Now he owns a team called Chelsea in the English Premiere League. I think Mick Jagger has a box there."

"After the communists, Abramovich was an orphan. He started with nothing."

Roxanne nodded and looked at Vince, and she knew he was thinking the same thing she was. That this Russian guy didn't have nothing — he had nerves of fucking steel and was ruthless.

He saw his opportunity and he took it.

Roxanne said, "So we agree this is good business and it's just going to get better. We've got an idea how this situation can help everyone."

Boris said, "I buy membership on the sites. I become a partner. Some of my girls," he motioned to the two sitting in Vince's chair watching the movie, "go on webcam sites."

"Essentially," Roxanne said. She kept looking at Vince, waiting for him to say he didn't need any partners, but he just sat there nodding. She said to Boris, "You might want to be a consultant, incorporate yourself, do it that way."

Boris said, "Maybe that, too. Maybe have an agency provides the girls."

Roxanne said, yeah, that could work, too.

Boris said, "How do you get the money online?"

Vince said he knew a guy, ran a cheque-cashing business. He could turn the cash into digital cash. "Is it Canadian?"

"American."

"That'll work."

"Works everywhere in the world," Boris said, "but this deal is getting crowded now."

Vince said, "Price you gotta pay."

Roxanne said, "Once it's digital money, that guy won't know what it's for, right?"

"No," Vince said. "He puts it into one account and

then the software turns it into thousands of memberships. It all ends up here, but it can't be traced."

Boris nodded. He looked satisfied. Roxanne was thinking it was almost too easy. She couldn't figure why Vince was just going along with everything. He had to know how this was going to change his business, change his life.

She was thinking more and more that he really was a guy with no plan, just floating along, things falling into his lap. She wondered how he'd react when Boris moved him out of the company completely.

One of the girls watching the movie said something in Russian and Boris said something back. He looked at Vince and said, "They like it. She said it's *Run Lola Run*."

"This one's actually *Come Lola Come*, but Garry, he does an even better job connecting the three versions."

Roxanne remembered seeing the original at the Festival a few years back. It was German, with the girl who was in *The Bourne Identity*, Famke or something. Roxanne remembered not liking it much. The girl in the movie, Lola, had to get a lot of money to save her drug-dealing boyfriend in a hurry, and the movie was really three short movies, each one her different plan, except all three plans were just to go and ask her rich Daddy. Her only problem was getting there.

And here they were. Roxanne said, "We should go to dinner, toast the beginning of a great partnership."

Boris said that would be good. He had to go back to the club, drop off the girls, do a few things. He'd be ready in a couple of hours.

Vince said, "There's a place near here, Rodney's Oyster Bar. What do you say, seven?"

Roxanne said, "Seven it is."

She thought Vince might be expecting her to stick around, spend some time with him and they'd go together, like it was a date, but he didn't say anything when she said she had a couple of things to do and left with Boris.

Driving back to her condo, she felt a strong itch between her legs, but it was just the Brazilian.

And now she didn't know who she wanted to show it to first.

CHAPTER NINETEEN

PRICE SAID TO LOEWEN, "You ask her out?" and Loewen said, no, she was trying to decide between the porno king and the Russian mobster.

Price said, "Good, because Constable Jen Sagar of the Mounted wants to talk to you."

Loewen figured she must have heard every joke there was about being in the mounted police. He said, "What's going on?"

"Ask her."

They had driven down Spadina, and Price turned left onto Lake Shore and got into the right lane to get onto the Gardiner. He told Price all about the real estate lady becoming a better liar, not talking to hear herself speak, and not worrying so much about filling in every silence.

"She's getting schooled by pros," Price said.

He stayed in the left as it turned away from the lake and became the DVP heading north. At the turn, they could see the three-storey BMW dealership with cars in the windows on every floor, like a 3D billboard.

Loewen said, "Nice cars. What do you think of that SUV?"

"I think if you want to drive that, you made the wrong career choice."

"On TV, the crime scene guys drive Hummers."

"They also carry sidearms and interrogate people of interest."

"Yeah, TV," Loewen said. "That's why the amateurs always think they have to talk, have to explain themselves, 'cause they always do on TV."

"But the pros know better."

"So you're sure this porno guy is a pro?"

"He's something."

"I'll ask Constable Sagar."

Price said, sure, you do that. "She might tell you."

• • •

Loewen walked into the Tim Hortons on Eglinton, out past McCowan in Scarborough, and thought right away there was something different about her. Constable Sagar had gotten a haircut, or she changed her hair colour, or something. Loewen wasn't exactly sure what it was, so he didn't say anything, but she looked a lot better.

Maybe it was the blouse and the skirt. And no sign of her gun.

He stood in front of the table and said, "There used to be a radio station played a game called 'Cop, No Cop.' They'd get someone on the phone and call a donut shop, and they'd have to guess if there was a cop in it or not."

"Anyone ever guess no?"

"You want a refill?"

She said sure, so he got two double-doubles and a couple of maple walnut fritters.

"What's going on?"

"I had a meeting with my CI and a bunch of names came up."

"You going to tell me whose?"

Sagar sipped her coffee and shook her head. "Of course not. But I'm going to tell you that your Russian is involved."

"I figured. And did your confidential informant mention that he shot someone on King Street?"

"Oddly, no. But I need to ask you a favour."

"Whoa," Loewen said. "The Mounties are asking a humble city cop a favour?"

Sagar said, "If you want to just forget it," and Loewen wished he hadn't said anything.

"No, no, go on, I'd be happy to oblige."

He watched her look him over, thinking she was trying to decide. He thought if there was anything he could say, anything to get back on track, but not saying anything was probably his best move.

Like the pros Price says you never see on TV.

Sagar said, "I want you to leave him alone."

Loewen said, "I don't think I can do that. We know he was driving the car, and his uncle's the shooter. We're just putting together the evidence."

"I know that," Sagar said. She took a bite of her fritter and Loewen noticed she was wearing lipstick. And looking closer he realized she had makeup on. She may have even had a facial, and he was flattered. There might even be more to her than to the real estate lady who, it seemed, liked to play with fire too much.

"If you could just stay away from him Sunday."

"Why, he going to church?"

She wiped her mouth with the little paper napkin, and Loewen was pissed at himself for giving her attitude. He was still worried he'd look like too much of a keener.

He said, "Okay, Sunday. But you have to tell me what's going on."

"I can tell you Monday."

Loewen shook his head and hid his smile with his coffee cup. "You got balls," he said.

Sagar said, look. She waited till he looked her in the eye then she said, "This is a big investigation, this has been building up for a long time. We didn't expect your Russian to be involved, we didn't expect him to kill somebody."

"But you're not investigating him."

"I can't tell you that."

"Well holy shit, you're not giving me anything."

"I've already given you more than I should."

"Given me? You're the one asking for the favour."

She nodded and drank some more coffee. Loewen noticed her fingernails. They were red and shiny, just been done. He wondered what she was getting all cleaned up for.

"Listen. It would be better for you not to be around. I'm telling you that because I like you."

Loewen leaned back in the little chair that swivelled halfway around and stared at her. "Well, I like you, too. Maybe we could spend Sunday evening together. Go out to dinner."

"See, that's why I like you. How about Monday?"

Loewen said, okay, Monday.

He was getting ready to leave and he couldn't help it. He said, "You look great today."

"You mean I looked like shit last time?"

Exactly why he didn't want to say anything. He said, "No, of course not. Must have been Greggs, brought the whole room down."

Sagar said, no, she did look crummy last time. "But I spent this afternoon in the spa. Had a facial and a maniped."

Loewen asked what that was and she said, "A manicure and a pedicure." She held out her foot from under the table, and he looked at her red toenails, the sandals with the little high heel, and her legs.

He said, "Wow, you Mounties do make the big bucks."

"It was company time."

"Nice work if you can get it."

They agreed on seven o'clock Monday night. Indian place on Gerrard. Turned out they both liked curry and English beer.

In the car on the way back downtown, Loewen told Price that she asked them to leave the Russian alone till Monday, and Price said, well, she really knows her stuff, so we might as well.

Then he said, "Besides, we got a call just down the street. Eighty-year-old man in an apartment building."

Loewen said, "Dead?"

Price looked at him sideways and said that was usually why homicide got called in, and Loewen didn't even care about the sarcasm.

He was just happy to be in homicide.

• • •

Vince was thinking how things were never going to be the same at VSF Online.

He thought Suss would be okay, he'd hang around and do his job and if things looked like they might get out of hand, he'd disappear. Garry was another story. Vince knew he'd have to talk to him, let him know what was really going on.

At the computer, Vince clicked through his playlists, Suss making fun of him using the Windows Media Player, but he'd copied a bunch of Vince's CD's to the hard drive and downloaded hundreds of songs.

Vince put on *Frampton Comes Alive*, man it'd been so long.

Summer of '76.

When Vince fell in love. With Liz Downey and with the movies. The only reason he'd kept Garry around this long was because they both loved the movies.

Vince sat on the soft leather couch in his office, listened to the guy say something about an honourary member of San Francisco society, and then "Something's Happening" came on loud.

Something was really happening. It had to be Roxanne that was making him so nostalgic, opening up about his past, she was so easy to talk to. Now he was thinking about what might have been.

Summer of '76.

His father's heart finally gave out after ten years of strokes and living half the time at the Royal Vic hospital. Brother Danny was overseas in the army, and his mother sold the house and went back to work and moved the two of them into that apartment in LaSalle.

Then he met Liz Downey. Hanging out in the park behind the Catholic high school with a bunch of kids, then walking her home. And she kissed him and that was it. Made him feel like anything was possible.

Lovestruck teenagers, sixteen, too young to get into bars, they went to movies. Liz went to concerts, too. She went to all of them, with her friend Louise. They saw Peter Frampton, Supertramp, Genesis, Nazareth; but with him, she went to the movies. *Close Encounters of the Third Kind*, *One Flew Over the Cuckoo's Nest*. When they walked out after *The Man who Fell to Earth*, she held his arm and said the movie changed him. Teenage drama, looking for drama. He was just wondering if it was weird that he thought Teri Garr was sexy. Liz liked *The Song Remains the Same* more than he did.

Vince sat there in the dark looking at the screen and loving it. *The Outlaw Josie Wales*. They went to see everything that came out, or he went by himself when Liz was with her friends. He went to the rep theatres, the Seville and Cinema V. What amazed him about *Taxi Driver* was that Travis Bickle was twenty-six. Just ten years older than he was, the same age as his brother Danny, off fighting for peace, which was, like he said, fucking for virginity. It made Vince feel like he was living in the shadows, like he had just missed out on something, on everything, just a little too late. Wrong time, wrong place.

That's what was on his mind in the spring, two months left in high school, when Liz finally had enough confidence to tell him she was looking for something more and dumped him. Sitting in her kitchen, it took him twenty minutes of her talking to figure out what she was saying, and then he just wanted to get out of there. Her mother came in and invited him to stay for dinner, and he said sure, he just had to go somewhere, he'd be right back. He went all the way to Alberta.

"It's a Plain Shame" was on, not one of the songs from the album that ever got played on Super Seventies Sunday, but a decent song, when Rosi popped her head in the office and said, “Hey boss, you want me to come in?”

Vince looked up and was about to say, no, not today when Rosi said, “It’s Friday,” and he said, “yeah, sure.”

She said, “Ten minutes,” and winked at him, playing.

Vince’s Friday bonus, his employee’s idea of sending him off for a good weekend. They didn’t even know it, but he’d been so young when he went to jail in Alberta, and then working for Travis driving the escorts as soon as he got out, this professional sex, as he thought of it, was about the only kind he’d ever had. The only time he didn’t go for it was when he was trying to date someone from the straight world, trying to figure that out.

So what was Roxanne?

At first Vince had thought she was a cool chick in the straight world, someone he could talk to. He’d told her his stories, didn’t leave much out, and it didn’t bother her, and he realized how much he wanted that. It had been so long since he could just talk to a woman and be himself. Shit, since Liz Downey. But then Roxanne jumped on this deal with Boris so fast he started to think she was more in the other world, the world he’d stumbled into and was still in after all these years of telling himself he was getting out. Just like all those escorts and dancers and Rosi.

He went to the computer and looked through more playlists, saw what he wanted, and put it on. He went back to the couch.

Couldn’t believe he was thinking about the old days. Or about dating. For a while he’d thought the only women he could ever get close to would have to be ones he knew before — before he went to jail, before he went to work for Travis, before he became Vince Fournier. But there was only one from before.

He lay back on the couch and almost laughed. It was like sex in prison — you just never thought about it, pushed any thought of it right out of your head the second it started to form, till it became pure instinct and the thoughts just never made it. That's what Vince did with the idea of living a normal life in the straight world, but now . . . now it was coming in like a fucking flood.

Rosi came into the office looking pissed off and said, "Sorry it took so long, shit. You okay?" She had her hands on her hips and was waiting. Cup of coffee? Make some photocopies? Blow job?

Vince was laying back, eyes closed. The T-Rex was on its last song, "Rip Off," imagine that. He opened his eyes and sat up, making room on the couch. "Sit down, here, okay?"

"Okay." She let out a breath and sat down. Then she said, "There were some Russian girls in here today?"

"Romanian. Don't worry about it."

Rosi said, "Everything's going to be okay?"

Vince looked at her, her little girl eyes and her big girl makeup. He'd seen so many just like her, and in the end, he never thought it would be okay. It might be for a while, but he could never really picture them at forty-five getting nostalgic for their high school sweethearts and sending their kids to school.

Some of them must, though. It must work out for some of them.

He said, "To tell you the truth, Rosi, things are probably going to change around here."

She said, "Oh."

Vince listened to "Rip Off" finish and then the CD started over again. It was just like being back in Liz Downey's living room, that last year of high school.

Liz would stack three or four vinyl LP's on the record player. Led Zeppelin, David Bowie, and maybe Heart, Liz liked that *Dreamboat Annie* album. They'd neck. Long deep kisses for hours. Tongues. She started to let him feel her up. Vince smiled thinking about it, those words, *feel her up*. His shaking hands inching up under that pale green T-shirt. It wasn't cropped in 1976, it always started out tucked into those brown cords. A real ritual, pulling it out, slipping his hands up, her skin so smooth and hot. He'd sit up on the couch and she'd put her head in his lap and look up. She'd take off her glasses, big plastic frames, and close her eyes. After a while, she even stopped wearing a bra.

"Why don't you just lay down here," Vince said, and Rosi did, but face down.

"You just want a blow job," she said.

He was looking at the back of her head. Liz Downey sure never asked him that.

Once he complained to his brother that he could never get below the waist, he wanted to get laid so bad, or get head at least. It wasn't that he wasn't grateful for what he was getting, Liz had the most perfect breasts, her nipples would get rock hard, and he could play with them for hours. It was just, you know. His brother was home on leave and he'd said yeah, he knew, but never underestimate a girl who's good with her hands.

"No, roll over," Vince said.

Rosi rolled onto her back and looked at him like she didn't understand. Her skin was so smooth and clean, not a blemish. Not a single zit. Her makeup was subtle. Dark curly hair. No glasses. Beautiful, really. A small silver hoop in her navel, tattoo of a vine with flowers on it snaked over her belly and disappeared into her thong.

"Sit up, okay."

Now she was looking a little worried. "Everything okay?"

"Yeah fine." It wasn't like he could tell her he was thinking about his high school sweetheart. "How about just, um, with your hand?"

"Okey-dokey." She smiled, probably more relief than anything. Everyone's worried when the boss starts acting weird. Her perfectly manicured nails scraped gently as she undid his pants and opened them up.

Vince closed his eyes and dropped his head back on the couch. "Jeepster" playing, I'm just a jeepster for your love, whatever the hell that means. *Electric Warrior*, he remembered how electric it was the first time Liz opened up his pants. He just about exploded when she touched him, or grabbed him was more like it. But he held it together. It became part of their routine. A bit of a race before her mother got home from work. From the second time they did it, Liz had a little white rag ready. She had green eyes.

Rosi didn't have anything ready so by the time "Bang a Gong" came on, she said, "Oops, I need some tissue," and jumped up and walked over to the desk.

Vince opened his eyes and watched her walking back, wiping off her hands, Marc Bolan singing, dirty sweet and you're my girl.

Rosi said, "How was that? You want the blow job now?" She wiggled her ass and said, "Or is it booty time?"

He said, no thanks, that was fine.

Dirty sweet and you're my girl.

Someone who knew him before.

• • •

Roxanne showed the Brazilian to Boris first.

He didn't even notice.

She figured it was probably the only way he ever saw women look. That was okay, at least he didn't look like he spent his teenage years listening to Jethro Tull albums and looking through his brother's *Penthouse* magazines. Guy was all business.

Which usually Roxanne was, too. Lately she'd been with a lot of guys Vince's age, in their forties — she even had that night at the airport Hilton with Maurice Abernathy, and he must be in his sixties — so she gave them a little taste of everything and they were in heaven. But Boris, he wasn't any older than she was, and he seemed to be going through the motions the same way.

When they were finished, and they both were, she said, "You ever think about getting a condo?"

Boris said, "That market is too unstable. I'm going to rent till I buy a house."

"Okay," Roxanne said, "but you don't have to rent here."

Bathurst and St. Clair. One street west, Raglan Avenue, an ugly fifteen-storey concrete slab apartment building from the seventies, filled with eastern European immigrants and eighty-year-old women.

Boris said it was okay for now. "Someday I get married, buy a house up past Lawrence, nice big place, 4000 square feet, indoor pool. Maybe tennis court."

Roxanne thought it sounded nice. She said, "Up past Lawrence."

"Yeah," Boris said turning sideways, looking at her. "Not in Little Israel like an immigrant, further out. Jewville."

That didn't bother Roxanne at all, she couldn't care less. She said, "That's what you want? Marry a nice Jewish girl, have kids, join the club."

Boris went back to looking at the ceiling and said she didn't have to be Jewish. "She just has to be smart, know what's going on."

"Know what you're going through, in case you bring your work home with you."

"I don't bring it home."

"It could follow you. She'd have to know what to do."

Boris said that's right. Roxanne thought what he meant was know where the money was offshore, know what lawyer to call, and to get out of the country. Get the kids out and know where to meet up.

Or how to be a good widow.

She sat up on the edge of the bed and asked him if he had anything to eat.

He was asleep.

In the kitchen, Roxanne found a box of Cheerios and some milk that smelled okay. It didn't look like Boris had cooked a single meal in the place since he arrived in Canada. Okay, so he didn't care too much about home cooking.

Wait a minute, Roxanne thought. Are you really thinking about this?

Five hours ago at Rodney's Oyster Bar, she was there with Vince. At least she thought she was, but he didn't seem to care. He was nice enough, polite, had a few Malpeque oysters from P.E.I. and a couple of glasses of wine, but she could tell he wasn't really into it. She'd suggested they go to the Drake after, and Vince said no thanks.

Boris said he'd go, and that was it. Vince went home and Roxanne was with Boris.

She ate the Cheerios and tried to think if she'd ever moved from one guy to the next in the same day, but couldn't remember a time.

She'd seen something in the paper on the weekend

about a new book, something about sex etiquette or bedroom etiquette, and it had given the slut formula. Roxanne thought it was cute but she hadn't worked it out. Still, it was easy to remember, it said take your age, minus fifteen, and times by five. If you've slept with more men than that, you're a slut.

Okay, so she was thirty . . . say thirty. Minus fifteen times five is seventy-five. Really giving you a lot of leeway on the slut factor. Did she know anybody who'd qualify?

Then she thought she'd only slept with three guys, and then Sammy till she was twenty, so that left seventy-one guys in ten years. Say seven a year. Now it didn't seem like so much, though she still didn't think she knew any women who'd actually qualify. She sure knew a lot of guys who would, if they counted sleeping with hookers.

And then she thought, she's going into business with the mob and she's worried about how many men she's slept with?

She stood up and put the empty bowl in the sink, next to two others. The apartment had one bedroom, a small bathroom, and a living room–dining room wrapped around the galley kitchen in an L. There was a balcony with sliding glass doors, and Roxanne stood in front of them and looked at her reflection.

She could see herself in a big house with an indoor pool and a tennis court. Take up yoga, buy her own mat. Maybe keep her real estate license, try a little residential, just to keep her hand in.

Like her hero, Madonna, out on her Reinvention tour, calling herself Esther.

Reinvent herself. A whole new life.

CHAPTER TWENTY

After Rodney's, Vince went back to his office and picked up his laptop. He checked his email, and there was one from Suss saying the software would be ready in the morning. They'd have a little time to test it, but not much. All day Saturday, anyway.

At dinner, Boris said he was picking up the money Sunday morning, but Vince knew he already had it. The cars were getting loaded Saturday night. Half the money, really, the rest when they got to Vilnius. Vince would go with Boris to Ravinder's place and make it digital.

Vince thought, man, the Drake Hotel. As soon as Roxanne mentioned it, he knew he was going home alone and he was all right with that. The place could be okay on a Tuesday, but Friday night it was everything he hated about Toronto. All the trendy people out to see and be seen. That wasn't such a big problem, every city in the world had plenty of people like that, but Toronto couldn't seem to tell the posers from the real thing. If it had the real thing.

The Drake was in Parkdale, or Crackdale as Suss and his buddies called it, an old fleabag with hookers out front till some dot-com millionaire bought it and made it a hobby.

Hobby art. That's what Vince hated, the way the most obvious attempt to buy cool worked in this town.

Yeah, right. Or maybe he just hated it because he couldn't fit in, he'd never be one of them. All those new art galleries along Queen West by the Drake, having openings and showings and whatever the hell they called them, and Vince knew he was always too old or too young, or too something.

The way he always was. Shit, something had really gotten into his head lately and he didn't think it was Roxanne. She brought him this new deal, was going to give him another five years at least. What he could skim off what Boris was going to move through, plus what he was already managing, it would really add up. No, it was good business.

It was this fucking nostalgia. Making him think that he was always just a little out of it.

Like back in Calgary, when he got out of jail and went to work for Travis. It was the eighties by then, Loverboy and everybody working for the weekend. Vince had a great apartment on 17th Avenue South West, a red brick building from the twenties called the Devonish. Had a Murphy bed pulled down from the wall in the living room, just like all those old movies he loved.

The neighbourhood wasn't the coolest then, hell there was an A&W drive-in you could actually park your car in front of and girls would come out with Teen Burgers on a tray, but it was getting started. 17th was the main drag in the South West, the dividing line between the old wood frame houses and apartment blocks of downtown, and the nice big houses up the hill they called Mount Royal. Back before Starbucks and mountain bike stores and great little Indian restaurants. Some good bars opened up, and a couple of decent coffee places, so when a developer bought the Devonish, kicked everyone out, and turned it into retail space, Vince sublet a condo a couple of blocks away in another old building, the Anderson. This one had been completely reno'd, had a brass birdcage elevator.

By the late eighties, Travis was gone and Vince was making real money running the escorts. By then he didn't even think of it as a decision, it was just his life.

He was hanging out at a bar, the Ship and Anchor, which was funny, a thousand miles across the Rocky Mountains from the coast, and listening to everyone else talk. He was ten years older than most of them, college kids, but not like the ones in Toronto now, these kids seemed to have more going on, they were always doing shit, and were a lot less self-conscious and didn't have so much of that phony irony.

It was really then that Vince started to know he was an outsider. There was another regular in the place about his own age, but this guy had long hair and wore T-shirts and shorts, and the mood in the place picked up when he came in. Vince liked to listen to the guy tell stories about working on Japanese TV commercials, shooting in the Rockies with Jack Nicholson, hear what crazy guys Tony and Ridley Scott really were.

But Vince knew he couldn't be in that crowd, any more than he could ask the blond with the one green eye and one blue eye out. What if she said yes, and halfway through the Phad Thai he got paged by one of the escorts like he knew he would? What would he say, can you just wait here while I go slap some drunk around to get the 150 bucks off him? Or, I'll have to call you tomorrow, I'm going to be up all night with a stoned, suicidal chick, talking her into going back to giving the biz boys blow jobs so she could pay her rent and keep her kid?

He hadn't even realized he'd turned on the desktop and started the media player. Eddie Money, "Two Tickets to Paradise," was playing. That was from before. Before he went to jail, before he was a complete outsider. Vince thought part of the problem was the technology made everything so easy now. He said to Suss, get me songs from the seventies, and the next day there were 300 on his hard drive.

No, Vince realized. He was an outsider before jail, before the escorts, before the online porn. Since Liz Downey dumped him. She was right, she knew. He laughed at himself and shut off the music.

He picked up the laptop and carried it out of the office thinking, the technology's not the problem, it's like opportunity, it's just there.

What matters is what you do with it.

• • •

Loewen thought he'd feel better to finally get one, finally close a homicide and arrest a murderer, but it was just sad. The eighty-year-old guy who'd been killed, stabbed again and again, it turned out his son did it.

Price asked all the questions at the scene, got the information from the neighbours about the old guy moving into the building less than a month ago, and the son visiting, the two of them fighting. Crime scene telling them no sign of forced entry. In fact, whoever left had locked the door, left blood on it.

Blood all over the kitchen where the old guy was on the floor. Half-empty bottle of rum, bunch of empty beer bottles. There was a grapefruit on the table, cut in half, but no knife.

Loewen said, "I wonder what they were fighting about," and Price said, what do they ever fight about.

They got an address for the son and drove over. Another apartment building a few blocks away just off the Danforth, across from the Victoria Park subway. When they knocked, a guy in his fifties wearing an undershirt came to the door. He tried to stare them down.

Price said they had some bad news, and Loewen could see right away the guy knew what they were going to say, could see the guy did it, and he could see Price knew.

The guy said, "What?"

Price asked him if he was Donald Killeen and the guy said yeah, so what, and he asked if his father's name was John.

"What'd he do now, the old prick?"

They were standing in the doorway of the apartment on the first floor. The guy looked past Price and Loewen at some kids playing basketball in the parking lot.

Price asked him if he wanted to come down to the station and the guy said, "What for?"

Loewen wasn't sure what Price was doing. He knew somewhere in the apartment were bloodstained clothes they'd need as evidence and probably the knife.

Price said, "You can put your shoes on, walk to the car, no cuffs. If you do it right now."

The guy nodded, beaten. He bent over and pulled on a pair of dirty white running shoes. Loewen saw the red stains all over them.

They walked out to the car, past the kids playing ball,

who all stopped and watched. The guy stared them down, waving his arms like he was free, getting into the car like he was going for a ride with his friends.

In the backseat he said, "Fucking nigger kids are everywhere. This city is gone to shit."

Loewen looked at Price and then at the guy, waiting for him to say something about the black cop arresting him, but he was staring at his hands.

Shit, Loewen actually saw blood on the nails. Guy didn't even clean up properly.

While Price took his statement, Loewen filled out the forms to get a warrant and went back to the apartment to find clothes — which was easy, they were right on the bathroom floor, and the knife which was just about as easy, under the sink. The guy had rinsed it off and wiped it down with the dishrag, which was also under the sink, but there was still blood everywhere.

That's when Loewen started to think how sad it all was. This old guy and his ancient father, both of them paying slumlord rent. Not understanding what was going on in their city, not understanding themselves anymore. Getting drunk and killing each other.

He made sure the crime scene guys tagged everything and took pictures, and he made a lot of notes. His first murderer.

It was hours later, almost midnight, when they finally finished booking the guy and he was transferred to the Don.

Loewen asked Price if he wanted to stop for a drink.

"Hey yeah, your first homicide collar," Price said, and Loewen couldn't tell if he was being sarcastic.

"It's not what I expected."

They'd processed the guy at 55 Division, on Dundas at

Coxwell, so they drove down to Queen and went into a place called Murphy's Law. It was trying to look like an Irish pub but it was too big, in an old bank building, and the people in there were too rowdy, volleyball players still out after an evening on the beach.

Price said Loewen did fine.

"Did fine. What'd I do? I didn't do anything."

"You didn't do anything wrong, that's the most important."

"What?"

"It's all about procedure, you know that."

"I guess."

"This the third dead body you've seen in less than a week, right?"

Loewen didn't say anything and Price said, "Right?"

"Right."

"And you didn't expect it to take this long to get someone."

"The guy in the boozecan's not ours."

"And you're pissed off, because you know who did the other ones, but you can't arrest them like you did this poor old bastard."

"Because they're actual killers. This Russian guy is a criminal and his uncle, the shooter, he's a pro. He got brought into our town to kill somebody and he's gonna get away with it."

"Why you say that?"

"Well, we don't have anything on him, and now it really is going to the task force like you wanted in the first place, and if anything happens it'll be the Mounties who get him."

"Because she told you to stay away?"

"Yeah."

"So you think we're going to?"

Loewen looked at him and thought again how Price was full of surprises.

Then he realized it wasn't a surprise at all. If he really thought about it, Price was always determined, in his own way, never showy or going on and on. Loewen was starting to think maybe that way was what you needed.

• • •

Suss was pounding on the keyboard like it was a drum, tapping out a rhythm as he edited.

Garry said, "Hold on that longer."

"It's a fucking bathroom, Fudge."

"Take your time, it's always such a rush with you. Enjoy the moment."

Garry was standing up, pacing behind Suss, staring at the monitor. On the screen two men were in the stall of a bathroom, one on his knees.

"They have their clothes on, still."

"Slow down, watch the zipper come down. Anticipate."

Vince walked into the room and said, "Hey Suss, did you install that new software?"

Suss kept looking at the screen. "It's not here."

"What do you mean? It was supposed to be here this morning."

On screen the standing man's pants were pulled down and his erection popped out. Suss hit a key and the image froze. He twirled around to face Vince and shrugged.

"They called, said it wasn't ready. They still adding some code."

"They called today to say it wasn't ready today?"

"Yeah."

"Assholes."

"Come on," Garry said, dropping his back and waving his hands around. "Too much anticipation."

Vince said, "Let's go for a ride, Suss."

He was standing up and walking across the room before Vince even finished speaking. "Thank you, man, these faggots are crazy."

"Hey," Garry said, "we're in the middle of something here."

Vince was already gone. Suss stopped in the doorway. "You finish it, Fudge."

"It'll take me all night."

Suss walked out, saying, "So don't stop to jerk off ten times."

"And don't call me that."

In the car Vince said, "Do you have any sunglasses?"

Suss, doing his best to look cool, pulled a pair out of his pocket. He had the look, the scowling black guy in the leather jacket wearing shades, but he really was just a computer geek. He looked at Vince behind the wheel and saw a guy with more edge than he'd realized before. He was the boss, he ran the place pretty loosely, but now as Suss thought about it, he'd never seen Vince take any shit. Clean shaven guy, casual clothes, top-end Eddie Bauer at least, but he wasn't soft. Shit, Suss thought, he'd seen plenty of old white guys trying to walk the walk.

The software place was on Cherry Street, down by the Docks nightclub in a building overlooking the water. A lot of movie companies had their offices there, and the parking lot was mostly empty except for a couple of old RV's and some sports cars. Vince pulled his SUV up in front of the doors and got out.

He said to Suss, "Don't say anything," and walked into the building.

The third floor, Eccentric Arts, was one big room. Hardwood floor, exposed beams and pillars, big windows looking out over the harbour, and desks scattered around in no particular order, every one of them with a laptop on it. There was a pool table in the middle of the room and pinball machines against one wall.

When Vince walked in, the president of the company, a kid barely out of school, stood up from behind his old wooden desk looking surprised but not unhappy. "Hey guys, cool, but didn't you get the message it's not ready? We're still checking the code."

He came around his desk, pointing to a bunch of computers against the far wall, but Vince walked past him to the pool table and picked up a cue.

There were two other guys in the place sitting on an old couch by the big windows. They both stood up. All the software guys wore concert T-shirts with bands Suss had never heard of, talk about obscure, and those long shorts down past their knees. Sloppy, but expensive sloppy.

Vince didn't stop, he picked up the cue and walked to the president's desk swinging it hard, slamming it down on the bright blue laptop.

"Hey! What the fuck!" The guy sounded pissed off, but he stepped further away from the desk as he said it.

Vince slammed the laptop a few more times and it fell off the desk. He pounded the butt end of the cue into it a couple more times smashing it into pieces. Then he turned on the guy and poked the fat end of the cue into his chest, high up near his neck.

"You say it'll be ready today, it's fucking ready today." He shoved him hard, and the guy banged up against the *Blow Up* poster on the brick wall.

Suss hadn't moved from the doorway. The two guys

who'd stood up hadn't moved from in front of the couch.

"Yeah, sure, today, it'll be ready today, this afternoon, man." He looked, bug-eyed, at the other guys and said, "How much longer it have to go, man?"

The two guys didn't move, they just stared, and finally one of them said, "Maybe an hour. Maybe two."

Vince dropped the pool cue and clattered around on the hardwood floor. He walked out the door, saying, "Bring it over in an hour."

He was shaking, but Suss knew the college boys couldn't see it. He was surprised none of them had wet themselves. He stared at the president, nodded as serious as he could, and walked out.

In the car, Suss was laughing. "Fuck man, in-tense. I mean, I'm never late, I say I'm going to get something done, I get it done. But now, man, I'm really gonna get it done. Shit. I say Tuesday, the shit will be motherfucking ready on Tues-daaay."

Vince said, "It's okay, Suss."

A couple of minutes later, Suss said, "Fuck man, they don't teach that shit at DeVry. That's some fucking advanced MBA management shit."

He looked sideways at Vince and thought, they were pumping it up now, bringing in the Russians and who knows what else kind of shit. Suss liked it, he thought it would be cool, great stories for the clubs, he was gonna be the man.

And he was never going to be late.

CHAPTER TWENTY-ONE

Roxanne said, "I'm beginning to see how serious this is," and Vince said, "Beginning to?"

She said, yeah, yeah, she knew, but on the way over, Boris had a little freak-out.

Vince said, "You came in with Boris?" and she said, yeah, and thought, oh come on, be a man. Then she thought it was good he seemed to care, that was more than she got from him last night, so maybe this hasn't totally played-out yet after all.

She said, "We went back up to his club and Boris parked in the back."

"Near the dumpster," Vince said. "By the no parking sign."

"Yeah, so a guy blocked him in. We came out and the guy was sitting in his pick-up truck, a big white one, talking on the phone. Boris doesn't slow down as he walks past the guy to his own car, he just says, 'move your truck,' as he passes."

They were sitting in Vince's office. Suss and the software guys were down the hall installing the new program, and Boris was with them. He was still deciding between being a partner or a consultant, thinking about which way the paperwork would look best, and Roxanne had kind of snuck Vince into his office to feel him out.

She said, "So the guy — a big guy by the way, like a construction worker or a contractor — doesn't say anything, he just holds up his hands, like, one minute okay?"

"Yeah."

"And Boris gets into his car and blares the horn. Have you ever heard the horn on an Audi?"

"No."

"Well, it's high-pitched. So the guy yells something like, 'Keep your pants on,' or something. And Boris honks the horn again."

Vince said, uh-huh, waiting.

"So the guy waves him off, you know, like he's not worth dealing with, like he's shit."

"Yeah."

"So this time when Boris honks, the guy just hangs his hand out the window and gives him the finger. He doesn't even look at Boris, he's looking at something on the seat."

"Probably his day planner. He didn't say anything?"

"Nothing. And neither did Boris. He just got out, walked back to the guy's truck, grabbed the finger and snapped it back. You could hear the bone break."

Vince shook his head and said Boris is in a mood.

"The guy jumps out of his truck, screaming at him, calling him a fucking jerk, saying how he's gonna kill him, and Boris just tells him to move his truck again. The guy runs around the back, grabs a piece of wood, and comes back swinging it like a bat." She paused for effect and Vince just looked at her. "He walks right up to Boris holding the wood in the air like he's going to swing it, slam it into Boris's head or something, when he sees the gun."

Vince said, "The gun," and Roxanne said, yeah, now I think I have your attention.

"He was pointing it at the guy's chest and he says, 'Move your fucking truck.'"

"So the guy moved his truck."

"Yeah, well, he walked back around it, tossing in the piece of wood, trying to be Mr. Bigshot, saying if this was supposed to scare him it didn't, and he might come back if he feels like it, and other shit I didn't really hear. Then when we got in his car, Boris says, I should have shot him, and I tell him it was good that he didn't, because we've got a deal to close."

Vince said, "You have to keep your eye on the prize."

Roxanne said, "So many deals fall apart at the last minute, people get scared, whatever. They're just afraid to do it, to commit, to make the decision and stick with it. It's always easier not to do it."

"You think Boris took the easy way out?"

"God no," Roxanne said. She'd already moved on, thinking about the deal. "The hard thing to do was not shoot him. I mean, the guy was really a jerk. And then Boris had to drive down here, convincing me he was still a tough guy. No, I'm sure he wanted to shoot him, it was harder not to."

She looked at Vince nodding, agreeing with her, but now she wasn't sure. Shit, it was so easy yesterday.

• • •

Denis said, "Where does he keep the cars?" and Nugs said what do you mean?

"After he picks them up, before he loads them. Where does he keep them, this guy all out on his own?"

"I don't know."

"Fuck, you got to think of these things."

The waitress came over and put down salads in front of them, the garden salad with cherry tomatoes for Denis, and a Caesar salad for Nugs. She held up the cheese grater and Nugs said sure.

"That stuff's all fat," Denis said.

They were sitting on the patio of one those Foxhound and Fricken places, this one out by the airport, so the only view was of an eight-lane highway and an endless stream of trucks. But patios were the only place you could smoke in this town now.

Nugs had said, "Montreal is more civilized, more European," but Denis said it was changing, too. All cities were starting to look the same to him.

Now Denis was looking around at the warehouses and hotels and bars that served the airport area. He said, "How did you guys ever let that club go?"

"The Galaxie? It was a piece of shit."

"Looks good now."

The waitress came by and asked if everything was okay, and Nugs said, yes, honey, if it isn't we'll let you know. Denis stopped her as she started to leave, and tried to smile politely, excusing his country cousin. He asked for another San Pellegrino, with lemon.

"What about the hotels?" Denis said. "You got girls working out of them?"

"Some of them. We got a few in the condos off the 427, too."

"How much is it to rent one of those?"

"The condo or the girl?" He looked at Denis like he might actually laugh at his joke. Then he said, "We own the fucking condos."

Denis nodded, right. Shit, they had so much business these days, he couldn't keep it all straight. It was so much more work than it used to be, him and Emile St. Croix on their bikes, selling coke and weed, four or five girls in that apartment building on Napoleon, back before the Plateau was the Plateau. A great house out past Candiac, man they had some great parties there, three, four days long, some of the best bands in Quebec, Stephen Barry Blues Band, Men Without Hats, Smiley's People. They never had money, it went as fast as they got it, not like now. Now they have investments, they own property, they're businessmen.

But it's so much work.

Nugs said, "You know, I think Henri told me the niggers steal the cars and they put them in long-term parking right over there."

"That works," Denis said. "Car can sit there for weeks, no one notices. If someone finds it, it's just one car, you don't lose the whole load. No warehouse to trace."

"Ronnie might just have got bored and left."

Denis couldn't believe it. Which was worse, Nugs's guy got taken out, or he fucked off on his own? "You put a guy on it would do that?"

"No, I'm just saying. Maybe nothing happened."

The waitress brought the bottle of San Pellegrino to the table. She put it down and then a new glass beside it, had a lemon wedge stuck on the rim, and picked up the empty bottle and glass. Denis watched her, thinking she was probably new at this, probably new to the city, couldn't be more than twenty years old. He figured all cities have country girls showing up looking for a good time, something new. Figured she'd go from the Fox and Fidget to Club International in no time. A couple of years ago, he would have started talking to her, seeing how much work it would be to set her up in an apartment across the highway. He was thinking maybe he missed that, too, that challenge, that payoff. It used to feel like he was *doing* something, now it just felt like he was managing.

"This fucking Russian is a lot more trouble than we thought."

Nugs said, "Guy all on his own, has one club and one connection back home buys a few cars."

"You sure about that?"

Nugs shrugged, but he didn't say anything.

Denis said, "I want that contact, I want to know who's buying twelve cars a month. We're going to take it over."

"We get the shipping."

"I want the whole thing." He finished his salad and pushed the plate away. He could smell chicken wings from another table, and nachos. Shit, they smelled so good. And the garlic bread. He was down about fifteen pounds since Christmas, almost four pounds a month, but man, he had a long way to go. He lit a cigarette and said, "Either we see who the Russian meets here, or we pick up the boat over there."

Nugs nodded, not too happy about it.

Denis looked at him and thought again how the guy lacked ambition. They had to take on so much useless shit when they patched over all these guys in Ontario, these guys who'd been sitting on their asses for years, not getting a tenth of what they could out of the territory. Let anybody walk in, Russians, Vietnamese, Tamils, anybody who wanted a piece. Fucking Jamaicans were doing more business than these guys.

Claude came onto the patio and sat down at the table. He said everything was ready.

The waitress came over again, this time looking to Denis like it might not be such a challenge after all, she looked so tired and ready for almost anything else. She had a nice rack under the uniform, too, covered in freckles and standing right up.

Claude ordered a bacon burger with cheese and fries.

Denis watched the waitress leave and thought he'd have to go for a walk when it came to the table. He said, "You checked it, inside and out?"

"Couple of VIP rooms, they only went into one. It's standard."

Denis nodded.

Nugs said, "You guys sure you want to do this?"

Denis said, "We don't have a choice."

Nugs leaned in close and practically whispered, "This isn't Quebec, you know. You go blowing up buildings it's going to be a big deal."

Denis said, "We want it to be a big deal."

Nugs sat back and crossed his arms over his chest.

Like a little kid, Denis thought, afraid. He looked at Claude and said, "You have everything?"

"My guys came in from Niagara Falls, they've got everything they need."

They talked a little bit about how the Niagara Falls chapter was really improving, and the new casino going in there. It looked good, they'd be able to double or triple their loan-sharking, and a casino always meant more speed, gamblers doing anything to stay up all night.

Denis said, "It was a good idea, bringing in Big Boy

from London," and Claude agreed. Denis looked at Nugs and said, "You know, Roy Berger."

"I know who Big Boy is," Nugs said, still with his arms crossed. "I don't know you had to bring him in."

Denis said, yeah, they did. "He really got things in shape, sent the right message."

"I still don't see who you're sending a message to now. This Russian is all by himself."

"And his fucking uncle," Claude said.

Denis said, "First of all, we don't really know that. And second . . ." He stopped and watched the waitress carrying the huge plate of fries and the hamburger, open faced, to the table. The patty covered with at least two kinds of shredded cheese and three strips of bacon. She put it down in front of Claude and asked the rest of them if there was anything they wanted.

Yeah, Denis thought, two of those with mustard and mayonnaise and you get on your knees and spread 'em, but he didn't say anything. He watched her blow some of her blond hair out of her face and then look at him.

She stared for a second and then left. He watched her, and then he said, "We need a show of force, and this fucking Russian is as good as any."

Nugs said, "I don't know," and Denis thought, of course you don't fucking know.

"One of the freelancers will put it in the locker room," Claude said. "It'll play after the place is closed. Just a demo, you know?"

Nugs said, "What about the porno guy? We've been looking for a web operation we could get a piece of."

Denis nodded, inhaling the bacon, and said, "So, even better. We take out the Russian, and we go talk to the porno guy. This puts him in the right mood."

Claude laughed, dipping a fry in the puddle of ketchup and putting it into his mouth.

There was no way Denis could sit and watch him eat any more. He stood up and said he had to take a leak.

On his way inside, he saw the waitress leaning back against the wall next to the open kitchen door. She looked up and saw him, took a deep drag on her cigarette and blew the smoke up to the sky. Denis figured he could at least show her one good time in the city.

• • •

They were walking on Gerrard Street, Roxanne saying the area was called Little India. Then she said, "Some people call it the India Bazaar."

Vince watched her and thought, yeah, or Pakiville or Raghead Town, even though there weren't many turbans around. This was her real estate personality, or her tourist guide, proud of her city.

Boris said, "I've never even been here, all the time I'm in Toronto."

All the stores were Indian — grocery stores, clothing stores with saris in the windows, places selling TV's and tape decks and Indian movies on tape, "PAL and NTSC," and CD's of Indian pop stars. A lot of windows had posters for concerts and appearances of Bollywood stars. Vince was surprised to see some of them were playing at the Air Canada Centre, the same place the Leafs and Raptors played. And restaurants, every block had two or three restaurants. They weren't just Indian places, now they all had specialities — vegetarian, Northern India, Southern India — and they weren't after tourists anymore, half of them didn't even have any English on the signs or menus.

Roxanne was telling Boris how the neighbourhood had changed, how it used to be Irish working class, bus drivers and transit workers, and there was still one hold-out, the Old Dublin Pub. She said, "There's still a lot of change going on here, renovations and new construction. There are a lot of opportunities here."

Boris agreed, but Vince thought, sure, if you were Punjab. But then he thought maybe Roxanne knew what she was talking about. Look at all the other neighbourhoods in Toronto that went through the same kind of changes, starting out working class from somewhere in the U.K., built up around some industry, little row houses and a couple of churches. Then it turned into Little Italy, and now there are a bunch of Italian restaurants and the green-and-white street signs in Italian, but the place was really mixed. Happened to the Greeks on the Danforth, happened in Little Portugal, the Polish on Roncevalles, all over town.

Roxanne and Boris walked right past the young Indian guy standing in front of the restaurant, and Vince stopped, shook his hand and said, "Russell."

The guy was in his late twenties, tall and good-looking. He was wearing a colourful silk shirt, a gold necklace, some kind of light weave summer pants, and sandals. Vince was pretty sure his sunglasses weren't knock-offs.

Russell had no accent at all, except maybe that East Toronto one, the same as Jim Carrey when he was being sincere in his Barbara Walters interview, and he said, "Vincent, how's business?"

Roxanne and Boris had turned around and come back. The sidewalk was fairly crowded, Saturday afternoon shoppers, whole families walking in bunches, Moms in their saris, kids in their jeans and Britney Spears T-shirts.

Vince said business was good, really good, and Russell smiled and said he wasn't surprised. "You work hard, you get ahead, right?"

Vince said yeah, right. He introduced Boris and Roxanne and Russell shook their hands, taking an extra moment to look at Roxanne. She did look good, new sunglasses today, her hair barely long enough for the ponytail, a light blue blouse you could see the frilly bra under.

Then Russell said, "Okay, Pops is inside, you hungry?"

Roxanne said, "I am now, smell how good that is," and walked into the restaurant. Boris followed right behind her.

Russell pulled his sunglasses down a little, he looked like one of the popstars on the posters, and said to Vince, "Who's with who here, buddy?" and Vince said he'd tell him when he found out.

After they got seated and Russell introduced his father, Ravinder Samanani, and the old guy said to call him Sam. The waiter brought them some pakoras and some bottles of Taj — Roxanne saying she'd never had beer from India before — and they got straight to business.

Sam said, in his Indian accent that Vince always thought sounded so fake, so much like Peter Sellers, "If you work with Vincent, then we know you are good people."

Vince leaned back in his chair, sipped his beer out of the bottle, and watched. He thought old Sam had come a long way in a few years, from back when he first approached Mickey Kennedy about running Indian girls out of the escorts. Sam provided the girls, and a lot of the customers, and Mickey got rid of the guys who thought they could just start up on their own. Russell was a teenager then, but the old man brought him along.

Vince also watched how easily Roxanne ran the meeting, talking about the ongoing possibilities, getting them right to the point.

"The money," she said, "gets transferred?"

"No, not transferred," Sam said. "Do you know what is a Hawala?" He looked at them all, nodded like he understood, no problem, and said, "It's a Hindi word, it means 'change,' and it also means, 'trust.' This is something we've been doing since before the British."

Vince watched Boris and Roxanne, saw them paying attention. He also saw two Indian guys sitting at a booth at the back of the restaurant, but they weren't sitting across from each other having a meal, they both had their backs to the wall, watching.

Sam said, "When I first came to Canada, I worked out of a restaurant, just over there. It's the way Hawala works, a back booth."

"A booth," Boris said. "Like Lloyd's of London."

Sam liked that. "Exactly, like Lloyd's of London. A customer comes to me, he wants to send money home to his family. He gives me the money, and I contact a partner in India and the family gets the money."

Boris said, "And no one knows."

"Why pay the bank fees? What's it to the government, what you do with your own money."

"Right," Roxanne said. "So the money isn't actually transferred anywhere, there's no record, nothing to trace."

Russell caught Vince's eye and leaned his head a little towards Roxanne, impressed with her.

Boris said, "But we don't want to give the money to someone in India."

Russell said, "Yeah, Vince said you wanted to get it online, turn it into digital cash."

"That's right."

"You see that place across the street, MoneyChangers? We own that."

Sam said, "Russell is bringing us into the twenty-first century."

"Cheque-cashing, payday loans, money transfers," Russell said. "All of your financial needs. Including digital cash to buy stuff online."

Everybody looked at Vince and he said, "You know, Ebay and stuff. There are a few different systems. They're all owned by the big credit card companies. The thing is, there's been a lot of pressure on them not to handle the transactions of adult content."

Russell laughed and said, "Like there's any other money spent online."

Vince said a little here and there, and more every day. "But, I know what you mean. So some of them set up subsidiaries, gave them a different name, and that seems to have shut people up."

"But it also left a little opening," Russell said, "for guys like us. We can get your money into the system, and all you have to do is spend it. You know what you're spending it on?"

Roxanne started to say something, but Boris cut her off. He said, "I'll think of something. What's your cut?"

Russell said, "The cost of the service is 2.9 per cent."

Boris said, "Two per cent."

"Over half a million?"

"Yes."

"It's a deal."

Vince watched the two guys at the back of the restaurant. They hadn't moved and they hadn't ordered any food. He thought Sam and Russell were getting a lot more independent since Mickey Kennedy got killed. He figured it could work, but maybe they were also starting to get too big. They might get noticed soon.

Boris asked exactly how the cash got turned into digital money, and Russell said not to worry. From the time he got the cash, it would only take an hour till the money was in an offshore account. From there, it was up to them.

Roxanne said, "We've got that covered."

Russell looked at Vince over his sunglasses and motioned to Roxanne and Boris.

Yeah, Vince thought, I can see who's with who.

CHAPTER TWENTY-TWO

SUSS SAID IT WAS INCREDIBLE, unfuckingbelieveable. "You should have seen him. That is one stone cold motherfucking faggot."

"I always figured that," Vince said. He took a drink of the Steam Whistle beer from the bottle and leaned back in the chair. They were in the editing suite, what Suss called his office.

"They come in here, freshies, still."

"They were from the islands?"

"No, shit, white guys, from someplace else. Had accents."

"French?"

"Could be."

Suss was going through video on the hard drive, mostly what Garry called twinkie stuff, young muscled guys with no hair on their bodies making out. Every once in a while, he threw in what he called a bear, a big burly guy with a beard, but it was usually just his own tastes.

Once in a while Vince would tell him he had to make stuff for other people, this wasn't just for his personal use, it was a business after all. But really he didn't care. It sold, and Garry was damned good at it, even Suss could tell that.

Still, he pounded on the keyboard till he had a scene of three women making out. It was shot in the studio next door.

"Here, we just finished this. Supposed to look like webcam chicks after work, they finish talking to the sweaty guys online and they still hot for each other."

Vince said how come Garry is only budget-conscious when it comes to the chicks. "The guys he has dressed up like cowboys and shoots it at Riverdale Farm."

"He did a lot of it hand-held, but he had the webcams on, said we'd edit it to look like they didn't know they was being filmed."

"Okay."

"Okay, so right, so we finishing up, and these guys come in, two of them. A short one and a tall one. They both fat."

"The cameras were off?"

On the monitor, two of the women were kissing, 'necking' Vince would have called it, and he had to admit it looked good, like they were really into it. Long, deep, passionate kisses, none of that phony lesbo stuff with their tongues sticking out. One was sitting in the chair and the other was in her lap, and they had their arms around each other. It was Rosi and Marissa, which surprised Vince, because he didn't think they liked each other or were good enough actors. That Garry might really be a filmmaker someday.

"Yeah, the cameras were off, but they don't know that. They come in like they bigshots, still, the short man doing all the talking. Saying shit like, who owns this place and how many memberships you have, like that."

"Did you tell them?"

"The fuck you think we are?"

Vince nodded, kind of apologizing. Suss was still getting used to the new feel of VSF Online, not yet realizing their days of flying under the radar were about over. Or what that really meant.

"We don't say shit. But Garry, man, little fucker, turns on the monitors so we all see ourselves everywhere."

Suss hit the keyboard again and there was Claude and Denis on his monitor, looking pissed off but not totally confident.

Vince drank some more Steam Whistle and waited. Suss was liking the story, trying it out, Vince knew, before he told his buddies. Vince would call them his homies and watch Suss shake his head at the sad old white man.

"So we all on the monitors, from about four different angles, webcams everywhere, and Garry says, 'Why don't you guys fuck off.' Not asking a question, but telling them."

"He could tell they were bad guys?"

"Fuck yeah, we both could man."

Telling it later, there was no way Suss would sound so scared. Right now, just a few hours after it happened, he was still freaked. Vince said, "But they didn't say anything threatening."

"Didn't have to, man. The way they was standing, the way they walked in, the way they talked, not what they said. Like we were shit and if they wanted anything they'd take it."

Vince looked at the faces on the monitor thinking, yeah, and they won't take no for an answer. With Boris on board it could be a real fight, but it could go on for a long time. He said, "Till Garry told them to fuck off."

"Like as if he said they had little dicks or were fags like him, or as if I was fucking they mama, you know?"

Vince said yeah, he knew.

"So the big one, he walks over to the monitor to smash it, but he sees his own face on it." Suss let the picture play. "Look at him, like where's the camera, but he don't see one."

Vince was looking at him.

"So that's when Garry says, yeah man, you being filmed. You don't even know from where, you dumb shit."

"He said you dumb shit?"

"Something like that."

Vince could see Suss already improving that line for later. He didn't think Suss'd try and take credit for anything, or tell anyone that it was him who did the talking. He might want to be the man, but he's not rushing into anything.

"So he stops, you know, looking around, seeing all the monitors with all the shots, all different angles." Suss clicked a few through from the stuff they shot, Marissa still on the chair, Rosi on her knees between her legs, and it really did look good. Linda sitting on the bed behind them watching, looking a little jealous. Four different angles, even Vince could tell it would cut together just fine. Damned Garry. Then all the monitors in the place had the bad guys on them.

"And Garry says, yeah motherfucker, you're on so many cameras and you don't even know where they are and what computers they recording to, and even if they in the building, so why don't you fuck off and get out of here."

"And they left?"

"They all tough and shit, saying watch your back, and using the N word on me, but yeah, they left."

"Shit, Garry."

"Shit yeah. And when they walk out I say to him, nice going Fudge, 'cause you know, I never thought he had balls of steel, and he just kept looking at the door and says to me, 'Don't call me that anymore,' and I'm like, you know what? I won't."

Vince said, "Balls of steel," and wondered how Suss would end the story for his buds? Maybe the way it happened. It was all right, didn't make him look too bad.

Suss said, "You know, that time he had the twinkies going at it by the skating rink at city hall? And the cops showed up? He almost talked one of the cops into joining in. Shoulda known."

Yeah, or not, Vince thought. He said, "So where is he now?"

"Had some shit to do."

"Why'd you stick around?"

"Had to get the software up and running. Working fine now. And I was gonna start editing the chicks."

"So it'll generate the accounts?"

"And spread the payments out over the month."

Vince said that sounded great, and then told Suss he should head home, too.

"Yeah, okay, you leaving, too?"

Vince said no, not right away, and Suss said he'd keep working on the edit, then. Vince was about to go back into his office, when he realized Suss was probably just afraid to leave the building on his own. He said, "Suss, they won't be waiting."

"Shit, that's not it."

And it didn't look like it. It really looked like Suss liked it at VSF, where else was he going get stories like this?

Made Vince wonder how he was going to tell him how much things were going to change. If there was going to be a place for either of them.

Shit, Vince thought, he should think about this a little more, instead of just letting it happen.

• • •

Claude reached up to the rear-view and said, "You know what that is?"

Denis said it was a Dreamcatcher, an Indian thing.

"It's probable cause." Claude pulled on the feathers hanging off the bottom of the thing and it came off in his hand. "It's what those mounted pricks used to pull over Dukey in New Brunswick. Everybody has something hanging, but there's a law against it, just an excuse."

Denis said, "Operation Pipeline."

"Those fucking Jew lawyers, sometimes I think they're worth the money. My first trial, lawyer was a chick, Jewish chick, she's just pounding on the asshole cop, 'Why did you stop the car, were the headlights not working?' Shit like that, on and on, finally the asshole says because he didn't think a guy looked like me could own a car like that."

Denis said, "I got pulled over once, the tailgate on my truck was down."

"Assholes."

They'd just left the house on Eastern Avenue and were heading downtown. All those shitty old houses and warehouses, and the big bakery where they made the fluffy white bread, smelled like yeast, and what they were trying to call the "Studio District" because a couple of old factories got turned into soundstages.

"Why didn't you just get a hangaround to drive us?"

They came off the overpass and took the Front Street exit instead of Richmond towards downtown.

Denis said, "I think you were supposed to take that."

"This fucking city." They drove along Front and Claude turned down Church, thinking it would get him to Lake Shore, but when he got to the bottom, he didn't know where he was.

Denis said, "Turn around."

Claude cut across two lanes and pulled into the parking lot, then backed out onto the street. Some guy in a Land Rover swerved around them and blasted the horn, leaning over, looking out the passenger window at them like they were idiots.

Claude said, "Keep driving, Tarzan, you want to keep breathing."

Back on the road, Claude asked if the guys from Niagara Falls were still in town and Denis said, yeah.

Claude didn't know which way to go when he got to Jarvis, but he could see the Gardiner Expressway to the right, so that's where he went.

"Maybe we'll use them on the porno guy."

"Let's get Nugs to send in some guys."

"Nugs. Fucking Nugs worries me."

"Everything worries you."

"He's going soft, he spends too much time on his boat with that chick."

Denis said, "She's hot that chick. And she's sophisticated."

"Where was she tonight?"

"I don't know, I didn't see her all day."

"Ah, fucking shit!" Claude pounded the wheel with both hands.

"What?"

"We're supposed to be up there," pointing at the Gardiner above them. "Did you see a sign?"

"There's always fucking construction on these fucking roads."

"Why don't they just build them right the first time. Shit."

"You can turn around here."

"We're going the same way."

"Yeah, but we have all these lights."

Lake Shore Boulevard, under the Gardiner, stop-and-go traffic. They passed the Air Canada Centre and could see the SkyDome ahead.

"We're supposed to take Spadina. Can we get to that from here?"

"I don't know. Fuck it, let's just go to the airport."

Claude said he still wanted to pass the place again.

"You're still pissed," Denis said, "at the fag. You're always telling me, don't make it personal."

"It's not personal. There." He pointed at an exit and had to cut across three lanes of traffic.

They drove around some, got lost a couple of times, Claude getting more and more pissed, until they finally found the Toy Works building. Claude drove around back and parked across from the parking lot.

"There," he said. "That's his."

"What is it, a Land Rover?"

"No, it's that Mercedes, looks like a Jeep it's so square."

"Why the fuck would anyone drive that?"

"Let's talk to the guys from the Falls."

Denis didn't like the idea, but he agreed. He said, "They could have something together in a couple of days."

Claude said, "Tell them to be ready. As soon as they see a chance, take it. Let's get rid of this asshole."

• • •

He sat in his office and thought about David Bowie. He was thinking about "Changes" at first, but then "Five Years" started playing in his head.

Five Years.

Could be a pretty good run. It was coming up on five years for VSF Online. Almost five years with Mickey and Carole Kennedy. A little more than five years in Millhaven, but put together with the two in Spyhill, it worked. Five years on his own with the escorts in Calgary.

"Five Years" was on that album he used to play after school in LaSalle with Liz Downey, something about that's all we've got, we've got five years. One of the records his brother Danny left behind when he joined the army.

Now it was dark out, and Vince hadn't put on any lights except the desktop monitor. He played the Bowie, on one of the playlists Suss called "Early Seventies Glitter," because Vince hadn't finished his rock'n'roll lessons. He could see his reflection in the office window, and he figured it looked okay. He had all his hair, he wasn't fat, well-dressed, casual.

Alice Cooper came on, "Is It My Body?" because Suss thought anyone with makeup was glitter and couldn't tell the difference between that and glam.

But Vince had heard a new Alice Cooper song on the radio a while ago and thought, man Alice, why bother, till he heard the words, all about how he couldn't feel anything anymore. The song was "Novocaine," or something like that, and Vince knew exactly how Alice felt. Couldn't really feel anything, not anything good, not anything bad. He sat there in the dark and typed, and thought how everything he'd worked for for the last five years was going to be taken away from him. Because he didn't care enough to fight for it, and because he wanted to get laid by the real estate lady.

What would his brother have said? Danny, home on leave in his fatigues, saying something like, "It's yours, bro, fight for the fucking shit."

Or maybe, "Caught between Russian mobsters, bikers, and cops? You gotta know when to fight and when to flee."

Who knew what Danny would say, why he did the things he did. One day he was having screaming fights with Dad about his hair — his greasy fucking hair halfway down his back — and the next he's home with a brush cut. He went down to the Canadian Armed Forces recruiting office on Ste. Catherine Street, the same one the FLQ bombed and killed the security guard, the Commissionaire, a few years before. What did Danny want to do in the army, piss off Dad? See the world? He saw Cyprus, the Golan Heights, and Africa. Stood there in his blue helmet between people who hate each other more than Vince could ever imagine, and he met the Frenchman. No one ever found out his name, Danny never said if he even knew.

Mott the Hoople going all the way to Memphis, and Vince thinking about growing up in Montreal, how the radio was all British prog rock, the word was always that the bands broke there first, then the rest of North America. Who knew if it was true, but Danny sure left a lot of those records behind.

Vince remembered playing them in the basement while his father read the letters Danny sent. Had no idea what they made him think. His own time in the navy during the Second World War? Probably. That Danny was doing something good and noble? Probably not. More likely that Danny was wasting his life.

Even when Danny showed up at the door in Greenfield Park in a brand new Corvette, throwing money around, everybody wanting to know where he got it, Dad knew. He never said anything, but he knew.

Six months later, Interpol identified the fingerprints on a headless corpse in the Ivory Coast, Danny running guns for the Frenchman. The Frenchman still unknown.

Vince wondered again why Danny was doing it. The money, for sure, but there had to be more to it. Excitement, power, taking the bad boy as far as he could. Who knew with Danny?

Or with Vince.

He stood up and walked around his office. Saturday night and the place was empty. He'd finally got Suss to leave, practically had to walk him to his car, and then decided to come back in. Really, where else did he have to go?

By now, Boris would be wondering why he needed Vince, the bikers were walking in the door, and the cops hadn't finished with him.

And Vince was wondering why he let it all happen. He walked back to the employee lounge and got himself a shot of Oban, which he found out was pronounced *O-bin* by the Scots, probably just to confuse the rest of the world. Bastards. He sat on the couch under the window and sipped. He left the bottle on the floor beside the couch.

The last time something felt like the end for him was

in '89 in Calgary. He was doing great on his own, had a half-dozen escorts — real pros, no kids in the bunch, good steady customers. He'd take on a few extra girls, out-of-towners or part-timers, for the big oil and gas conventions or the Stampede — or the playoffs, the Flames won the cup that year, beat Montreal right in the fucking Forum. Vince liked that but it did make him a little homesick.

It was great for business, though.

So great that after the last game, he took his regular girls to Vegas for a vacation. He laughed about it at the time, like taking popsicles to the fucking Arctic, taking hookers to Vegas, but they had a great time. Maybe too great, because when they got back, a couple guys came up to Calgary and offered to buy the escort agencies.

Guy actually said to Vince, "What's the leaving fee on the girls?" like he was a street pimp. Vince was a businessman, like his customers. The Vegas guys, though, they weren't.

Threatened the girls, beat up a couple, scared them away. The cops Vince was paying off didn't do shit — not that he really expected anything, but you never know — and then they cut up Erin.

She was a plump redhead, seemed to be always happy, telling jokes and getting along. Nice. Harmless really, which is why it really pissed Vince off when he saw her chest all slashed, long red lines on her pale white skin, not deep enough for stitches, but dozens of them all over her big tits. Every one of the cuts would leave a mark.

She said to Vince, "Next time it's my face," and tried to smile.

Looking back on it now, Vince was trying to figure out what was going through his head. He should have sent her back to Sarnia and taken off. But he had nothing. His condo, his car, everything he had was leased, and he took in just enough money every month to make his payments. After all these years, if he was really going to be honest about it, he could have easily put away a lot of money, but when you make it like that, you spend it just as fast.

But he never even thought of that. He never thought about why he was where he was, why that was his life. He did what he did.

He called up a couple of Travis Goodeagle's cousins from the reserve, and they went after the guys from Vegas. Vince could have just paid the Indians a grand and let them do it themselves, but he wanted to be there, be part of it, he wanted to see them go down, and he did. They followed them out of Caesar's steak house on 4th Avenue to the parking lot and went after them with baseball bats.

The Vegas guys were a lot tougher than they expected, and it got a lot messier, a lot louder. The cops got there quick and the reservation crew was gone. Vince was the only one the cops picked up, standing there with a bloody bat in his hand and two dead guys on the pavement.

He might have gotten off if he'd had a decent lawyer. Killed a couple of pimps from Las Vegas in self-defense after all. But he didn't, he had some guy named Aull, called himself Aull That and a Bag of Chips.

There was an Aull Building on Centre Street downtown, built in the twenties, but this guy, Patrick, blew what was left of the family fortune. Thought he was a deal-maker. The best he could do for Vince was second-degree murder, two counts, fifteen to life. Maybe Vince's 'lifestyle' was the problem. Maybe a better lawyer could have kept a lid on it. Maybe if the cops hadn't been so worried about their names showing up in his books.

He poured himself some more Scotch, but he didn't get

off the couch. Back at his trial, just before, Patrick Fucking Aull That convinced him he was lucky that he wasn't getting charged with all his crimes; five years of living off the avails, the stolen construction equipment no one ever found out about, an ever-widening assortment of assaults. And he figured, yeah, it's true, he was living this life, this life that didn't seem like his own. He'd just kept digging himself in deeper with no way to get out. He was almost glad someone stopped it.

But then he did five years in Millhaven Maximum, as the song goes. A third of his sentence. Maybe he was lucky, maybe it could have been a lot worse.

As it was, that was where he met Carole Kennedy, in visiting her useless brother, the guy a career fuck-up, but small-time till he went down for killing a cop. A big kid, really, talked too much, easy to mess up. He wasn't in for a month when he was on the phone to Carole, crying like a baby. If she didn't deposit five grand into an account number he gave her, they were going to kill him.

Vince remembered Carole showing up in the visitors room, tall and thin, model good-looking with her blond hair and blue eyes, tight Levis and leather boots, sitting down with Tommy and telling him to go back to these assholes and tell them to fuck off, because she was Mickey Kennedy's fucking wife and she wasn't going to pay off some half-assed extortion from some fucking loser in Millhaven. Vince, by himself in the visitors room, smiled and made eye contact.

Carole rolled her eyes and said, "You believe this shit?" and Vince said, "What are you gonna do?" and she asked him what his name was, and for the first time in his life he said, "Vince," because he was never going leave himself with no back door again.

She came to visit her brother once a month and spend more time with Vince. He started a computer course through correspondence at Thousand Island College and got into html at the very beginning. The first time he filled out a form online, he put down the name Vince Fournier and got himself a Hotmail account. When he got out, he went to Toronto and started working for Mickey. Well, really, he started working for Carole, it was almost completely her show by then, and she liked the idea of going high tech. They were the first ones to start putting escorts up on the web, and it really took off. By the time Carole killed Mickey, Vince was on his own running his Internet company with Suss and Garry.

• • •

Sitting behind the wheel of his Jag, Cohiba in his hand, Henri said, "Now that would make a nice grow op." He pointed to the old silos on Lake Shore, the ones with the real estate guy's name on it saying he sold it, the land the tent city was on till the cops rolled in and threw all the homeless out.

Nugs said, "Take too many people, too hard to keep quiet," and Henri thought there he was, afraid to think big.

"Look what happened to Angelo up in Barrie."

Henri thought, yeah, what happened? He turned the old Molson Brewery into a gigantic grow house, had a dozen guys working it full-time, pulling out a million bucks a month in crops. Henri said, "It worked great. Who'd have thought? Canada a dope-exporting nation. Cops spend all their time worrying about what's coming in, they never think about what's going out."

Nugs said, “Let’s hope,” and looked at the containers being loaded onto the ship. They were near the end of the load, the sun was starting to come up over Lake Ontario, and the sky was clear.

“Nobody tipped this,” Henri said. “Did they?”

He watched Nugs not even realize what he said for a second and then shake his head. Nugs said, “You were always a hard-ass.”

Henri thought about that and decided, yeah, he was always a hard-ass. Good.

Nugs said, “Those giant operations, Angelo’s obsessed. I mean it was a pretty good gig, 150 trucks a day taking Toronto garbage to Michigan, tons of it, couple times a week one of them is packed with homegrown.”

“All B.C. Bud?”

“Some of it, some Little Dragon, Bubble Ton-ton, Shiva Skunk. They even had some M-39 and Double 07.”

“Angelo’s brother has the garbage-hauling contract?”

“Brother-in-law. Who cares? Someone got pissed at someone higher up than we’ll ever be, leaked the fucking shit. By the time the cops got there, three Vietnamese guys were the only ones left, sleeping on cots. They got nothing.”

“A million bucks worth of equipment. The place was engineered.”

“Yeah,” Nugs said rolling his eyes, “and Angelo paid straight up for that. You’re right, though, he’s probably got another one going. He’s always talking about abandoned hospitals out in the boonies, old factories. He talked about a whole apartment building, and factory farming up in the Bruce.”

Henri watched the big forklift roll over the mud and scoop up another container, another car heading off to Serbo-fucking-something-istahn. He said, “There’s only two left, we'll be out of here in half an hour."

"So where are they?"

"They'll be here."

Nugs stewed. Henri knew he wanted to ask where they kept the cars, picking them up all month and bringing them in on the day, no warehouse, no property out in Uxbridge. Does he work for a lonely Russian guy, or is he part of something big? Henri thought about telling Nugs he was thinking of getting rid of Boris, that he actually ran the show himself. Tell him that, see how hard-ass he thought he was then.

Nugs said, "But shit, the small operations are no easier. You ever try running a grow house? Find someone who can do that? Sounds easy, sixty-eight days from bulb to harvest. Set up a bunch of plants, watch them grow. They're fucking weeds after all."

Henri looked at his watch and wondered where the last two cars were.

Nugs said, "The right temperature, the right humidity. Hydrogen peroxide and sodium hydroxide, 1000-watt bulbs, fans, hoses. All that shit costs money. Fucking plywood tripled in price, it's sixty bucks a sheet now, you know."

"Plywood?"

"You close the curtains, then you put up a sheet of poly, and then plywood to keep the condensation off the windows in the winter. Looks pretty fucking bad, all your windows covered in a sheet of ice. And someone has to make sure all the shit is working, check on it every day. Empty the mailbox."

"It's not that easy," Henri said.

"No," Nugs said. "It's not."

Fucking lazy piece of shit. Really, though, Henri didn't

give a shit, just another reason why he'd wanted out of the gangs. Go legit. One thing the biz boyz dropping two hundred bucks for a hand job in the VIP room proved to him was that the real money was made legally. Why break the law when it's really on your side all the time?

Henri said, "Oh well, weed'll be legal soon, then you won't have these problems."

"Not if Angelo has anything to say about it."

Jesus, these guys have no vision at all. "Then he could buy those silos, start really producing."

"And competing with the fucking cigarette companies?" Nugs shook his head and said, "I'd rather deal with those assholes from Montreal."

You mean work for them, Henri thought. He said, "What about Angelo?"

Nugs looked at him sideways and said, "Come on, you know the Hells do what Angelo tells them to. You and the Russian ever get big enough, you'll do what he says, too."

"You don't know who's behind Boris."

Nugs nodded, but Henri couldn't tell if he believed him or not. Who gives a shit, really, go legit, get a bank behind you. That's the biggest, best-armed gang in the world, no one touches you.

Nugs said, "You remember when we were kids, when it was fun? Ten bucks an ounce for Mexican grass. Put a baggie in the palm of your hand, eyeball it. You remember the Green Moroccan Hash? Three bucks a gram."

Henri didn't remember any of that. By the time he came up it was a business, and people didn't share. It was a product moved for profit no different than Big Macs, and the people moving it were just as ruthless. Henri saw the future even then, though. The future is business. The future is money.

He said, "Fuck, finally," and opened the car door.

Mud all over the ground, April in Toronto, they were lucky it wasn't pouring rain. Or snowing.

A BMW X5 drove in way too fast and stopped close to Henri's Jag. The black guy with the yellow dreads got out in a haze of smoke, looking serious. Then a black Excursion with tinted windows all round drove in, and the other guy got out, the tall skinny one with the short dreads.

Henri said, "The fuck took you so long?"

They didn't say anything, they just leaned against the X5 and lit cigarettes.

Henri looked at the Excursion and said, "That's not what we ordered."

The skinny guy leaned his head back and blew smoke. He said, "It's extra. My gift to you."

Yellow dreads said, "Got some wet work in the trunk," and they both started to laugh.

Henri said, "What the fuck?"

Nugs had gotten out of the car and stood beside Henri, waiting.

The skinny guy said, "We were picking up the cars, in the lot, you know?" He looked at Henri. "And some white dude pulls up in this piece of shit." The Excursion. "He's all, that's my car, you stole my fucking car." Meaning the X5.

Henri said, "So?" and he could tell Nugs was starting to enjoy himself for the first time tonight.

The skinny guy said, "He's all like, my girlfriend works for Boomerang GPS Systems and she located my car." Even Henri found his white-guy accent funny. Nowhere near the way a white guy talks, but probably the way this guy hears them.

Henri said, "What did you do?"

"So, he's all like, this is my car, right? So Gee here says, this car? This not your car."

Yellow dreads started to smile, thinking how cool he was.

"We behind the car, still, so Gee, he pops the trunk, says this not your car, look, see what's in the trunk."

Now they're both laughing, half the weed they've been smoking for hours, half how fucking funny they think they are. Skinny says, "He comes right over says," almost doubled-over laughing, doing his serious white guy now, "This is my car, there's nothing in my trunk." Now he can't even get the words out.

Yellow dreads, Gee, gets it together, no more laughing, cool, so cool he won't say anything.

"So, Gee says, no look, and the dude leans way into the trunk."

Henri said, "Shit," and Nugs started laughing.

"Gee pops him three with the .22, back of the head motherfucker, says to him, yeah, they's some dead white guy in here."

They give each other fives and turn halfway around, it's so fucking funny they can't even look at Henri and Nugs.

Henri said, "Well, get this piece of shit Ford oughta here and bring down the other Beamer."

Yellow dreads said, "We done, man."

And that's when the cops rolled in.

Hundreds of them. They were on the boat, and behind the stacked containers, and in cars that were all over the place. They had helicopters and floodlights everywhere.

Yellow dreads was too cool to run, he just stood there. Nugs was too fat. The skinny black guy took off, but he didn't get far.

Henri said, "You fucker, you amateur fucking dickwad."

Nugs said, "This is bullshit."

The forklift guys disappeared.

Greggs, wearing a track suit and shades, cuffed Henri himself and said, "You just can't trust anyone can you?"

"Fucking assholes."

"The walls have ears, my friends, the walls have ears."

Sergeant Jen Sagar pushed Nugs to the waiting van, and he said, "You never took security seriously you overgrown fucking bouncer. I fucking told you."

Henri watched the cops, so fucking happy because they got ten lousy cars and a couple of stoned Jamaicans, and he knew Nugs was the leak. Whether Nugs knew it or not.

Greggs looked at Henri and said, "Don't worry, we're picking up your boss right now. You having fun yet?"

Henri said, "Fuck you."

Greggs laughed loud and long.

CHAPTER TWENTY-THREE

BORIS SAID IT WAS ALL ABOUT the money, and Roxanne said, "No kidding."

"No," Boris said, "it's actually about the money, the cash."

They were on the 401, Boris driving the Saab. "One of the reasons people, Europeans and South Americans, like Canada is because it's an easy place to launder money."

He changed lanes, looking in the rear-view and hesitating, and Roxanne thought how uncomfortable he looked behind the wheel. She stared at the red tail lights ahead and thought about the money, the cash.

"The biggest problem anyone has these days is getting the cash into a legitimate business. A lot of these guys, they think so short term, they just cover their expenses."

"That's most people," Roxanne said. She'd have to talk to Angus soon, tell him she had some money coming in. Then she thought of something. "You ever think about putting your money in real estate?"

"In land, sure." Boris nodded up and down. "Another thing about Canada, you can still buy land. Nova Scotia and the other one, what's it called?"

"Newfoundland?"

"The other one, the one nobody knows about."

Roxanne wasn't thinking about some dirtpile out in the sticks. She didn't mean land, she meant real estate. She was already seeing how it could work with Angus, how Boris could buy the Toy Works. How she and Boris could buy it, once they got rid of Vince.

"New Brunswick," Boris said. "Like in New Jersey. Everything in this country is named after something else. There's still lakefront property there, oceanfront. You people have no idea how rare that is in the world, that just anybody can buy property on the ocean."

Roxanne said, "A lot of it is being bought by Germans."

"Sure it is. And Americans. Like always you Canadians are giving it away."

"Selling it."

Boris shook his head and she wanted to smack him. "Selling for nothing. Yes I want to get into real estate."

She'd have to wait to mention the Toy Works, but she was already starting to put it together in her head. She wasn't exactly sure how much Angus was really into it for, the guy never gave up numbers, but she was pretty sure he'd want out.

"You sure about these Pakis?"

They turned onto the 427 north to the airport, Boris not watching the road and almost hitting the guardrail, and Roxanne didn't even know what he meant at first. Then she said, "The digital cash guys? Sure, they're taking a decent cut."

"Something we could look into later."

Roxanne figured sure, why not, look into everything. They'd just dropped off a little over 400,000 dollars in cash with Russell Samanani, and then Boris picked up a bag from a guy she would swear looked like a diplomat. She was pretty sure it was another payment on the cars, now that they were being loaded, but Boris wasn't telling her.

Not yet, anyway, but he was on his way.

They took the Dixon Road exit and Boris pulled into the parking lot of the Club International. He said, "Okay."

She said, "Okay, what?"

"I'll be right back."

"Good."

She watched him look like he was making up his mind, and she thought maybe there was something to say to push him into it, but she knew she didn't have to. One thing Roxanne knew was men. She knew this was a guy out all by himself, he started to confess his business to her way too soon, and she knew that only came from desperation.

And like all desperate men she had known, Roxanne could get what she wanted out of him. She was starting to feel good, like she was finally getting her real price.

"You come right back, baby," she said and leaned over and kissed him.

Like a kid, he got out of the car and walked to the back door of the club, unlocked the door, and went in.

• • •

Inspector Nichols called Price just after midnight and asked him if he and the new guy, Loewen, wanted to be in on the takedown at Club International. "I know you're working on something there."

On the way over, Loewen wasn't too happy, saying how he knew this was gonna go task force from the very beginning, and Price had to tell him that's what he'd said.

"You wanted to work it."

Loewen said, "Yeah."

"So now you're working it. This is part of working it. It's all about getting the bad guys."

Loewen said, "I guess."

Price figured he was getting the full introduction to homicide. Phone calls in the middle of the night, Tim Hortons coffee, and the wife gone to work by the time you get home.

At 23 Division they met up with a few Mounties, and a few Halton Region guys and some OPP. The Mounties were in charge, of course, and one of them, looked like he just joined up a few weeks before, gave them the speech about this being an integral part of a large operation, each section of which was just as important as the others.

One of the Halton guys said, "But the TV cameras'll be at the strip club, right?"

Price watched and figured the Mounties taught their guys an official smile along with an official everything else.

The young Mountie said, "This investigation has been ongoing for some time, and we just want to the thank the other forces for such good work and cooperation. It's only right that we're all involved in the takedown."

Only political, Price thought, but he admitted he wanted to be there. He did want to see the look on that Russian's face.

The Mountie said, "We've had various homes and businesses under surveillance for some time now." He looked at his watch and Price thought he was going to say something about synchronizing, but the Halton guy beat him to it, saying, "The big hand is on the twelve."

"This unit will be divided into two. Some of you will be going to a residence, an apartment, and the others moving on a business, the Club International. Some of you are familiar with the layout."

A few guys looked at the two women cops, both OPP, and one guy said, "Sheila, you can tell us what the locker rooms look like, right?"

Sheila said, "Fuck off."

They were loaded and ready to leave, and the Mountie got a phone call. He looked pissed off and said, okay sure, a few times and hung up.

"A slight change of plans, people. There's been an explosion at the Club International. We're still going to move on the residence, but as I understand it, the person of interest was in the club at the time."

• • •

The bomb blew a huge hole in the back of the club, and debris landed all over the parking lot and on the Saab, lighting the roof on fire. Roxanne got out and just stood there, watching it burn. There was smoke everywhere and all she could think was how fucking loud it was, there was noise everywhere. The explosion, the fire, then the sirens.

There were fire trucks all over the place, and guys grabbing Roxanne and pulling her in different directions. Then a fireman got right in her face and said, "Come with me," and Roxanne said, "Boris."

"What?"

"Boris is inside, he went in."

The fireman pulled them behind a truck and took off his helmet, and Roxanne saw it was a woman fireman, firefighter, she couldn't really concentrate. She said, "Boris went in to get . . . something."

The firefighter, the woman, said, "The club's closed."

"Boris is the owner, he went in."

She had long blond hair in a ponytail, the firefighter, and it spun around when she turned and ran, yelling to the others about someone inside.

Roxanne sat down on the edge of the truck, she thought that's what the firefighter told her to do. The smoke was still everywhere, she couldn't breathe, and the flames were making the whole place red and yellow. More fire trucks arrived and there was more noise.

The next thing Roxanne saw, someone was in her face, calling her name, calling her Ms. Keyes. She squinted in the smoke and stood up, let herself be led to an ambulance by the paramedic. And some guy in a blue track suit. She thought she knew him, but she couldn't say from where.

In the ambulance the paramedic got a mask on her, and the air was cold and fresh and she sucked it in. Her eyes were watering from the smoke, but they started to clear up and she looked at the guy in the track suit. He was talking to the paramedic, who was saying there were no injuries, just shock. She was probably in the car when it happened.

She nodded, tried to tell them, yes, that's where she was, and the guy in the track suit said, "Shit, there's nothing left of that car. You think she got out by herself?"

"No one else around. We found an arm and a foot, guy must have blown up."

"You think?"

The paramedic opened the door and jumped out of the ambulance.

Roxanne realized they meant Boris, he'd blown up. She looked at the guy in the track suit and he said, "We have to stop meeting like this," and her head cleared enough to realize he was a cop. The cop she met when Boris killed that guy on King Street. A couple of days ago, but it sure seemed longer. She couldn't remember his name.

"I'm Detective Loewen."

"How you doing?"

He laughed and said better than she was. "What were you doing here?"

"Boris came to pick something up."

"Yeah, pick up what?"

She said she didn't know, they'd been out, had dinner, went to some clubs. She couldn't really remember. "He was just going in for a second, I waited in the car."

Loewen asked if he could have been picking up cash.

Roxanne knew her reaction gave it away, but still she said, "Cash, what do you mean?" and expected Loewen to keep asking her questions, but he just nodded and looked away.

Roxanne said, "I could have been killed."

Still not looking at her he said, "You have to be careful the company you keep."

She thought, yeah, thanks for the advice, pal. Like all those jerks on that TV show, *Cops*, always yelling at the losers, chewing them out for being losers. She was going to set him straight, let him know what she was really doing, how it was her plan coming together, when the bald black cop walked up to them.

He said, "The only real damage was to the change-room. The fire's under control."

Loewen said there were a lot of firemen around, and the black cop, Roxanne couldn't remember his name, said they were going to wait till the place was scheduled to open so they could be heroes for the strippers.

Loewen told the black cop that it looked like Boris was just stopping off to pick up some cash.

"This stuff," the black cop said, "that's raining down on us?"

"The firemen got it all?"

"Crime scene picked up a lot, said it's evidence."

"I'm surprised Burroughs isn't here from narcotics."

Roxanne watched them joke around. She started to cough and choke, and the female firefighter gave her a bottle of water and told her to drink slowly, it was the smoke in her lungs.

But Roxanne knew it wasn't, she knew it was her plan, her whole life going up in flames. Shit. She drank the water slowly and tried to think. Okay, get it together.

Something's going to come out of this. Maybe it wasn't over for her and Vince.

• • •

The brand new terminal, and Vince didn't know if he should get in line or take a piss, the place looked like a toilet. All grey on grey. The big pillars that looked like unfinished concrete were grey, the carpet that was so hard to pull a suitcase on was grey. He walked through the arrivals level, just looking around, watching people get off planes, making sure every security camera caught him. People came through the sliding doors from picking up their bags and had to come down a ramp — either left or right — and it looked like they were walking out on stage, the sea of faces waiting in a mob. Vince thought they should put in bleachers, show a movie.

Up on the departures level, Vince walked up to the Air Canada desk.

The woman asked him if she could help, and he said, "You'd think with all the airports in the world, someone would figure out a better system than this maze of poles and ropes everyone knocks down."

The woman, probably Vince's age or a little older, but not yet fifty, with streaked blond hair and a very pretty face, smiled at him and said, "Sometimes we arrange them so they don't actually lead to the counter."

Vince said, "I think I've been in that line."

The woman said, "What I like is that they still put in the temporary poles, like this time they weren't expecting any lineups."

Yeah, Vince thought, there'd be a few things he'd miss about Toronto, like these easy conversations with strangers. He knew no matter how hard he tried to learn the language where he was going, he'd never be this comfortable with it. He said, "I need one ticket on the eight-fifteen to San Jose, Costa Rica."

She asked him when he was returning, and he said he didn't know, he was going to drive around Central America for a while, maybe fly back from Honduras or Belize.

She was still friendly with him. She said, "Most people do that in the winter."

"You've got to go when you have the chance."

It was almost exactly what he'd said in Terminal Three when he bought the ticket for Argentina and the one for Australia. He didn't think the cops would come looking, but they might, even if they were just after a witness. But the other guys — he didn't think they'd just let him walk. Not with what was on his laptop.

The ticket agent handed him the ticket and his credit card, a gold American Express, and said, "There you go

Mr. Leach, you've got about a half-hour to get through security."

He thanked her, said he'd probably need every minute of it, even though all he had was carry-on, and then he went to the British Airways desk.

All his tickets bought, his face shown all over the airport, Vince went back out to the brand new parking garage. Everything was automated now, getting the ticket on the way in, paying at the machine and getting out. There may not have been another human being in the place.

He opened the trunk of his new car, a Subaru Outback, dark green with the full sport package and roof rack, backed into the parking space when he heard the voice, the French accent.

"Hey porno man, where you going?"

Vince, his back to the concrete wall, looked around the open trunk and saw them, the two guys Garry told to fuck off, they looked just like they did on the monitors back at the office. The whole floor of the garage was quiet and empty except for all the cars. Vince was parked between a minivan and a Volvo station wagon. He said, "You guys had enough of Toronto?"

Denis said, "Come on over here, we want to talk to you."

Vince dropped his bag in the trunk and unzipped it. He pulled out the .38 he'd taken off Gord, that poor guy whose girlfriend was probably in a gang bang at that very moment, and held it in front of his stomach. He didn't close the trunk.

Denis said, "This is a lucky break for you, running into us. You not going somewhere, are you?" and Claude laughed. They were on either side of Vince's Outback, coming down between the cars, blocking any way out.

Vince watched them, seeing how they were so used to taking up all the space in a room, so used to people getting out of their way. He was thinking he'd like to get out of their way.

He raised the .38 and shot Denis in the chest, knocking him back against the minivan, then he turned fast and shot Claude in the stomach — guy was even taller than he thought.

Then Vince moved fast, right into Claude's face as the big guy was getting out his own gun, a much bigger .45, and he rammed his shoulder into the big guy's head, knocking him backwards, and Vince came away with the .45. He shot Claude again as he staggered back, right in the throat.

Denis was up on one knee, the door handle of the minivan in one hand, raising his other, saying, "Wait a minute, fucker, we can work this —" and Vince shot him in the back of the head.

Neither body was even blocking his way, so Vince got into his car and drove out of the garage. He slipped his paid ticket into the machine, the bar lifted, and two minutes later he was on the 401.

Shit, his heart was still pounding. He took a few deep breaths to calm down. It wasn't the way he would have planned it at all, but sometimes things just work out. He turned on the radio and pressed the buttons till he found the Hamilton station and the Super Seventies Sunday.

A few minutes later and he was just one of a million cars on one of the busiest highways in the world. The radio played a lot of ads, but by the time he cleared the city limits he smiled at "Bang a Gong."

She dances when she walks, take a chance.

Vince nodded in time with the beat. Take a chance, that's right.

Dirty sweet and you're my girl.

He could drive all night.

CHAPTER TWENTY-FOUR

"They said the biker dudes killed Vince?"

"That's what they said," Roxanne said.

Suss said he knew they were pissed at Garry, and Roxanne said they didn't really give a shit about Garry, they were after the top guy.

"And they killed Boris?"

"Looks like they picked Vince up here, his Mercedes is still out back. The cops figure the one they got with the cars, Frantisek somebody, they call him Nugs, probably took Vince out on his boat to the middle of Lake Ontario and dumped him. Then they planted the bomb at Club International."

Suss watched Roxanne take another hit on the joint and said, "So who killed them?"

"Boris's uncle." She exhaled a long time, pushing it all out of her lungs and said, "Well, he's not really his uncle, he used to be his father's partner. Boris knew him his whole life, called him Uncle Khozha. He flew back to

New York, the cops figure he just ran into them in the parking lot."

"Right place at the right time," Suss said.

"Luck," Roxanne said. "Preparation meets opportunity."

Which Suss thought might be true, but in this case he knew was bullshit on account of the email he got from Vince that morning. No way to tell what else was wrong with the cops' theory, but he didn't really give a shit.

"You know who Vince Fournier is?"

"The cops said they have no idea."

Suss took the joint from Roxanne, the Blueberry, kind of a chick weed, and took a hit. "No," he said, exhaling slow, taking his time, "in real life. It's Alice Cooper."

"The rock singer with the snake?"

"His real name," Suss said. "Some of that shit I downloaded, 'I'm Eighteen,' 'Cold Ethyl,' 'Dead Babies,' some of that shit was cool." He watched Roxanne hold the joint between the tips of her fingers, her red fingernails close together, and inhale. He noticed her lips, the same red as her nails. "All these other names, Reg Dwight, David Jones, they all famous rock singers."

"Davey Jones was in the Monkees," Roxanne said. "Not exactly a rock singer."

They were standing in Vince's office by the fire escape with the window wide open. Suss took another hit and offered it to Roxanne but she waved him off and he stubbed it out on the sill. Was decent of her to offer it up to begin with.

Suss said, "David Bowie's real name was Jones, I think that's who it's for. He even had one in Norma Jean Baker."

"Marilyn Monroe?"

"You like that video Madonna did, about the diamonds, looked like a Marilyn Monroe movie?"

Roxanne said, yeah, "Material Girl," and Suss could tell she was impressed he knew his shit. There was no way he was going to tell her about the email from Vince with the password that got him into the company's real books. Let her think he was a genius, hacking his way in, finding dozens of employees going back years, all of them turned out to be Vince.

When Roxanne had arrived at VSF that morning, no one really knew why. No one knew what they were going to do. Ella at reception was freaked out, crying, and the webcam girls — Vince always called them that and Suss did too, even though most of them were older than he was — they were all worried about losing their jobs. At first, Suss thought he could just take over. With the email from Vince he had all the info he'd need, but these people just treated him like a kid, and when Roxanne came in, he didn't know why, she just looked like she knew what she was doing, so he took her aside and told her the situation.

She'd said, "You mean he was stealing from himself?"

"Skimming," Suss said. "Putting it away for a rainy day. Like the mobsters, you know, escape money, cash they can get at anytime. This be the new digital version."

Roxanne said, yeah, like the women she knew married to developers twice their age, all signed pre-nups so they had to skim as much of the household money as they could. It never seemed to amount to more than a few grand, ten or twenty maybe, after ten years.

"Well," Suss said, "It's hard to tell here, some of these employees only on the books a few months, some maybe a year, but he's probably up to a million." In fact, Suss was able to find almost two million in the last year.

"Plus what he got from Boris last night." Almost half a million.

Suss closed the window and stepped back into the office nodding. "Some of it, the program is set up to make recurring payments for memberships so he only got the first month's worth. Less than a hundred grand."

"So the program's working?"

Suss could see right away she was moving on. "Yeah, there's no problem with the program," and he watched her nod, working it out. He was thinking it was a good idea that he told her.

Garry knocked on the open office door and stepped in. He said, "So, are we still in business, or what?"

Suss shrugged, looked at Roxanne.

She said, "What's up?"

"I know this guy, he's a location manager on big-ass Hollywood movies shooting in town. He's working on some piece of shit action movie, *SkyBlast*, or something."

Roxanne said, "Yeah, so?"

Suss liked the way she was calm about it. She walked from the window and sat down in Vince's chair. It was a little too low, but she leaned back, put her feet up on the desk. Man, her toenails matched her fingernails.

"Well, they're wrapping out of the Dome, you know, and my guy says if we keep it really quiet we can shoot there."

Suss said, "Shoot what?"

"*The Pinch Hitters*, *Double Play Boys*, I don't know, I'll think of something, but we have to know right now." He looked at Roxanne and said, "This is a great opportunity."

And she said, "Yeah, okay. Put it together."

Garry said, "Fantastic."

As he was leaving, Roxanne called him back and said, "Take some girls along, shoot something with them. Guys love the lesbian stuff."

Garry said okay, he'd see what he could do but he didn't know how long he'd have the location for, and he was out the door.

Then Suss looked at Roxanne and said, "So, you want me to put you on the payroll?"

He waited for it, and she said, "I'm thinking of the name. Louise Ciccone, maybe."

Suss said, who Madonna? We can use that, sure.

He watched Roxanne turn on the desktop and he thought he'd have to start downloading a whole bunch of new music. She might even like some of the same shit he did.

CHAPTER TWENTY-FIVE

Standing in the first bank he'd ever opened an account in, back when he was a teenager, he gave the teller his real name. It felt weird after all these years. He was amazed the bank was still there, in the shopping centre on Champlain Boulevard in LaSalle. Then he said, "I had an account here a long time ago. I don't think I ever closed it."

"More than seven years?"

"Yeah."

"It's closed by now then."

"I guess I better open a new one."

He gave her the rest of his information, and when the account was opened, he transferred in nine grand from another account and went for lunch. He could transfer the rest from home later. There was a brasserie in the mall that wasn't there when he was in high school, and then he went for a drive.

He knew where he was going, but he didn't go straight there. He drove along Lakeshore, almost all the way to

Verdun and then back along the aqueduct, over the bridge on Bishop Power, and past that Catholic Church that looked like the top of a rocket ship. Seventies architecture, man, the whole neighbourhood.

He drove by the old high school, LaSalle Protestant High. There was a cement slab in front of the red brick building — looked more like a red bunker — with the name spelled out in metal letters. He'd never seen the sign with more than a couple of letters. Now it didn't have any. Another sign, smaller and bolted to the slab said something about an adult education centre. He didn't slow down enough to read it.

The houses in the whole area, for miles, were all the same. Two stories, four units each, balconies up and down, flat roofs, driveways sloping down to garages in the front. Four feet to the next house. They looked like Soviet-era housing. And the people who moved in from the Point or Little Burgundy thought they had it made.

After driving past the apartment building where he'd lived with his mother so many years ago, so many lifetimes ago, he finally gave in and drove the couple of blocks to 12th Avenue. You couldn't tell it from 11th or 15th or any of the other streets for miles. In fact, when he'd first moved in, that first night he'd walked Liz Downey home he had gotten lost in that maze of streets all lined with the same houses.

The Downeys' place was in the middle of the block. He slowed down and stopped right across the street. He wondered who lived there now. Probably a French family. LaSalle had a lot of English and Jamaican and Italian back in the seventies when he'd lived there, but it was mostly French now.

Twenty-five years ago. Closer to thirty, really. Sitting in

the Outback looking at those concrete steps, that wrought-iron railing, every detail came back. Him and Liz stopped in front of the house. Awkward. He'd never stood that close to a girl he liked so much before. Could smell that Herbal Essence shampoo in her almost blond hair. Down past her shoulders. He finally said, "well," and she said, "yeah, well," and he just kept staring at her till she tilted her head to one side a little and grabbed him by the arm and pulled.

They kissed.

Right there on the sidewalk. He remembered thinking, wow, this feels great. He hugged her, held her tight, his hands on her back low, squeezing. Felt great.

Then she pulled away and turned and ran up those concrete steps. He stood there watching. When she got to the front door, she turned around and said, "See you tomorrow." They'd made a date, they were going downtown to a movie. That was when he got lost trying to find his way back to Bishop Power.

Now he had to laugh. Stupid nostalgia.

Well, he had his chance with her, a long time ago.

Then the door opened and Liz Downey stepped out.

She had a small dog on a leash. Her hair was dark and thick and fell to her shoulders, and she was wearing sunglasses. She came down the steps and walked the dog right past him.

He watched her go, looking at her Levis, and it was like he'd just seen her yesterday, man, she could still do it to him. He got out of the car and walked after her.

She stopped and bent over with a plastic bag in her hand to pick up the dog shit and heard him on the sidewalk. She didn't stand up, she just turned her head and looked at him.

She said, "Ryan Doyle." Then she stood up.

He said, "Hey."

She stared at him, and he couldn't think of anything to say. He liked the way she looked at him.

He said, "You still live here?" and she said God no.

"My Mom broke her leg, I'm walking her dog."

She walked past him, back towards her house, then looked back at him and said, "You coming? You said you'd be back for dinner, my Mom's been waiting."

Ryan said, yeah, sure, and walked beside her. This was more like it, he thought, this is more like my real life, like Ryan Doyle. He didn't know what else to say, but he didn't feel like he had to say anything right then and neither did Liz, which was great.

Then she stopped and said, "Oh shit."

Ryan saw it, a beat-up Ford Explorer in front of her mother's house, a guy getting out of it trying to look tough.

Liz said, "Asshole. I've got a restraining order against him, for all the good it does."

Ryan said, "I'll talk to him."

"You? What'll you say to him?"

Ryan started to walk towards the Explorer, half turned around, and saw Liz looking at him, smiling now, wanting to see what he was going to do. He thought there were a few things about being Vince Fournier he wasn't going to give up right away.

"I'll think of something."